Tea & Treachery

Treachery

VICKI DELANY

KENSINGTON BOOKS
www.kensingtonbooks.com

This book is a work of fiction. Names, characters, and incidents either are products of the author's imagination or are used fictitiously. Any resemblance to actual persons living or dead, or events, is entirely coincidental.

KENSINGTON BOOKS are published by

Kensington Publishing Corp.
119 West 40th Street
New York, NY 10018

All Kensington titles, imprints, and distributed lines are available at special quantity discounts for bulk purchases for sales promotion, premiums, fund-raising, educational, or institutional use. Special book excerpts or customized printings can also be created to fit specific needs. For details, write or phone the office of the Kensington Special Sales Manager: Attn. Special Sales Department. Kensington Publishing Corp., 119 West 40th Street, New York, NY 10018. Phone: 1-800-221-2647.

Library of Congress Card Catalogue Number: 2020931305

ISBN-13: 978-1-4967-2506-6
ISBN-10: 1-4967-2506-9
First Kensington Hardcover Edition: August 2020

ISBN-13: 978-1-4967-2508-0 (ebook)
ISBN-10: 1-4967-2508-5 (ebook)

10 9 8 7 6 5 4 3 2 1

Printed in the United States of America

To Alex, who loves a perfect afternoon tea

Acknowledgments

Afternoon tea, done properly, truly is an experience, and I'd advise everyone to give it a try at least once in your life. But remember, it is a treat and an indulgence. Thanks to my daughter Alexandra Delany, who enjoyed afternoon tea with me in places as diverse as the National Portrait Gallery in London and the Prince of Wales Hotel in Niagara-on-the-Lake in order to assist with my research, as well as tossing around ideas for the story and the characters in the car.

Karen Owen, tea lover extraordinaire, took the time to answer my tea-making and serving questions and gave me a tour of the marvelous delights (and a perfect cup of tea) to be found at Murchie's shop in North Vancouver.

Many thanks to my good friend Cheryl Freedman, who brought her ever-keen editor's eye to the manuscript and advised me to tone some things down a bit.

Thanks to the gang at Mystery Lovers' Kitchen for giving me a forum to express some of my foodie ideas and challenging me to expand my usual repertoire. I'll be posting some of the things I learned, in writing this book, to that blog.

Thanks are due also to Wendy McCurdy for loving the idea of this series, and to my superagent, Kim Lionetti, of BookEnds, for bringing us together.

The right to name Rose's cat was won by Linda Torney at a charity auction. I hope you like what I've done with Robert the Bruce, Linda.

Chapter 1

"Creamy Earl Grey."

"Darjeeling."

"English breakfast."

"Darjeeling. Doesn't the name say it all? The romance of travel. Misty hillsides and light, warm rain. Green plants and fragrant leaves."

"We're drinking tea, not writing a novel, Bernie."

"I like to think I can do both. At the same time."

"Very well. Two Darjeeling, please, Cheryl."

"You could have ordered a pot each, you know," the waitress said as she went to place the order.

My friend and I grinned at each other. "You sure you want to do this?" I asked her.

"Drink tea?" she replied with a wiggle of her eyebrows.

"You know what I mean, Bernie. Completely and totally change your life in order to pursue your dream."

She threw out her arms. "Absolutely completely and totally. Lily, this is the moment I've been waiting for my entire life. The point at which everything I've been learning, everything I've been doing, converges into one great promise."

"Your entire thirty-two years of existence has come into focus at this moment?"

She beamed at me. "Exactly."

I didn't say I'd been joking. This wasn't a joking matter. Not to Bernie, anyway.

And neither was the matter of what beverage to select for afternoon tea.

Bernie glanced over my shoulder, and her face lit up. She gave a squeal of delight, leapt to her feet, and held her arms out wide. I twisted in my seat to see my grandmother coming into the tearoom. I was pleased that she'd brought her leopard-print cane with her today. She insists she doesn't need help walking, but I worry about her on the long driveway between her house and the tearoom and on the rough flagstone path in the garden.

The two women hugged each other. My grandmother's a great deal tougher than she looks, but I'm always afraid Bernie will crush her one day. They're about as opposite as two women can be. Bernie, whom I called the Warrior Princess when we were kids, is six feet tall, lean, and smooth muscled, with an always out-of-control mane of curly red hair, a complexion dotted with freckles, and green eyes. Rows of silver hoops run up both of her ears; her long thin fingers are covered with silver rings; and colorful tattoos grace her upper back and shoulders. My grandmother, on the other hand, is barely five feet tall and as thin as the cane she held in her knurly hand. Her short gray hair stands up like a halo of spikes around her head, and intelligence and wicked humor shine from the depths of her wide blue eyes. Despite the network of fine lines and deep folds on her face, her porcelain complexion is one women decades younger might envy. This afternoon she wore a long, loose dress in every shade of purple imaginable, with earrings made of purple feathers, and a long double strand of purple beads. Her eyes were outlined by black liner; her mascara thick; and her mouth, a slash of bright red lipstick. My grandmother is a woman who likes color in her life.

"Good afternoon, Rose." Cheryl put the pot of Darjeeling on the table, along with cups, saucers, matching plates, a milk jug, and a sugar bowl. I'd asked Cheryl to use my personal dishes—the Royal Doulton Winthrop set of white china with a deep red border with delicate gold leaves running through it, and gold trim on the base of the cups and decorating the handles. The china had been given to me by my maternal grandparents, Rose and her husband Eric, on my sixteenth birthday, and it was now kept on a shelf at the back of the kitchen, to be used on very special occasions. Such as welcoming my best friend to Cape Cod.

"Will you be joining us for tea, Rose?" Cheryl asked.

My grandmother took a chair. "I will." She sniffed the air. "Not Darjeeling, though. I'm in the mood for Lapsang souchong. No food for me, thank you. I had lunch earlier." Rose had lived in the United States for almost sixty years, but her accent still carried memories of her native Yorkshire.

"Oh!" Bernie said, "I should have had that. Lapsang souchong is an even more exotic name than Darjeeling. What's the difference?"

"Darjeeling's from India and Lapsang souchong's from China, for one thing. Lapsang is smokier and has a slight sweetness, whereas Darjeeling is slightly muscatel, like the wine." I gestured toward the pot. "Darjeeling first flush was once called the Champagne of teas. Shall I pour?"

"Let me, let me." Bernie clapped her hands together, and I smiled at the memories of our childhood. "Enthusiastic" could have been Bernadette Murphy's middle name.

"So," my grandmother said as Bernie carefully allowed a stream of dark, fragrant liquid to fill my cup. "Tell me what you're doing here, Bernadette. Lily says you've quit your job and have some mad idea of making it as a writer."

"I didn't say it was a mad idea," I protested.

"You didn't have to," Bernie said. "Everyone else does."

"Including me," Rose said. "A job's a valuable thing to have. One doesn't give up a good job for no reason."

"I have a reason," Bernie said. "I'm writing a book, and Cape Cod is the perfect place to do it."

Rose's expression indicated exactly what she thought of that. As though her expression wasn't enough, she added, "Rubbish."

Bernie threw me a glance. I shrugged. "I'd forgotten," my friend said, "just how blunt you can be, Rose."

"Never paid to beat about the bush when I was a girl. My parents were plainspoken, and they taught me to be so, too."

"I doubt you were plainspoken, as you put it," Bernie said, "to your employers in that stately home in Yorkshire."

"I can hold my tongue," Rose said. "When I need to. Thank you, Cheryl. And you brought my favorite cup, as well."

Why a souvenir of Prince Charles and Lady Diana Spencer's wedding was my grandmother's favorite cup, I never did understand.

Along with the fresh pot of tea, Cheryl placed a three-tiered tray on the table. Freshly made scones on the middle tray, a selection of thin sandwiches on the bottom, and delicate pastries on the top.

"Wow!" Bernie said. "This looks so fabulous. You made all this, Lily?"

"I did, but I have to confess that at this time of day, all you get is leftovers."

"I'll eat your leftovers anytime. Everything looks so delicious. Where should I start?" Without waiting for an answer, she selected a plump raisin-dotted scone. She cut it in half, slathered it with butter and strawberry jam, and topped it off with a huge dollop of clotted cream.

I took a salmon sandwich for myself and watched Bernie take the first bite of her scone. Her eyes rolled back in her head, and she moaned happily.

Rose caught my eye and gave me a wink. Even after all these years and all the sandwiches and pastries I've made, I still get a flush of pride seeing the fruit of my labors so beautifully presented and enjoyed.

It was after four thirty, and Tea by the Sea, my tearoom, would be closing soon. The last few customers of the day were finishing their tea, scraping the bottom of the jam jar, licking clotted cream or sandwich crumbs off their fingers. Most of my work was finished for the day, except for the clearing up, and so I'd invited Bernie to come in for tea. She'd arrived last night from New York City to spend the summer on Cape Cod

"You're renting the Crawford place, I hear," Rose said.

"Yup," Bernie replied. "I was lucky to get it for a reasonable rent."

"That might be because it's falling down." Rose sipped her tea. "Not to mention falling off the cliff. I trust you're aware they couldn't get any vacation rentals this year."

"Uh, yes, they told me that." I've known Bernie since we were in kindergarten. I can always tell when she's lying: she'd known no such thing. "It's going to be the perfect place to write. In the big sunroom that looks out over the sea."

"If you have good binoculars," Rose said, "you might catch a glimpse of the ocean on an exceptionally clear day."

"Well, uh, yes, but it's very quiet."

"Because no one risks their undercarriage on that laneway," Rose said.

Bernie threw me a panicked look.

Rose leaned across the table and put her hand on Bernie's. "Don't listen to me, love. I know what rents are like on the Cape in season. You were lucky to get any place at all at an affordable rate and wise not to spend all your savings on something nicer than you need. I'm delighted that you found someplace so close to us." My tea room's situated on the Outer Cape, the peninsula part of Cape Cod curling north and west. We're close to the vacation town of North Augusta, south of North Truro, facing west, looking over Cape Cod Bay, rather than the open Atlantic Ocean.

Bernie grinned at her. "Thanks, Rose. You know I value your opinion. That house will be perfect for me. I'm going to be able to get so much work done there."

"Which you'll never find a publisher for," Rose said. "And that's if you ever finish the thing."

Bernie's smile faded, and she blinked.

"That's rather harsh, isn't it, Rose?" I said. "Bernie has talent, tons of it. She just needs the time to get her book finished."

Bernie nodded enthusiastically as she spread a thick layer of jam on the second half of her scone.

"I believe in speaking the truth," my grandmother said. "At all times. Such as telling you, Lily, that that cucumber sandwich has too much color."

"I added a touch of curry powder to give it some punch."

"A cucumber sandwich does not need punch. A properly made and sliced cucumber sandwich speaks of tradition. There's a chip in Bernie's cup."

"There is not."

"Opposite the handle."

Bernie held up the offending cup, and we both peered at it.

"So there is," I said. At eighty-five, my grandmother has better eyesight than I do. "Don't change the subject. Bernie wants to take a shot at her dream. Reach for the brass ring. I say go for it."

"I say rubbish."

I glanced at Bernie. She looked rather stunned. People often do after my grandmother says what's on her mind. Not more than ten minutes ago, I'd been thinking Bernie was making a big mistake, quitting her job as a forensic accountant at a big Manhattan corporate law firm, cashing in her savings, and coming to the Outer Cape to work on her book. Now, in the face of Rose's opposition, I was firmly on Bernie's side.

What's the point of having dreams if you can't strive for them? I glanced around the tearoom. My tearoom. Owning my own place had always been *my* dream. That the dream came with a well-meaning, loving, caring but opinionated and always interfering grandmother might not have been part of the plan. But sometimes we have to settle for what we can get.

Rose finished her tea and reached for her cane. She wobbled slightly as she got to her feet. Bernie leapt to assist her. "So nice to see you, love," Rose said. "Never mind what I said earlier. I'm delighted you're here, and I hope to see you regularly over the summer."

"You will," Bernie said.

"Come for dinner one night soon. Tomorrow would be good. Nothing fancy. Lily, you'll come also. Seven o'clock. A bottle of that nice New Zealand sauvignon blanc you brought last time would be lovely. Oh, that nasty man was back just now, with his binoculars and his clipboard. He waved at me as I walked over here. I did not return his wave. I'm not happy at him poking around. See you in the morning, love." She walked away, her cane tapping at the wooden floor.

Bernie dropped into her chair. "I'd forgotten what a force of nature your grandmother is."

"I can never forget. No matter how much I might want to."

Bernie studied the sandwich selection and helped herself to a cucumber one, made in the traditional way, with thin slices of the vegetable served on white bread spread with a layer of cream cheese and cut into fingers. I'd added a sprinkling of curry powder to the cream cheese for a modern touch.

"I don't like the taste of curry on this," Bernie said as she chewed. "It's overpowering."

"It is not. You've let Rose influence your thinking," said I, who'd only seconds ago changed my mind about Bernie's venture, not wanting to agree with Rose.

The chimes over the door rang as the last customers, a table of six women, left. Cheryl swooped down on their table with her tray and began clearing it off. I was pleased to see that scarcely a crumb remained.

My other waitress, Cheryl's daughter Marybeth, came in from the garden, also laden with a tray. She'd earlier taken a double tea stand outside, and only a single tiny strawberry tart was left. I smiled to see it: the guests had been too polite to take the last one.

"That's the end of them," Marybeth said. "And I'm beat. It's been a good day."

For most of the day, every table in the tearoom as well as those outside in the garden had been full. It was late spring in Cape Cod, the weather was perfect, and the tourists were out in force.

"What did Rose mean, a man with binoculars and a clipboard has been nosing around?" Bernie said. "That doesn't sound good."

"It's none of our business, but I'm afraid Rose is going to make it so. He isn't interested in our property. The house next door's for sale. It has been for some time."

"Have they been having trouble selling? It's a fabulous location," Bernie said. "Almost as good as Rose's house."

"It's a marvelous old house, yes, and in a great setting, but it needs an enormous amount of work. Or so I've been told. I've never been inside. It's been owned by a wealthy local family for generations. They used to use it as a summer home, but the family lost interest years ago, and it's been falling slowly into disrepair for decades. They need to bring the price down—a lot—if they're going to attract a buyer who just wants a nice house to live in. In the meantime . . ."

The chimes over the door tinkled.

"I'm sorry," Cheryl called, "but we're about to close."

"We won't be long," a deep voice boomed. "I hope you can rustle up a cup of coffee and a couple cookies for two hardworking men."

I turned to check out the new arrivals. They were both middle aged, but the similarities ended there. One was tall and round bellied, with chubby cheeks, a nose crisscrossed by a network of red lines, and thin strands of hair stretched into a comb-over. He wore jeans that looked as though they'd been recently ironed, a blue button-down shirt with the top button undone, and steel-toed boots without a trace of dried mud on them. He had binoculars around his neck and an iPad tucked under one arm. This must be the man Rose had seen. She'd mistaken the iPad for a clipboard. The other man was short and thin, with close-cropped hair and black-rimmed eyeglasses. His pants were part of a business suit, and the sleeves of his white shirt were rolled up.

"You're in luck," Cheryl said. "I haven't emptied the coffeepot yet." Tea by the Sea is strictly a tearoom, but we have to make accommodation for guests who (shudder!) don't care for tea. "How about two strawberry tarts to go with it? That's about all we have left."

"Sounds good," said the larger man.

"Maybe the house needs—" Bernie started to speak, but I cut her off with a touch to my lips and a shake of my head. She opened her eyes wide but said no more.

"Nice place you got here," the smaller man said.

"Thank you." Cheryl poured the coffee into takeaway cups. "Cream? Sugar?"

"Two of each," the bigger man said.

"Nothing for me, thanks," the other one said. "You been here long?"

"If you mean me, my entire life," Cheryl said. "If you mean Tea by the Sea, this is our first summer."

"I bet the tourist ladies love it."

"They do."

Tea by the Sea specializes in traditional afternoon tea. In keeping with the theme of the menu, the restaurant's decorated as though it were a drawing room in a castle in Scotland or a stately country home in England. Paintings of British pastoral scenes and horses at the hunt are hung on pale peach wallpaper with clusters of pink and green flowers. The wide-planked wooden floors are polished to a high shine; the chairs upholstered in peach and sage green; the tables laid with starched and ironed white cloths and either a single rose in a crystal vase or a lush flower arrangement, depending on what's currently available in the garden. Several small alcoves, similarly decorated, are tucked into corners, providing space for small parties or intimate gatherings. In the main room, a large antique sideboard, bought at a good price and carefully restored with a lot of elbow grease on my part and advice on Rose's, exhibits some of the china tea sets we use. The opposite wall has a real fireplace, at this time of year filled with flowers. A small room next to the kitchen displays items for sale—teapots and matching cups and saucers; tea accessories such as infusers and strainers, timers, and tea cozies; several varieties of prettily packaged tea bath salts I make myself from fragrant tea leaves; and locally made jams and preserves. The waitresses wear knee-length black dresses under starched white aprons and small white caps. As I stay strictly in the back, doing the cooking, I usually come to work in jeans and a T-shirt.

"Do you do a good business here?" the larger man asked.

Cheryl threw me a glance. "We do, Mr. Ford."

His back was to me, so I couldn't see him smile, but I heard it in his voice. "You know me. Then you know I care about the success of small independent businesses, such as this one."

I sipped my tea and listened. Bernie filled her plate with more sandwiches and tarts.

"If you're a local," he continued, "you must realize this place won't get a lot of business over the winter."

"No," Cheryl admitted.

"You're out here in the middle of nowhere. Nice location, close to the sea, fabulous views, but nothing much else around. Am I right?"

Another flick of Cheryl's eyes toward me. I still said nothing.

"Same with the B & B next door. What capacity do they have? Five guest rooms? Maybe six?"

"I'm not sure." Cheryl put the strawberry tarts in a paper bag and handed it to him.

The shorter man said, "Can't be much more than that. Not enough, really, to keep the place going year-round."

He pulled out his wallet, but Mr. Ford said, "Put your money away, Roy. This one's on me. I can buy you a coffee, I think, without anyone accusing you of taking a bribe." He laughed heartily. The smaller man, Roy, didn't return the laugh.

"We do okay," Cheryl said.

"This is your restaurant's first season," Mr. Ford said. "Soon the novelty will wear off, winter will set in, and customers won't be able to sit out in that nice garden." He handed her a twenty-dollar bill. "You need to keep the customers coming in, isn't that right, Roy? Keep the change. Nice talking to you. I'm sure we'll be seeing a lot more of each other."

They walked away. As they passed my table, Mr. Ford turned his head and looked directly at me.

He hadn't been talking to Cheryl, I knew. But to me.

Chapter 2

"What was all that about?" Bernie asked after the men had left, Marybeth started stacking the chairs onto the tables, and Cheryl got out the vacuum cleaner.

"The bigger man was the one Rose was talking about earlier I think. The house next door isn't selling as a house. There's talk that a hotel chain wants it."

"They want to use it as a hotel?"

"They want to turn it into a hotel, which isn't the same thing. Not just a hotel, but a hotel and conference center. Maybe even a golf resort."

"It's big, but it doesn't seem that big . . ."

"It's not, and that's the point. Right now the property's zoned residential and small business, same as Rose's property. There's some talk of rezoning, so the old house can be gutted and a big new extension added on."

"You're talking as though that's a bad thing," Bernie said. "Is it?"

I let out a breath. "To Rose, it is. I believe the phrase she used is 'over my dead body.' You see, what we have here . . ."

"Nicest piece of private property in this part of the Cape."

"Precisely. Peace, quiet, serenity. I don't know how

much of that we'll lose if they go ahead with the development, but I'm thinking a lot. Hotel, golf resort, conference center. All of which need parking and round-the-clock staffing. A full-service restaurant and bar means delivery vehicles up and down the driveway all day. No, Rose isn't at all happy."

The vacuum cleaner started with a roar. I held up one hand, asking Cheryl to turn it off. "You know who those men are?" I asked her.

"The one who did all the talking is Jack Ford. He's a big-time developer. Does work all over the Outer Cape."

"Does he, now?"

"Yup. And he's as nasty and crooked as they come."

"Strong words."

Marybeth joined us. "People have strong opinions about him. The old-timers, like Mom and me and the rest of our family, hate him. The newcomers, the big property owners, and the developers love him."

Cheryl nodded. "He thinks he's charming. They say some women fall for that."

"Who was the man with him?"

"Roy Gleeson. He's a town councillor," Cheryl said.

"Thus the comment about not offering a bribe. What do you suppose he was doing here?" I asked. "Not interested in supporting my small business, I assume."

When Tea by the Sea had its official grand opening in the spring, plenty of officials from North Augusta and other towns in the Outer Cape came, but Roy Gleeson hadn't. The mayor of North Augusta had made a speech. Or so I'd been told. I'd been in the kitchen, frantically trying to save a batch of brownies burning in the unfamiliar oven.

"If Jack Ford wants the property to be rezoned," Cheryl said, "someone on council has to propose it. Roy's checking things out. I bet Ford's courting them all. He'll be trying to find someone he can pay under the table for it."

"Roy'll get a kickback if the property's rezoned," Marybeth said, "and the development project goes ahead."

"Do you know that for sure?" I asked.

"No, but . . . ," Marybeth said.

"Everyone knows," Cheryl said.

"Meaning no one knows," I said. "Not for sure."

Cheryl shrugged, and the vacuum started with a roar. Marybeth returned to stacking chairs.

"I'll take that as a subtle hint you're closing." Bernie tossed the last bite of her pistachio macaron into her mouth.

"Yup. See you tomorrow night. You know Rose's dinner invitation is a command appearance, right?"

"I wouldn't dare miss it." She got to her feet, and I walked with her to the door. We gave each other enthusiastic hugs.

"I am so glad you're here," I said.

"I'm glad I'm here, too."

Bernie left, and I went into the kitchen. One thing I've learned in owning my own restaurant: service might be over for the day, but prep for the next day was always waiting to be done. And those dishes weren't going to wash themselves.

I was at work again at six the following morning. My morning job isn't at Tea by the Sea, but in the kitchen of Rose's B & B, Victoria-on-Sea.

My labradoodle, Éclair (so named because a streak of cream runs through the curly brown fur on her chest and belly), waited impatiently as I unlocked the back door. To my surprise, Rose was already seated at the cracked and fading Formica table, cradling her first cuppa of the day, with her big black cat, Robert the Bruce, curled up in her lap. Robbie gave me his habitual snarl of welcome.

I like cats just fine, but I don't believe they belong in

kitchens. On that, as on many things, Rose and I disagree. On that, as on many things, she won the argument. Robbie knew I'd confine him to Rose's suite if I had my way. But I didn't have my way, and the cat enjoyed the run of the entire house. Guests occasionally complained that he got into their room, and sometimes into their suitcase, but they couldn't protest too much, as the web site for the B & B plainly said a cat was in residence.

More like boss of the place than in residence.

As usual, Robbie ignored Éclair. I don't believe dogs belong in kitchens, either, but as long as Rose's cat was allowed in, so was my dog. *So there!*

I didn't, however, ever take her into the tearoom, and letting her have some extra time with me in the morning helped assuage my guilt at leaving her alone for a good part of the day, although I paid the housekeepers a bit extra to take her for a short walk and refresh her water bowl twice a day.

Given that I was American, not English like my grandmother, my first task was always to put the coffeepot on. While I did that, Éclair greeted Rose, and my grandmother patted the dog lightly on the top of her head. Greetings over, Éclair settled herself under the table and watched me with her keen brown eyes. She'd already had her breakfast, and she was never fed in the kitchen, but she never gave up hope.

Rose's house is one of the gems of this stretch of the coast. A marvelous Victorian mansion—white, and multileveled, with a gray roof; numerous turrets and dormer windows, and lavishly adorned with gingerbread trim. A wide verandah running the length of the house; which had been built in 1865 by a wealthy Boston family who wanted privacy and sea views. Except for the bathrooms, every guest room and the public areas were lovingly decorated almost exactly as they would have been when the house was originally built.

Every room, including, unfortunately, this kitchen. At least I didn't have to cook over an open fire or pump water by hand. Somewhere back in the fifties, the owners had made *some* improvements. The kitchen was dark and tiny; the appliances old and dated. Back then, the well-being of the kitchen staff wasn't considered worth putting a window in for, and whoever designed the kitchen clearly never worked in one: the sink was on the far side of the room from the cutlery drawers, and the island so close to the fridge no one could get past when the door was open. But these days, the only meal actually cooked in this kitchen was breakfast. Rose might have invited Bernie and me for dinner this evening, but she didn't intend to cook. My grandmother didn't cook—she reheated. The day after my grandfather's funeral, following a lifetime spent over a stove, Rose hung up her apron forever.

This morning she was dressed in her tattered red-and-purple-checked dressing gown and fluffy woolen slippers. Her thick gray hair stuck up in all directions, and she hadn't yet put her makeup on.

"You're up early," I said. "Problem sleeping?" She didn't usually come down until eight thirty or nine, when she'd pass through the dining room, graciously greeting her guests. Even then she complained—if only to me—about early mornings.

"I got an unwelcome phone call." She rubbed the fingers of her right hand together, as she always did under stress.

I hid a grin. My grandmother had smoked a pack a day every day of her life since she was fourteen, until five years ago, when she'd given it up under doctors' orders after a heart attack scare. It hadn't been her heart, just indigestion and heartburn, but her doctor had torn a strip off her. My mother said she'd never be able to kick the habit, but Rose had gone about it the way she did everything in life once she'd made up her mind: with determination and a will of iron.

She hadn't had so much as a puff since, although her hands obviously still ached to feel the thin, firm roll resting between her fingers.

"Bad news?" I asked.

This morning I was making bran muffins to go with the traditional full English breakfast—eggs, sausages, grilled tomatoes, sautéed mushrooms, baked beans, and toast—which was one of the features of the B & B. For those who didn't want such a substantial start to the day or were watching their weight but still wanted a hot breakfast, I'd make an egg-white omelet. We also served an assortment of cereals and yogurt and a huge bowl of fresh fruit every morning.

Rose didn't answer my question, so I said, "As long as you're up, you can start slicing the fruit." I put a paring knife and a bunch of bananas on the table in front of her.

She gave me a look. The very look that must have intimidated legions of young kitchen maids. "Really, Lily. I don't employ you so I can *work*."

"If by *employ*," I said, "you mean pay a living wage, you're failing on that account."

"I allowed you to rent that old cottage, didn't I?" she said, as though she'd done me a big favor by letting me save her from bankruptcy.

"Whatever. What's the bad news?"

"Gerald has quit."

"Oh, no. That is bad news. What happened? You didn't criticize the hostas again, did you? You know how sensitive he is about them."

"No, I did not criticize the hostas. I learned my lesson the last time. I didn't say they're a thoroughly common plant that anyone can have in their garden."

"Glad to hear it."

"I did think it, though. I considered mentioning that at Thornecroft we had—"

"Yes, yes. I know all about Thornecroft. I also know Gerry refused to even attempt to re-create the Thornecroft gardens here. Not with all the sand in the soil. What made him quit?" I stirred muffin batter as I talked. Rose had pushed the knife and the bananas to one side.

"*Quit* might not be the correct word. He decided to retire and move to Florida."

"Florida? He's Cape Cod born and raised. He always says he's never lived anywhere else in all his fifty-seven years and never intends to."

"It seems he met a lady." Rose sniffed with disapproval.

"Ooh, a lady. Do tell. I suppose this lady is from Florida?"

"Yes. Highly inconsiderate of him, to my mind."

"When does he finish? I hope he gave you enough notice to have time to find someone else."

"Yesterday."

I stopped stirring. "Yesterday?"

"His last day at work was yesterday. They're driving to Florida this morning. He called me from the car." Rose sniffed once again. "At least he was considerate enough to think of me at the last minute."

"Hardly considerate. We'll never get anyone else in the middle of the season."

The gardens at Victoria-on-Sea are large and lush and beautiful and are one of the highlights of the place. It's not easy maintaining an English country garden on the bluffs overlooking Cape Cod Bay, but Gerry and generations of skilled gardeners before him had accomplished miracles. The Victoria-on-Sea gardens occupy almost half an acre with neat hedgerows, carefully placed boxwoods and perennials, tall, swaying grasses, a rose garden, and the occasional statue or little folly scattered about to create interest. Gerald, whom everyone except Rose called Gerry, had worked four days a week, eight months of the year, to keep it all under control.

"Do you have much of a green thumb, Lily?" Rose asked.

"If you're asking me to take on the job of head gardener, along with everything else I do around here, the answer is a firm no. I grew up in an apartment in Manhattan, as you well know. Not much call for gardeners there. Mom didn't even have herbs growing in a pot on the kitchen windowsill."

"Your mother didn't do a lot of things."

"Why don't we not go there? You might be able to get a landscaping firm to come out once or twice a week to at least keep the weeds under control and cut the grass."

"I hope that won't be necessary."

I finished pouring batter into the muffin tins and popped them into the oven. This was a mighty big house, with eight rooms for B & B guests and a private suite for Rose. As she did every evening, last night Rose had left a note tucked under the saltshaker telling me how many to prepare breakfast for. We were almost full today, meaning fourteen meals.

"Not necessary? You'll be surprised how quickly a garden can get out of control. By tomorrow the foxgloves will be waging war on the portulaca."

"Portulaca. Such a lovely word, isn't it? It feels nice in the mouth. Port-chu-laca."

Muffins in the oven, I got the sausages out of the fridge. Whenever possible, I try, here and in the tearoom, to feature locally sourced and produced Cape Cod ingredients. The sausages were handmade by a local butcher. Guests had their choice this morning of pork sausages with spices and hot pepper, hearty German bratwurst, or a mild chicken sausage. In case any of our guests were vegetarians, I kept nonmeat versions in the freezer. Rose's instructions for this morning hadn't said anything about special dietary requirements.

"Are you going to abandon the gardens, then?" I asked. "I know they're an incredible amount of work, but I don't think that's a good idea. Some garden clubs stay here just to spend time in them."

"Gerald has a nephew, newly arrived from England, prepared to take on the job."

"Does this English nephew know one end of a rake from the other?"

"He is, according to Gerald, a professional horticulturalist."

"I wouldn't read too much into that," I said. "Gerald has been known to embellish the truth on occasion."

"Quite. It was difficult to hear him over the roar of the wind as he sped out of town in his new girlfriend's convertible, but I think that's what he said."

"When does this nephew arrive?"

"This afternoon. He's driving in from Boston. You can interview him in the tearoom."

"Me?"

"You manage the staff, love."

"Since when?"

"Since now. I'm promoting you."

"With commensurate pay, I hope," I said, knowing I was wasting my breath.

A tap on the kitchen door and Edna came in, giving us a cheerful "good morning," as she wrapped the strings of her apron around her waist. At least I didn't have to wait tables as well as do all the cooking. Edna was one of my grandmother's bridge partners, and not much younger than her. She'd been complaining at bridge one day in the spring of being bored since her daughter and the grandchildren moved away, and before she knew what was happening, she'd been hired. She also makes many of the delicious jams and other preserves I use and sell in the tea-room.

"I see you've laid out bananas. Shall I start on the fruit?" she asked.

"Seeing as how no one else is slicing them, yes, please." I checked the clock. Six thirty. We start service at seven. "Do you know anyone who's looking for a landscaping job?"

"No," she said, "but I know plenty of people looking for landscapers. Why?"

While Rose filled Edna in on Gerald's romantic entanglements, I poured myself a second cup of coffee. Sausages sizzled on the stove, and the room was full of the aroma of brewing coffee, spitting fat, and warm baking.

"Heads-up," Edna said. "Frank told me the proposal to rezone the property next door is going to a vote the week after next."

Judging by the look on her face, if my grandmother didn't consider herself to be a lady, she'd have spat on the floor.

"Already?" I said. "That was quick. A developer was poking around yesterday."

"Was it Jack Ford by any chance?"

I nodded. "He was with some guy named Gleeson."

"Roy Gleeson's the councillor sponsoring the motion. Jack knows there's opposition, and he hopes to push it through while everyone's busy with their summer businesses."

"Jack Ford can—" my grandmother began.

"Careful, Rose," I said. "My delicate ears."

She poured the last of her tea into the saucer and placed it on the table. Robert the Bruce leapt off her lap, landed lightly on the table, and began to drink. He loved his tea, Robbie did.

"Bad enough feeding the cat *at* the table," I grumbled. "Never mind *on* the table."

"You better hope the health inspectors never pop in unannounced," Edna said.

"You do get the most ridiculous ideas." Rose pushed herself to her feet. "I didn't pour my husband's and my life savings into this place, work my fingers to the bone . . ."

I took the hot muffins out of the oven while checking the condition of the sausages and trying to decide if I had enough tomatoes and mushrooms, calculating if I needed to run to the grocery store before opening the tearoom at eleven or if I had enough flour to last until tomorrow, and instructing Edna to add oranges to the fruit bowl this morning.

"To see some upstart property developer ruin everything," Rose finished.

"Don't do anything rash," I said.

"Really, love. When have you ever known me to be rash?"

I was tossing sausages with my back to my grandmother. "Every single time," I said under my breath.

Edna laughed.

"If you enjoy working here, Lily, best not to make fun of your employer." Rose tapped herself out of the kitchen. Robbie leapt nimbly from the table to the counter next to the stove and eyed the sausages.

Chapter 3

Breakfast finishes at nine. The last guests came down at quarter to; I plated the final two meals, and Edna carried them into the dining room.

Rose had prepared a proper English breakfast—called the full English—for my late grandfather every Saturday, Sunday, and holiday of their married life. A traditional full English has everything except the baked beans fried in a couple of inches of bacon fat: eggs, bacon, sausage, tomatoes, mushrooms, even the bread.

With a nod to modern ideas of healthy eating, I prepared each guest their choice of eggs, fried the sausages and lightly sautéed the tomatoes and mushrooms in olive oil, and toasted the bread in the toaster. No one ever complained they wanted more fat.

Except for Rose.

But Rose never eats breakfast, anyway, so I ignore her. She pretends not to notice.

I checked the clock on the wall and was pleased to see that breakfast had ended early enough to allow me time for a short break before I had to walk up the driveway to the tearoom.

I have the world's best commute. I live in a cottage on the grounds of the B & B, close to the bluffs overlooking Cape Cod Bay, between Rose's house and our nearest neighbor, the property to the south, the one I'd been telling Bernie about yesterday. My cottage would have been a guesthouse or perhaps a residence for the family of a senior member of staff back in the day. It's tiny—one bedroom and a small living room—but I've lived in apartments in Manhattan, and I can handle tiny. The kitchen isn't much more than a sink, a microwave, and a two-burner hot plate, but as I make my living cooking for other people seven days a week, I don't cook much for myself.

The cottage's best feature is the wide porch that runs across the front of the building, overlooking the bluffs and the waters of the bay crashing onto the rocks below. I hadn't brought much with me from New York, and once I arrived, I'd bought the best outdoor furniture I could afford. White wicker chairs, all-weather blue-and-white-striped cushions, a small iron bistro table painted turquoise with two matching chairs. I got several large terra-cotta pots and filled them with an abundance of colorful annuals and tall grasses. A small enclosed yard is off the side door, where Éclair can be let out without needing supervision. She was well trained and generally good around the guests, but I didn't let her run free on the property without me.

I poured myself one more cup of coffee, grabbed a muffin, hung my apron on the hook by the door, and shouted good-bye to Edna. I slipped out the kitchen door of the main house and climbed the three steps up to the ground level. It was a day full of promise: the sun was a huge yellow circle in a pale blue sky, and the lightest breath of wind carried the scent of salt off the ocean.

I planned to go home and finish my coffee and eat my muffin on the porch while watching the activity on the bay. The tearoom opens at eleven, and if I get enough prep done the night before, I look forward to a precious half hour of peace and quiet before leaping back into the fray of a busy kitchen: rolling dough, stirring batter, slicing fruit, icing cakes, making sandwiches. As I got closer to home, I heard shouting. Rose's tiny figure stood at the edge of her property, not far from the bluffs, her long multicolored skirt blowing in the wind as she waved her cane in the faces of the three men facing her.

Oh dear.

Instead of going inside, I broke into a run and headed for the neighboring property. Happy for the exercise, Éclair ran on ahead. Two of the men arguing with Rose were the ones who'd come into the tearoom yesterday, but I didn't recognize the third. He was older than them, well dressed in the Tommy Bahama–type clothes wealthy New Englanders wore on vacation. He had a deep tan, his thick gray hair was expensively cut, and his nails manicured.

"Please calm down, madam," he was saying as I ran up.

I could have told him that was a mistake.

"Calm down!" Rose waved her cane with renewed vigor. "Don't you give me that cheek, you patronizing little twit. I'll calm down when you've taken your ridiculous plan and driven away."

Éclair sniffed at the men's pant legs. They ignored her.

Three vehicles were parked in the weed-choked driveway at the side of the neighbor's house: a gleaming blue Audi, a sleek Lexus SUV, and a black Toyota Camry. The house itself could be used for a Halloween display. The windows were covered in plywood; the Victorian gingerbread trim ripped and sagging, the paint coming off in strips; some of the gutters threatened to crash to the ground; and weeds invaded the cracks in the porch and foundations of the house. A privet hedge lined most of the property line, keeping the house out of view of many of the rooms in Victoria-on-Sea. The hedge was neat and trimmed on one side, a ragged mess on the other.

The hedge ended close to where the land dropped to the beach as well as at the point farther toward the road where the two driveways almost touched. Grass as lush and well cut as could be seen on a golf course was on our side; the weeds and beach grasses on the other were as high as the men's knees.

The weeds reached my grandmother's thighs. Meaning she was on their property.

"What seems to be the problem here?" I asked, trying to keep my tone light and friendly.

"Allow me to handle this, Lily," my grandmother said.

One of the men held his hand out to me. "You were in the tearoom yesterday. Sorry we didn't get a chance to chat. I'm Jack Ford."

I took his hand in mine. His grip was strong, too strong, as though he was engaged in some sort of dominance display. He held my hand a fraction of a second too long as he stared into my face in a way that made me feel uncomfortable. I pulled my hand free. "Lily Roberts. This lady is my grandmother. What's going on here?"

"You need to take your grandmother home," the third man said.

Rose drew herself up to her full five feet, two inches. "I am not a dog nor a small child, to be taken home so the adults can talk in peace."

"Peace," the third man said, "would be nice."

Bored with the lack of attention she was getting, Éclair wandered off to sniff at her surroundings.

"The issue of this property'll be coming to council shortly," Jack said. "I wanted to have another look at it. I haven't come to any final decisions regarding putting an offer in on it yet."

Rose harrumphed. She pointed a finger at Roy Gleeson. "Paid you off, has he?"

Roy stiffened. "That's an insulting accusation. I'm acting strictly in the best interests of the people of North Augusta. It is not in anyone's interest if this property continues to remain an eyesore. Not to mention dangerous."

I couldn't help but glance at one of the gutters, swinging cheerfully in the breeze. "It doesn't have to be rezoned to be sold. Perhaps someone would like to buy it as it is. They could fix it up to be a nice house again."

"Are you interested in purchasing it, miss?" the third man asked.

"Me? No. I don't want anything that big, and I couldn't afford it even if I did."

"Which is exactly my problem," he said. "No one wants a house that big, certainly not one that needs work before it can be inhabitable. I'm Lincoln Goodwill. This is my property. Your grandmother is trespassing, and I have asked her to leave."

"You should be ashamed of yourself," Rose said. "Selling off your family's land to a common hotel chain. What would your ancestors have to say about that?"

Lincoln turned around. He studied the house, slowly crumbling into the sandy soil, the gardens, nothing but tough weeds, wild beach grasses, and stunted bushes. "I doubt my ancestors would like to see it drop off the cliff."

"If the property's developed to its full potential," Jack Ford said, "the benefits to the entire community will be enormous. That includes your B & B and charming little teahouse."

Patronizing twit, indeed.

"This is a delicate stretch of oceanfront environment,"

Rose said. "The cliffs are fragile. Birds nest there and in the trees surrounding."

"The town will take all of that into consideration when . . . I mean if . . . we decide to rezone," Roy said.

"You've obviously already made up your mind," Rose said.

"Nothing to decide," he said. "The rezoning is in everyone's interest. Almost everyone."

"If you'll excuse us. I'm a busy man." Jack turned to the others. "Let's have a closer look at these cliffs. We'll need to take their fragility into account."

"I'm thinking the clubhouse could go there," Lincoln said. "Nice view out to sea."

"Clubhouse!" Rose yelled.

Jack lost his patience, and the fake neighborly smile was instantly replaced by something very nasty indeed. "Mrs. Campbell, your opposition to this project is indefensible. You can't expect to live in solitary splendor the remainder of your days."

"I see no reason why not," Rose replied.

"Your neighboring landowner disagrees."

Rose waved her cane in the developer's face. "This project will go ahead over my dead body."

"Don't tempt us," Lincoln muttered. Jack laughed.

"Watch it," I said.

Startled by my tone, Éclair lifted her head and barked. Lincoln had the grace to flush and duck his head.

"Come on, gentlemen," Roy said. "We can't stand around chatting all day. We've all got work to get back to."

"I suggest you don't make idle threats, Mrs. Campbell," Jack said. "That cane can be turned into a weapon."

"I assure you," Rose replied, "I never make idle threats. If not my dead body, perhaps someone else's."

I touched her arm. "This has gone far enough, Rose. Let's go back to the house."

"I'm not moving." She planted her cane and her feet firmly among the long grasses and the weeds.

"You're trespassing," Jack said. "If you don't leave, Mr. Goodwill is within his rights to call the police and have you removed."

"I don't want any trouble," Lincoln Goodwill mumbled.

"Whether you want trouble or not, you've got it," Rose said. "Trouble and more, if you go ahead with this project."

"The project isn't up to me," he said. "I don't care what anyone does with the property once they own it. All I want is to sell this eyesore my father saddled me with. No one in our family has come here for years, but my father had sentimental reasons for keeping it. And so he kept paying the property taxes on it. I don't want it, and I can't afford to repair it. Mr. Ford here"—he nodded toward the big man—"is considering buying it as it is. A win-win. The entire community will benefit—"

"It is not a win-win for me," Rose said. "I will not benefit."

"Please, Rose. This isn't doing anyone any good." I took her free arm and tucked it into mine. "Let's go home. Maybe you can start making some phone calls. Ask the neighbors for their support at town council."

"Neighbors. That's the entire point. I don't have any neighbors. And I don't want any. Much less a golf course! If I find one golf ball on my property, or a single spare nail, I'm calling the police."

She wrenched her arm out of mine, spun on her heel, and marched away, shouting over her shoulder, "Mark my words! You haven't heard the last of this! I will stop this project. One way or another."

I called to Éclair and started after Rose.

"I don't want any trouble," Lincoln repeated to his companions.

"Don't worry about that one," Jack said. "She's nuttier than an English fruitcake. And she'll crumble like one."

I decided it would be best not to mention that English fruitcake does not traditionally contain nuts. Or that my grandmother never crumbled in the face of opposition.

Chapter 4

I made the mistake of trying to argue with Rose. "The property is a shambles. The house looks like the set of *Night of the Living Dead*. Is a conference hotel and golf course really going to be so bad?"

She glared at me. "I came to Cape Cod in search of peace and quiet for my declining years. I am not going to have dump trucks and jackhammers breaking the silence at all hours of the day and night, and then corrupt politicians and crooked businessmen in ghastly pastel trousers and checked shirts yelling, 'Fore,' and knocking my planters over with their golf balls. I will stop this development, Lily."

"Plenty of nice people golf, you know."

"I am making a point, Lily."

"So am I. If you want peace and quiet in your declining years, as you call them, going up against town hall isn't a good way to go about it. I doubt you'll get much support, if any, when the vote comes up to change the zoning. The project will bring jobs to the area, and it won't ruin the view of anyone except you—us. You might even benefit from overflow business from the hotel. The tearoom will."

"Whose side are you on, Lily?"

"I'm on your side, Rose. In everything. And because I'm on your side, I'm asking you to face facts."

She harrumphed. No one but my grandmother could put so much disapproval into a single sound.

We turned at the beep of a horn. A dusty red car was turning off the main road. Cheryl tooted again and waved.

"Time to go to work." I was still holding my coffee mug and uneaten muffin. So much for a relaxing break before plunging into a day in the kitchen.

"Don't do anything rash," I said to my grandmother.

Once again, I might have saved my breath.

It was almost eleven: opening time. Cheryl was in the tearoom's enclosed patio, putting the finishing touches on the tables, Marybeth was starting on the sandwiches, and I was up to my elbows in shortbread dough when the swinging half doors opened and Bernie's tousled red curls popped in. "Knock, knock," she said. "Can I come in? Cheryl told me you were here."

"Sure. I'd tell you to take a seat, but we don't have one." The kitchen was barely big enough for me and one helper as it was.

Bernie leaned against the counter next to the sink and studied my domain. "So this is where it all happens, is it? It's . . . uh . . ."

"Small?" I said.

"Small."

"I prefer to say compact. I know where everything is, and I can put my hand on anything I need in a moment."

Bernie sucked in her stomach and moved aside to let Marybeth get to the fridge. "I suppose there's that. What smells so nice?"

"Miniature cinnamon buns for the children's tea." I slipped my oven mitts on and lifted the baking sheets out of the oven. A wave of warm sugar and spicy cinnamon goodness washed over me, and I almost groaned in pleasure. No matter how many pastries I've made over my lifetime, I never get tired of these scents. Or of the pleasure in producing beautiful food and having it enjoyed.

I put the little buns on cooling racks as I said, "How are you today?"

"Terrible," Bernie said.

Once I had the shortbread dough rolled out to a suitable size and thickness, I patted it into the baking sheet ready to be popped into the waiting oven. I was working at the square butcher's block in the center of the room, the top of which was devoted exclusively to rolling pastry and dough. Today we'd be serving traditional English shortbread, made from a recipe that supposedly came from the kitchens of Buckingham Palace itself. Shortbread is normally a Christmas treat, but my customers love it no matter the time of year. It's the perfect accompaniment to a cup of fragrant tea and the centerpiece of our featured light tea offering for those with smaller appetites.

"Are you sick?" I glanced up from the dough and studied my friend's face. She looked okay. "If you're coming down with something, I'll have to ask you to leave the kitchen."

"Not sick, no." She threw up her hands and moaned in despair. "My life is a disaster! Everything I touch leads to failure!"

I left the dough—it wouldn't hurt it to sit a few minutes—and hurried to wash my hands. I dried them on my apron and then gathered my best friend into my arms as she started to cry. "What's happened? Is it your mom? You said she wasn't doing too well."

Bernie sobbed into my chest. "Mom's fine. It's . . . it's my book. I'm stuck!"

I released Bernie and turned my attention back to the shortbread.

"You don't understand," Bernie cried. "I have a terrible case of writer's block. I can't come up with a single decent idea. My characters are boring. I keep peeking over my shoulder, expecting to see them standing there, accusing me, blaming me for their dull lives."

"What happened since yesterday?" I finished patting the dough into place in the baking sheet. "I thought the change of environment was unleashing your pent-up energies and freeing your imagination."

"It didn't," she moaned. "I sat at my desk at seven this morning, excited and ready to start work." She pulled a tattered tissue out of the pocket of her shorts and wiped at her eyes.

"And . . . ?"

"And nothing. Nothing came to me. Not one single word." She blew her nose. "I might as well go back to New York. Not that I have a job or apartment to go back to, and I've paid two months' rent on the place here in advance."

I refrained from saying, "I told you so." But I thought it. "Maybe you need to give it time."

I'd read the short stories Bernie had had published over the past few years. They were good—more than good. She had genuine talent; her writing worked on the reader's emotions in a way I'd rarely come across. But three short stories in five years do not a writing career make. She'd been writing a novel for more than two years now, and I no longer asked how it was going. Not since the first time I'd done so and then spent the next hour trying to comfort her. Whenever she had talked about it, she'd said it was taking so long because her mind was always too occupied with her accounting job and she couldn't focus properly.

I'd been hoping the move to the Cape would give her the time and the headspace she needed. Apparently not.

"I'm kinda busy," I said to her now. "We have reservations for a full house this afternoon. Let's do an exchange. You tell me about the book—talking about it might open your imagination—while you take over from Marybeth and finish that lot of sandwiches."

"I suppose I can do that." Bernie gave her eyes a final wipe and stuffed the tissue into her pocket.

"What do you want me to do instead?" Marybeth asked.

"Ice the cinnamon buns, please. They should be cool enough by now."

"I don't know what you want me to make," Bernie said.

"First, wash your hands. Second, assembly and arrangement instructions are in that folder on the top shelf. It looks as though Marybeth has started the curried cucumber. You can finish them. Next, we need egg and roast beef."

"Egg and roast beef? That doesn't sound very good."

"Egg sandwiches and roast beef sandwiches, Bernie. The egg salad mixture is prepared and in the fridge. The roast beef will be open-faced, with spicy mustard underneath the meat and arugula on top."

The chimes over the door tinkled, announcing the arrival of the first customers of the day.

Bernie set to work. Cheryl came into the kitchen to place an order. Cream tea (meaning just tea and scones) for four, with two pots of tea: Creamy Earl Grey and English breakfast. Marybeth began arranging the scones on flower-patterned china plates and preparing the tea. Shortbread in the oven, I started on today's batch of pistachio macarons. Bernie talked as she worked. Her novel had potential, I thought. It was to be a multigenerational historical saga beginning with a family that set sail from Ireland for New York in the late seventeenth century.

"That sounds good," Marybeth said. "I'd read that."

"Thanks." Bernie worked slowly and methodically. It was taking her forever to assemble the sandwiches, but she was giving me free labor, so I wasn't going to complain. "I know what I want to happen overall, but I'm stuck on this important scene, and I can't see a way through it."

"Stop right there," I said. "The women are shipwrecked, is that right?"

"Yes. When Esmeralda is fleeing her abusive husband. I'm having trouble generating the feeling of panic."

"First, drop the name Esmeralda. Second, go for a walk on the beach. Right now. Do you have your phone on you?"

"Of course."

"Take pictures. It's a calm day, and the beach is on the bay, not the open ocean, but you can use your imagination. Smell the sea, feel the sand between your toes, watch the waves, observe the birds. Ignore the tourists. Open your mind."

Bernie threw down her knife and threw up her hands. "You are a marvel, Lily Roberts, a marvel. That's a fabulous idea." She pushed the doors open and ran through them. She was back before they stopped swinging. "Where's the nearest beach?"

"You can get to it from the back of the B & B, the far side of the house from my cottage. It's a steep drop, so there are stairs leading down. Take care on the steps. They need some maintenance."

The doors swung again, and she was gone.

They continued swinging, and Cheryl's head popped into the kitchen. "We've got a sudden rush out there. Three tables arrived at the same time. They should be finished when the people with reservations start arriving."

"Marybeth," I said, "finish those sandwiches, please." Bernie had left behind a mound of neatly sliced cucumber.

The bell on the oven beeped, and I checked the shortbread. Absolute golden perfection. I took the sheet out and sprinkled the hot shortbread lightly with sugar to give it a bit of crunch.

"Someone to see you, Lily," Cheryl said from the doorway. "A man. He says he has a job interview?"

"A job interview? I'm not hiring."

"That's good," Marybeth said, "as I don't plan on leaving."

I mentally slapped my forehead. The gardener position. Gerald's English nephew.

Timing was not good. We had reservations that would give us a full house from one until four, and I still had a great deal of baking to do. Marybeth was a good kitchen assistant, but she was not a pastry chef, and she doubled as a waitress when we were busy.

"I guess I have to see him if he's come all this way. I'll try to make it quick. Do we have an empty table?"

"The tables for two in the tearoom are all taken," Cheryl said, "and you don't want to use a bigger one, in case we get more drop-in customers. A couple of tables outside are still free."

"Thanks. I'll take one of those. I'll try to be quick. The scones are baked, and most of the pastries are ready, so we should be good for now unless we get some picky eaters. Marybeth, can you slice the shortbread, please? It needs to be done before it cools." I washed my hands, didn't bother to take off my apron, and went into the dining room.

Tables of women were sipping tea, nibbling sandwiches and pastries, and laughing. A pink-cheeked baby sat in a high chair, banging his spoon on the tray while his mother tried to ignore him. Looking totally out of place, a young man dressed in jeans, T-shirt, and heavy work boots stood facing the wall, studying a painting of a fox hunt.

"Hi," I said. "I believe you're looking for me?"

He turned and held out his right hand. I took it in mine. His greeting was firm, but not aggressive. "I'm Simon McCracken. Here about the gardening position."

"Lily Roberts. I own this tearoom, and I assist my grandmother, Rose Campbell, with the running of her B & B. Pleased to meet you, Simon. Shall we go outside for a few minutes? Would you like a cup of tea? I can promise you it will be made exactly as you'd get back home."

He grinned. "I'd love a cuppa. Thank you."

His accent was fresh from London. Upper middle class, maybe a private school, maybe not. I signaled to Cheryl to bring two teas and led the way outside.

The cottage that's now the tearoom is built of stone and wood and is about a hundred years older than the house. When we turned it into my restaurant, I planted climbing vines around the base, hung a swinging sign over the door, and laid a flagstone floor in the yard, which was now dotted with tables and chairs, some of them under pink and blue umbrellas. Masses of terra-cotta pots overflowing with red and white geraniums, purple lobelia, white bacopa, and trailing sweet potato vines lined the stone half wall enclosing the patio. On the branches of an old oak in the center of the garden, I'd hung a multitude of cracked and mismatched teacups from brightly colored ribbons, which had already faded in the sun.

Simon and I took a seat in the far corner of the enclosed patio. He smiled at me. He was around my age, early thirties, about six feet tall, lean but well muscled, with sandy hair streaked by the sun, blue eyes, and prominent cheekbones. His face and his arms, thick with muscle, were heavily tanned, as befitted a man who worked outdoors.

"Nice place," he said. "I had a quick look around when I got here. You've done a good job with a harsh environment."

"We're proud of it. Tell me what experience you have with ocean-side gardens."

Fifteen minutes later, I had a gardener. We shook hands on the deal and exchanged contact information. He said he'd start work at six tomorrow morning, and I went back into the tearoom. Before going to the kitchen, I stood in the doorway, watching Simon leave. A motorcycle was parked in the lot, a leather jacket tossed over the seat. He put on the jacket, untied a black helmet and placed it on his head, climbed onto the seat, kicked the engine to life, and roared away. He didn't look back.

As I turned, I caught sight of a short, chubby figure in a flowing cotton dress walking at a rapid clip through the gardens in the direction of the Goodwill house. She did not stop to admire the flowers. The blue Audi that had been there this morning was now the only car in the Goodwill driveway. I gave the woman no more thought and went back to work.

We ate dinner at the kitchen table. Bernie arrived bearing a chilled bottle of white wine and a huge grin. She hugged me and then hugged Rose with such enthusiasm, Rose said, "What's gotten into you?"

"Thanks to Lily, I have had the best idea ever!"

"What's that?" I asked as I twisted the cap on the wine and poured two glasses.

"I'm abandoning Esmeralda and the saga of the O'Brian and Escalada families and Manhattan itself and starting over. My new book will be set on Cape Cod. Isn't that absolutely fabulous?"

"What about all the work you've done so far?" Rose asked.

Bernie waved her hand in the air, dismissing two years' worth of effort and an ocean's worth of tears. "It wasn't coming along very well. I'm going to start researching the settlers on the Cape. Their stories must be absolutely fascinating. The ocean—and this was Lily's idea—will play a huge part. My novel will be about the relationship of the people to the sea. I started it this afternoon, as soon as I got home from a walk on the beach. All these ideas kept flooding into my head, and I wrote up an absolute storm. That's a pun. Do you get it?"

"I get it." Rose sipped her gin and tonic. She enjoyed one G&T every evening, the habit of a lifetime. Robert the Bruce watched the activity from the comfort of her lap, and Éclair snoozed in front of the stove. "You have one flighty idea after another. If you want to have a book published, Bernadette, you need to finish it. Not start another."

"But this one's sure to be a huge success." Bernie beamed. "People are really interested in the history of Cape Cod."

"And that is why—"

"I'm pleased for you," I said quickly. I lifted my glass. "Cheers." Bernie and I clinked glasses. "Whenever you feel writer's block coming on, you can step out the door and drink in the atmosphere."

"Exactly!"

"Stuff and nonsense," Rose said.

I glared at my grandmother. She gave me a sweet smile in return.

"You'll be proud of me, Rose," Bernie said, "when I hit the *New York Times* bestseller list."

"Which won't happen if the book is never finished."

Bernie grinned at her. She never took offense when Rose was being forthright. Rose and Bernie had been close since we were seven years old and my grandparents had visited Manhattan. It rained on and off the day we went on an excursion to Central Park, a cold, dark rain warning of winter soon to come. My mother and I cowered in the shelter of the steps of the Metropolitan Museum of Art, while Bernie and Rose cavorted in the rain, loving every drop and splashing through every puddle.

I might look like Rose, but when it came to personality, anyone might have thought Bernie was her granddaughter, not me.

"Maybe you should check the pie, Rose," I said. The grocery-store box the meat pie had come in was sticking out of the trash can.

She didn't move. "It's fine. You can start the salad, love. Ingredients are in the fridge."

I checked the pie, noticed the crust was blackening around the edges, and turned the oven off. I then opened the small fridge, the one used for Rose herself, not B & B cooking. It contained nothing but a loaf of bread, a stick of butter, a container of milk, a handful of condiments, and a package of presliced salad ingredients, complete with dressing.

"It's June in New England. You should be buying fresh ingredients from the farm markets. Better for you, far better tasting, and you'll be supporting your neighbors at the same time."

"Why should I support my neighbors?" she said. "They're not supporting me."

"Supporting you in what?" Bernie asked.

"Don't ask," I said. But I was too late.

"I submitted an article to the local newspaper this afternoon," Rose said. "It was returned to me as unacceptable. Imagine the cheek!"

I groaned. I had no doubt what this "article" was about.

"What do you mean, they returned it to you?" Bernie asked. "If they didn't want it, they wouldn't publish it, not get into a discussion."

"They said it was libelous. Stuff and nonsense. Email makes things happen too fast. In my day, it would take a day for the letter to get to its destination, the recipient would take time to consider it and to write a polite and appropriate response, and then a day for the return letter to arrive in the post."

"Whereupon you'd have waited three days, rather than ten minutes, to be rejected," Bernie pointed out.

Éclair jumped to her feet and let out a soft bark. Moments later, a light tap sounded on the door, and Edna peered into the room.

"Sorry to bother you. May I come in? I don't want to interrupt your dinner, but . . ."

"Of course," I said. "Is everything okay?"

Edna glanced at Rose, calming, sitting at the table, stroking Robbie with one hand and sipping her G&T with the other. "It depends on what you mean by okay. As long as I was coming, I brought you some jam." She put a bag on the counter. From inside came the sound of glass jars bumping together.

"I'm running low on your tomato salsa," I said. "The guests love it."

"Nothing I can do about that until tomato season."

"Fair enough. Can't rush a tomato. Would you like a glass of wine?"

"Thanks, but no. I won't stay long. Frank suggested I drop by and have a word, Rose."

"I'm sure he did," Rose replied.

"A word about what?" Bernie asked.

I had a bad feeling about this. Edna's husband, Frank, was the editor in chief of the *North Augusta Times*. "You're here about a letter Rose wrote to the paper?"

"Not a letter, but an op-ed article she wanted him to print." Edna turned to my grandmother. "You can't be libeling people, Rose."

"I speak my mind."

"You might, but my husband isn't going to print it."

"Coward," Rose said. "I thought better of him. Whatever happened to a free and independent press?"

Edna looked at me. "I thought you should know, Lily, in case she . . . uh . . . tries another avenue to get her opinions out."

"Tell me," Rose said. "Are your husband and his newspaper also getting kickbacks from this scheme?"

"That's ridiculous," Edna said.

"Is it?" Rose asked. "Didn't the paper run an editorial recently saying the Goodwill property was too valuable to be allowed to fall into ruin? To continue to fall even further into ruin?"

"A great many people in town think the same," Edna said. "That doesn't mean we're all being paid to think so."

"You include yourself in that number?"

"I do."

"Then you're fired," Rose said.

Robert the Bruce hissed and leapt off Rose's lap.

"You can't fire me," Edna said.

"You are not fired," I said.

"Yes, you are," Rose said.

"You can't fire me, because I quit." Edna spun on her heel and headed for the door.

I threw up my hands. "Please, don't leave mad, Edna. I need you. You work for me, not my grandmother."

"She pays my wages, not you." Edna opened the door and stepped into the soft glow of early twilight.

"I need you," I repeated.

"Good night, Lily." Edna climbed the steps, her back straight and her head high.

"Now you've done it," I said to my grandmother. "Be here, in this kitchen, promptly at six thirty tomorrow morning. I cannot cook and wait tables at the same time. How many rooms do we have tonight?"

"As it's a Friday, we are full. Sixteen adults and five children."

"Twenty-one breakfasts. You'll have to help."

"Really, Lily. I told you when I hired you, I do not wait on tables."

"Someone has to."

"Even if I wanted to, which I do not, I'm too unsteady on my feet to be carrying trays of hot tea and taking food from the oven." She attempted to look frail.

Whether that was true or not, Rose had made her point. She would not back down, not even to do so much as supervise the making of the toast. I turned to Bernie. "Six thirty. On the dot. We start breakfast service at seven."

"That's early. I hope . . . Oh, you mean you want me to help?"

"That's right."

"I wish I could, but I can't. Morning's my best working time. That's why I moved here, right? To get an early start. Sorry."

I took the pie out of the oven. It looked highly unappetizing. "You're doing a historical novel, right?"

"Yes. Parts of it, anyway. I'm thinking of weaving the present and the past together. It might have a supernatural aspect, as one woman tries to—"

"Hold on a sec." I tore open the bag of premixed salad ingredients and dumped the contents into a bowl. Equally unappetizing. "For a historical novel to have an authentic feel and atmosphere, you need insight into the lives of the common worker of the times. Your characters can't all be from the upper classes. You need to bring maids, servants, kitchen workers to life. As they would have lived their working lives in a grand old house. Say, one built on Cape Cod Bay in the eighteen sixties. Be here at six thirty on the dot."

"I get the point," Bernie said.

"Excellent," Rose said. "I told you not to worry, Lily.

As Mrs. Harrison always said at Thornecroft, these things have a way of working themselves out."

Despite the bad start—and the poor food—dinner was a pleasant affair. Rose chatted gaily about news of family members (every one of whom had told me I was crazy to even consider going into business with her) and told us she was considering taking a cruise over the winter.

I told them I'd hired a gardener and he'd be starting tomorrow.

"On a Saturday?" Bernie said.

"One day blends into another around here. The only difference on the weekends is we're busier in both the tearoom and the B & B. If he wants to work weekends, that's fine with me."

"I hope you didn't offer to pay too high a wage, Lily," Rose said.

"He's getting the same as Gerry."

"That's ridiculous. Gerald had been in the employ of this house for many years. Long before I bought it."

"Yes, and he treated it like his own private garden, so he didn't mind that you paid what he probably made back in nineteen seventy-eight, when he started."

"He worked here that long?" Bernie said.

"I'm guessing," I said. "If we want a young, qualified gardener with seaside experience, at the height of the season, we have to pay accordingly."

"What's for dessert?" Rose asked.

"You invited us for dinner," I said. "What did you make?"

She pushed her nearly empty plate to the side of the table. Robert the Bruce made a flying leap across the room and landed nimbly next to it. He bent his head, and his little pink tongue flicked across the plate, scooping up the last of the beef and gravy.

"You shouldn't feed the cat on the table," Bernie said. "The health inspectors won't like it."

"Do I see any so-called health inspectors in my kitchen? I do not. I shall therefore continue to do what I want in my own house."

Robbie lifted his head and threw Bernie a self-satisfied smirk.

The phone on the wall rang. It was an old-fashioned thing, bright pink with big square buttons and a receiver you shouted into at one end and listened from at the other. As Rose made no move to get up and answer, I did so.

"Victoria-on-Sea Bed-and-Breakfast. Good evening."

"Oh, hi, Lily. It's Cheryl here. I was calling Rose."

"I'll get her."

"Hold on. It might be a better idea to run this past you first."

"Who is it?" Rose asked.

I gave her a wave. "What's up?"

"My sister's daughter Andrea works at the courthouse. She isn't really suitable for that job, being somewhat of a gossip, but tomorrow it'll be common news, anyway."

"What will be common news tomorrow?"

"Who is it?" Rose shook her hand at me. "Give me that."

"Andrea knows I work at the tearoom," Cheryl said, "and everyone knows you're Rose's granddaughter, and . . ."

"And . . . ?"

"Jack Ford has filed papers suing your grandmother for slander."

Chapter 5

Because I didn't trust Bernie to remember she was supposed to be working at the B & B this morning or to not make an excuse if she did remember, I sent her a text as soon as I woke up.

When I came out of the shower, towel-drying my hair and mentally inventorying the contents of the tearoom freezer, she'd replied: **I'm up. Now. You owe me. Big-time.**

At five to six, Éclair and I made our daily commute across the yard toward the house. The property is perched on the west side of the long curving peninsula that makes up the Outer Cape section of Cape Cod, overlooking Cape Cod Bay toward the mainland. The sun doesn't rise over the water, but the morning view is still spectacular when the long rays of light creep slowly across the bay. There was no wind this morning, and the surface of the water was as smooth and shiny as the surface of the glass tray we served breakfast muffins on. By Cape Cod standards, we're pretty high here, about a hundred and twenty-five feet above sea level, giving me a nice view of the morning's activity on the bay. Working fishing boats, charters, and sailboats dotted the calm blue water. In a few hours the whale-watching boats would pass by, heading for the top of the Cape and the open ocean and the animals' feeding grounds. I stood at the edge of the bluffs, and leaned on the fence protecting walkers from the sharp drop-off. I breathed the sea air and felt the soft, salty wind caress my face, while Éclair ran in circles, sniffing at the ground. I could think of no better place to start the day. Whenever I began to regret leaving Manhattan, I came here, stood still, and simply breathed.

"Good morning. Hope I'm not disturbing you." I turned to see Simon McCracken coming toward me, dressed in brown overalls, a white T-shirt, and high-laced brown boots. The wind ruffled his hair, a pale lock fell over his forehead, and he was smiling broadly. "Beautiful day."

"You're not disturbing me," I said. "When I can, I like to take a moment on my way to work to admire my surroundings. I'm happy to share the view with anyone who appreciates it."

"This high up, it must be one of the best views along the coast."

"It is."

Éclair sniffed at his boots, and he bent over to give her a hearty pat. "Nice dog. My parents are looking after my two chocolate Labs while I'm away. I miss them a lot. What's this lady's name?"

"Éclair."

He laughed as he straightened up. "I should have guessed. She looks like one with that coloring."

I didn't tell him I hadn't named her. I inherited the dog from a roommate, also a pastry chef. My roommate went to Los Angeles on vacation, got a job, fell in love, and never came back to Manhattan. She asked me to pack up her clothes and mail them to her. I considered sticking a stamp on the dog's nose and sending her by the US Postal Service, but that didn't seem terribly practical. Rather than search for another roommate, I decided to rent a smaller place, and I intended to find another home for the dog. But somehow, slowly, she worked her wiles on me and wormed her way into my affections, and we'd been together ever since. My mother told me I was insane to keep a dog in Manhattan but, as usual, if my mother said it, I had to do the opposite.

Which, come to think of it, was part of the reason I was here in Cape Cod, in business with Rose.

"Come into the kitchen," I said to Simon, "and I'll get you the key to the garden shed. Everything you need should be in there. If you have to buy anything, keep the receipts and we'll reimburse you. Gerry had me save coffee grounds and used tea leaves from the tearoom for him to use in the garden."

"I'll take them, too. Plants love them. Plus any kitchen scraps I can use for compost."

"In exchange, if you can bring us fresh flowers in the morning to put on the tables, I'd appreciate it. Don't decimate the plants. Just cut any extras they can spare."

"It's a deal," he said.

"One more thing. You're welcome to pop into the kitchen here and make yourself a tea or coffee at any time. The doors are only locked at night."

"Thanks, Lily. I know I'm going to enjoy working here. If you don't mind my saying, that looks dangerous." He pointed to the steep staircase leading down to the beach. Some of the boards were cracked or tilting ominously, and the railing had come unfastened in places. A few steps were missing altogether. The gate at the top of the steps rattled on its rusty hinges.

"I know. It's but another thing we need to get done. Gerry was supposed to fix it. He'd been saying for months he'd get around to it. He never did."

"I saw kids playing near here yesterday, when I was

poking around. You don't want any accidents. I'll do it this weekend if you want. I can fix the gate for a start."

"That would be marvelous. Thank you." The last thing we needed was a lawsuit. Another lawsuit, I should say.

I smiled at him. He smiled at me.

"Good morning!" Two women crossed the lawn, heading for the stairs. They were dressed in khaki shorts and sturdy shoes, with binoculars around their necks and hiking poles in each hand. They walked with firm, determined strides and looked as cheerful as only people on vacation could. They unlatched the gate, stepped through it, and carefully closed it behind them.

"Careful on the stairs," I called after them.

"Let's get that key, shall we?" Simon said.

By six thirty, I had two types of muffins in the oven—banana chocolate chip for the children and bran and walnut for the adults—and sausages sizzling on the stove. I was grating cheese for the herb and red pepper frittata, which would be an optional extra this morning, when the kitchen door opened.

"Spot on time," I said. "First, lay out the cereal with milk and the pots of yogurt in the dining room in case anyone comes down early, and then start cutting the fruit for the salad."

"I know what to do, Lily," Edna said.

I turned around. "Oh. Good morning. I wasn't expecting you today."

"Why not?"

"Because last night you were fired and then you quit. Or did you quit and then were fired? I forget the exact order of events."

She shrugged and took her apron down from the hook. "Life goes on. Rose says things she sometimes doesn't mean. I have to admit that I do, too, on occasion."

"I'm glad you're here. Before you start, something upsetting happened last night I'd like to ask you about. Did your husband show Jack Ford the letter Rose sent to the paper?"

She twisted her mouth into a moue of disapproval and took the cheese grater and the cheese from me. I started cracking eggs.

"I assume by your question that someone did," she said. "I can assure you it was not Frank. He wouldn't have done that, particularly if he didn't intend to print the letter, but he has a summer intern working at the paper, and I don't approve of her. She's far too ambitious and far too impulsive. I wouldn't put it past her to have sent Rose's email to Jack, hoping for a reaction."

"She got one. Why does your husband keep her on if she's not working out?"

"One, she's free. And two, she's our niece. Frank's brother's daughter Ilana."

"Oh."

"Oh is right. Ilana intends to be the next Rachel Maddow. Frank's too kindhearted to fire her. I hope he does if he finds out she did what you think she did."

"Jack has filed papers to sue Rose over that letter."

"Sorry I'm late." Bernie burst into the room. She wore a calf-length black dress with long sleeves and a stiff white collar, thick black stockings, and black flats. She'd tied her mane of curls into a severe bun at the back of her head, removed all the hoops from her ears, and her face was clear of makeup. "Hi. I thought you were fired?"

"I unfired myself," Edna said.

"Why are you dressed like that?" I asked.

Bernie held out her arms and twirled around. "Like it? I'm getting myself totally into the part. I want to *feel* the oppression of the working classes, so I'm dressed like a footman."

"Footmen are men."

"Not much I can do about that," she said.

"I guess not, but if you want to truly feel the oppression of the working classes, you should try running a restaurant in the tourist season."

"Or working for Rose Campbell." Having grated a mountain of cheese while we talked, Edna took containers of yogurt out of the fridge, poured milk and orange and apple juice into jugs, and got down cereal boxes.

I laughed. "I'm glad you're here. We'll be busy this morning, and Edna can use the help."

"I certainly can," Edna said. "But what's this about suing?"

"Oh, yeah," Bernie said. "That. You probably heard Rose yelling all the way in town. I learned some new English expressions last night."

"Jack has to have seen the email Rose sent to the paper," I said. "He's suing her."

"Have you seen this letter?" Edna placed everything on a tray.

"Sadly, yes." After Cheryl called last night, I'd insisted on Rose taking me to her computer. I searched the sent folder and found the email. It wasn't, to say the least, flattering to the property developer. She didn't actually come out and say he was working for the mob, but it was implied. She did more than imply that he was either accepting bribes from members of town council or bribing them.

"Suing her over an unpublished letter seems a drastic step," Edna said.

"It's a good way of ensuring everyone in town reads the contents of a letter that was going to otherwise remain unpublished," I said.

"Jack's a local boy who's done well for himself," Edna said. "Some say not entirely by following the letter of the law. He has his enemies around here, for sure. Maybe he's expecting someone else to come out against him soon, and he decided to send them a message."

"And Rose just happened to be the nearest target. She's going to have to back down. We can't afford to pay him a cent or to hire a lawyer to fight this for us."

"Do you think she will?" Bernie asked. "Fight it?"

Edna snorted, and I said, "Rose back down? Not a chance. She's going to push forward more than ever, guns blazing. What a mess. Nothing we can do about that right now. I'll have a talk with her later and try to talk some sense into her. Last night she was almost gleeful at the thought of taking him on. Bernie, get to work. You can slice the tomatoes and mushrooms. If we're lucky, the suit won't go ahead. He's only trying to intimidate her."

"Little does he know," Edna said, "that Rose doesn't take terribly well to intimidation."

"Guaranteed to rile her up and get her even more firmly on the warpath." The sausages were perfectly browned, and I turned the heat off.

"Has she come in yet this morning?" Bernie asked.

"No. I hope she sleeps in until I can make my escape," I said.

"Good morning!" a voice called from the dining room. "Anyone there?"

I glanced at the clock. Ten to seven.

Edna picked up the tray. "And so the oppression of the working classes begins."

"What do you want me to do?" Bernie asked.

"First, slice those mushrooms and tomatoes and toss them into that pan with a splash of olive oil and give them a light sautéing. Then be ready when Edna comes back with the breakfast orders and assemble the plates accordingly."

* * *

The final guests didn't come down until one minute to nine, so it was nine twenty before I hung up my apron. We were expecting another busy day in the tearoom; I'd have to miss my relaxing time-out on the porch this morning.

"You can run along now," Edna said to Bernie. "I'll clear up and set the tables for tomorrow."

"Thanks. I can't wait to get home and back to my laptop. I've got great ideas for the scene where Tessa O'Flannahan is fired for spilling the soup in Lord Blackheart's lap."

"Tell me you didn't name a character Lord Blackheart," I said.

"I didn't, but that's what I'm calling him until I think up something better. This is the opening scene of the book. A fancy dinner party, and poor Tessa is trying to avoid Lord Blackheart's wandering hands when she spills the soup, but she's fired for it. Tossed out on her ear to fend for herself."

"Women didn't serve at table at fancy dinner parties," I said.

"They do in my book," Bernie said.

I poured myself a cup of coffee and took off my apron and hung it on the hook by the door. Éclair knew what that meant, and she got to her feet with a mighty stretch.

"That's that done," I said. "On to the next job. What are you up to for the rest of the day?"

"Writing, of course. I'm so excited about the scene where Tessa's fired. Having no other options, she decides at the last minute to join her aunt and uncle and take sail to America. They think they're going to Boston but end up on Cape Cod."

I opened the kitchen door, and Bernie and I stepped outside. Éclair ran on ahead. "You might want to do some historical research before you get too far into it. That way you won't have to make a lot of changes later." Such as not having Tessa be a footman. We climbed the three steps to the ground level. Bernie threw out her arms and took several deep breaths.

"This is so great. I'm so glad I came. All I need is some peace and quiet. Manhattan was too noisy and crowded."

"I have a book I'll lend you. It was in the house when Rose bought it. Some great pictures and drawings of the early days on the Cape. You can come and get it now."

"Pictures are good." Bernie fell into step beside me. "I wish I had a sea view like this one. Anything that overlooks the water is way out of my budget."

"You can come here anytime," I said. "Take a seat on a bench and just enjoy, or have a walk on the beach."

"I'll do that."

Before I could turn and lead the way to my cottage, something moved in my peripheral vision and caught my attention. "Oh, no. I was just talking about that blasted gate and the stairs this morning. Looks like it's finally given up the ghost."

"You need to get that fixed," Bernie said. "It's a long way down."

The post securing the gate to the ground leaned at a crazy angle, and shards of shattered old wood hung by one hinge. I ran for the stairs. Éclair streaked past me. I needed to put some sort of warning up to keep people away. I should be able to find ribbon in the tearoom to string across the gap until we could get it fixed. I'd ask Simon to do that right away.

When I reached the top of the stairs, I realized that more than the gate itself was broken. Portions of the railing had come away, and bits of rotting wood littered the sandy soil. This was more than just a broken gate; the staircase was now dangerous. Éclair stood at the edge of the bluff, peering over the edge and barking furiously.

"Shush," Bernie said to her. "Stop that!"

"Stay here," I said. "I'm going to put the dog in the

house and get something to block this off and warn people away. Someone might get hurt if they try to go down."

Bernie clutched my arm. "I think you're too late."

The scattering of freckles stood out on my friend's pale face. Éclair's barking was getting louder and more urgent. Bernie's hand shook as she pointed down the slope.

A man lay at the bottom, staring up into the blue sky. His arms were flung out to one side, and his body lay half on, half off the staircase. I charged through the broken gate and took the stairs as fast as I dared as they shook beneath my feet. Éclair sped past me, and I felt Bernie close behind.

I tripped and stumbled but managed to keep my footing. Bernie grunted and swore.

I dropped to my knees on the rocky sand beside the man. Empty eyes stared into my face.

I touched his neck and felt nothing move beneath my fingers.

"Is he . . . ?" Bernie asked.

I swallowed. "Yes."

It was Jack Ford.

Chapter 6

"Everything okay down there?" a woman's voice called.

I glanced up to see two faces peering down at us. A man and a woman, almost certainly B & B guests.

I pushed myself to my feet. Bernie took out her phone and called 911.

"You stay here," I said. "Wait until help arrives. I need to put the dog away, keep people back, and check on Rose."

"Okay."

I called to Éclair. She hesitated, and I called again, more sharply this time. She gave Jack Ford one last sniff and then came to me. We scrambled back up the stairs. More people had arrived, and anxious faces studied me when I reached the top.

"There's been an accident," I said. "Please keep back, everyone. The emergency services have been called."

"Cool." A small girl pushed herself forward. "Can I look?"

An arm yanked her back. "You most certainly may not."

"Please go back to the house and carry on with your day," I said.

No one took my advice; instead, more people began to

arrive. I didn't know what to do. Someone had to stay here and keep these people off the steps, but I needed to make sure Rose was okay.

"Is he dead?" A man leaned over the fence to see better.

People threw each other questioning glances and murmured.

"Please take care, sir," I said. "You can see the gate isn't stable."

"Is it anyone we know?" a woman asked. "Can you see, Brian?"

"Can't tell from here," the man said. "He's not moving, though."

Simon McCracken appeared at my side. "What do you need, Lily?"

I sighed with relief. "Nine-one-one's been called. We don't want anyone else falling. I need to check on my grandmother, and I should get Éclair out of the way."

"Leave it with me," he said. "Sir, would you mind stepping back a few steps? Thank you. And you, young lady, need to do what your mother tells you."

I slipped away, and Éclair followed. I listened for the sound of approaching sirens, but other than the voices of people gathering, calling questions to each other, and the murmur of waves crashing on the rocks below, I heard nothing. First, I went to my cottage and shut the protesting dog inside; then I returned to the house and entered through the French doors leading into the dining room. Edna was setting tables for tomorrow with our pink and red china, sterling silver flatware, and white linens. She didn't look up when I came in.

"What's going on out there? Are there whales in the bay?"

"There's been an accident on the stairs. Have you seen Rose this morning?"

"No, I haven't. I don't think she's come in yet. What sort of accident? Is everyone okay?"

"No. Not okay." I lowered my voice, even though no one else was around. "A man's dead."

Edna dipped her head.

I let out a relieved breath when I heard a steady *tap-tap* on the old wooden floor of the hallway and Rose came into the dining room with her leopard-print cane, dressed for the day in red Bermuda shorts and a purple T-shirt dotted with orange flowers. Black socks were pulled up to her calves, and her feet were in sturdy Birkenstocks.

"There's been an accident outside," I told her. "A man fell down the steps." At last I heard the faint sound of sirens approaching. "An ambulance has been called, but I wanted to give you a heads-up."

Rose's eyes widened in shock, and she lifted a hand to her mouth. "Oh dear. Not one of our guests, I hope." The top of the bluffs was on our property, but hikers often didn't worry about such things and tried to keep as close to the cliff's edge as possible. We never asked them to leave if they weren't causing trouble.

"No," I said. "Not a guest . . ."

"How dreadful. Don't worry about me, love. You go out and supervise."

"It's Jack Ford," I said. "He seems to have fallen. He's dead."

Edna sucked in a breath.

Rose's eyes narrowed. "Jack Ford? What do you suppose he was doing here this morning? Trespassing on my property." She walked across the room and took a seat at a table next to the windows. "Edna, I'll have my tea here this morning."

"Only because you seem to be in such a state of shock," Edna said, "I'll make it. But just this once. Don't let it become a habit."

"You'll either have to make your own tea or wait for it," I said. "I have another job for Edna. Run up to the tearoom and take some cookies out of the freezer. The spare key is on the hook in the kitchen. Lay out coffee and cookies in here. If the police have questions for our guests, we need to give them something to keep them happy."

People in uniform ran past the windows. Edna headed for the kitchen to get the key to the tearoom.

"Your job, Rose," I said, "will be to keep the guests from speculating as to what happened. We don't want any talk of unsafe conditions."

"I can't entertain without first having something to wet my whistle."

"Stiff upper lip and all that. Pretend it's the Blitz and you're in a tunnel in the London Underground while bombs drop overhead."

"Really, love. I am not *that* old."

"Use your imagination."

I went back outside. Most of our guests had come to see what the fuss was about and were being kept away from the gate and the steps by a scowling uniformed police officer. Simon and Bernie were standing to one side, talking to a short, round man. I walked over to join them, and the newcomer turned toward me. His face was flabby; his jowls loose; his nose covered with a network of fine red lines. Strings of long greasy black hair were plastered across the top of his head in a failed attempt to appear as though he wasn't going bald. He wore a cheap, ill-fitting suit and a plain tie with a coffee stain on it.

I held out my hand. "I'm Lily Roberts. My grandmother is the property owner here."

He glanced at my hand, hesitated just long enough to seem rude, and then took it in his. I've felt firmer dead fish.

"Detective Chuck Williams. North Augusta PD. I've been told this is a bed-and-breakfast establishment."

"That's right. These people"—I indicated the watching crowd—"are our guests." Whether they were all staying at the B & B, I didn't know. Other than cooking the breakfasts, I didn't have much to do with the running of the hotel.

I didn't want to look, but I couldn't help myself, and I threw a quick glance over the fence. A woman crouched beside Jack Ford, while a uniformed officer watched. Two medics were climbing the steps.

When they reached the top, Detective Williams said, "One moment, please. You people wait here," and went to speak to them.

"You okay?" I asked Bernie.

She gave me a weak smile. "Yeah. Tough way to start the day." She turned to Simon. "Hi. I'm Bernadette Murphy. Everyone calls me Bernie."

"Pleased to meet you, Bernie. I'm Simon, the new gardener." He eyed her totally out-of-place clothes. "Do you work here?"

"Not if I can help it," she said. "I hope we don't have to stand around outside much longer. I'm getting hot."

"If you didn't dress like the bride of Dracula, you wouldn't be," I said.

"I thought I was getting in the mood." She glanced behind her and shuddered. "This wasn't the mood I was planning on. Do you think I can go home?"

"Better wait until the detective says we can leave. They'll be sure to have questions for us."

The paramedics and Chuck Williams talked in low voices. But not that low, and I was able to catch a few words, including *coroner* and *autopsy* and *head*. The medics walked away, taking their equipment with them. The woman who'd been studying the body appeared at the top of the stairs. She was about my age, attractive, with olive skin, dyed blond hair cropped short, and large dark eyes that seemed to take in everything at once. She was slightly taller than me, about five foot nine, and as lean and toned as a racehorse, with all the suppressed energy of that horse when it was about to leap out of the starting gate. Her very presence screamed "cop."

She gave Williams an abrupt nod and they joined our little circle.

"You were with Ms. Murphy when she found the body," Williams said to me. It was not a question.

"Yes, I was. I noticed the gate was broken and wanted to have a look at it. We saw . . . him and ran down to try to help." I swallowed. "We could tell right away it was too late."

"Doctor, are you?" Williams asked.

"What? Uh, no. I'm not a doctor."

"But you knew he was dead."

I glanced at Bernie. She shifted her shoulders in the slightest of shrugs, and I said, "I did."

"Did you have a dog with you?" the woman asked. "There are prints in the sand."

"Yes. I've put her in the house. I didn't let her . . . touch the body."

"What do you do for a living, Ms. Roberts?" she asked.

"I'm a pastry chef. I own and run the tearoom near the road. You would have passed it on your way in."

"Do you live nearby?"

I pointed. "That's my cottage over there. We'd been in the kitchen of the main house, preparing breakfast for the guests, and I was on my way home when I noticed the broken gate."

She turned to Simon. "What brings you here? You don't look like a B & B guest."

"I'm not. I'm the gardener."

The edges of her mouth turned up ever so slightly. "Is that so?" She studied him, and I got the impression she liked what she saw. He must have thought so, too, as he flushed and looked away.

"Where are you from?" Detective Williams asked.

"England," Simon said. "I'm here for the summer. I have a work visa."

"I'll want to see that visa."

"Sure."

More police began to arrive, uniformed officers and people in plain clothes. They struggled into white suits and put booties over their shoes and hairnets on their heads and carried bags of equipment down the stairs. The onlookers murmured excitedly and tried to get closer to the edge of the bluff for a better look.

"Cool," the little girl said again. I thought her mother should take her away.

"Did you know the deceased?" Williams asked me.

"We've met, but only twice and then casually. His name's Jack Ford, and he's a property developer."

"That's the name on his driver's license," the blond woman said. "He has a North Augusta address."

"I know Ford," Williams said.

"He was interested in buying the house next door," I said. "I assume that's why he was here this morning, but I don't know why he'd be on our property."

"Here comes Rose," Bernie said.

I turned to see my grandmother crossing the lawn. Her steps were hesitant; her liver-spotted hand quivered on the head of her cane; her back was bent; and she carefully watched where she placed her feet. Edna hovered slightly behind her, as though ready to catch her employer should she falter.

Rose had decided to appear as a feeble, frail, and probably confused old lady in need of assistance. I threw Edna a glare. She wisely avoided looking at me.

"What seems to be the problem here?" Rose's voice shook. Her accent was still English, but she'd added some upper-class notes in case anyone here watched *Downton Abbey*.

"Sorry to bother you, ma'am." Williams all but tugged at his forelock. "I hate to tell you this, but there's been a death on the beach below."

She touched the approximate vicinity of her heart. "Oh dear, I am sorry to hear that. People often don't take the care they should when out in nature, do they?"

"No, ma'am," he said. "Are you Mrs. Campbell?"

"I am she."

Williams looked over Rose's shoulder and spoke to Edna. "Did you or Mrs. Campbell see what happened here earlier?"

"No," Edna said. "I was in the house, working in the dining room. I didn't look outside. Mrs. Campbell only just came in. Her suite faces east, not over the bay."

"Why don't you take Mrs. Campbell back to the house?" Williams said. "I'm sure I won't need to bother her with this. I'll speak to you in a few minutes."

"Most upsetting," Rose said.

"Uh, perhaps not so fast," the policewoman said. "Didn't I see you in town recently, Mrs. Campbell? Weren't you at that protest over the visiting Russian fishing boats last week?"

"I . . . might have been," Rose admitted. "My memory isn't quite what it once was."

I figured it was time for me to intervene, before Rose was arrested for impersonating an elderly person. "Why don't we all go inside? We have coffee and cookies laid out."

"Sounds like a good idea to me. I didn't have my breakfast this morning." Williams patted his more than ample stomach. "Let's leave these people to do their work."

"I'd like to ask about—" The blond officer was cut off when a group of men pushed themselves through the circle of onlookers.

"Detective Williams, what's going on here?" Roy Gleeson asked.

"Morning, Councillor," Williams said. "Unfortunate accident at the bottom of the cliff."

"I don't think—" the female detective began.

"It's not Jack Ford, I hope," Lincoln Goodwill said. "We've been looking everywhere for him. His car's parked in front of the house, but he's not around."

"I'm afraid so," Williams said.

"Jack Ford?" From the depths of the crowd of onlookers, a woman snorted in laughter. "What do you know? Glad to hear it."

I didn't have time to wonder what that meant.

"Did you have plans to meet Mr. Ford this morning?" the policewoman asked.

"We did," Lincoln said. "We'd arranged to meet here—I mean next door—at nine o'clock. Who are you?"

"Detective Amy Redmond. North Augusta PD."

"You must be new," Roy said. "I don't think we've met. I'm Roy Gleeson, North Augusta town councillor." They shook hands.

"Detective Redmond joined us only last week," Williams said. "From Boston. She's brought her big-city way of doing things to our quiet little town."

The words were said in a light banter, but I sensed a thread of underlying hostility. If Amy Redmond had brought fresh new ideas, they were not welcome in Chuck Williams's patch.

"This is dreadful news," Lincoln said. "What do you think happened?"

"Good question." Roy Gleeson lifted his hand and pointed directly at Rose. "Whatever happened, you can be sure *she* had something to do with it."

Chapter 7

"Another cookie?"

"Why, thank you." The guest smiled at me. " Those are delicious. Can I have the recipe?"

"I'm afraid not. Family secret." I smiled, but it wasn't easy. I took my tray of offerings to the next table.

Even Detective Williams had had to stop thinking about accepting my offer of a snack when Roy Gleeson practically accused Rose of shoving Jack Ford over the cliff.

Whereupon the scene had descended into something out of a French farce.

Roy Gleeson accused Rose; Rose in turn accused Gleeson and Lincoln Goodwill; Edna told Gleeson his mother would be ashamed of him if she could see him badgering an elderly lady; Williams told Bernie to stop taking pictures; Bernie told him she was a writer and asked if she could interview him one day, and he said yes; Lincoln Goodwill had said he was going home; Williams said that was okay, while Redmond said it was not; the curious little girl asked Redmond if she'd ever shot anyone; and one B & B guest insisted he wanted to check out *immediately*.

And then the coroner arrived.

Amy Redmond stood back and put her fingers in her

mouth. She gave a whistle that was so loud, birds lifted from trees.

"If we can have some order please. Thank you." She turned to me. "Detective Williams would like to interview you and your coworkers and Mrs. Campbell in private. Do you have a room available in the house we can use?"

"Yes, we do."

"Thank you. You mentioned something about coffee and cookies. Perhaps these gentlemen and anyone else who has something to tell us can enjoy refreshments in your dining room while they wait their turn." She smiled at me. I cracked a smile in return.

No fool, this one.

She nodded to the uniformed officer who'd been watching the proceedings.

"Inside, everyone," he said. "You'll be spoken to in turn." Like a sheepdog herding sheep, he moved the whole motley crew toward the house.

"Me first," shouted the little girl. "Take me first!"

"Shush," her mother said.

"I'm sure you have a room in a house this large where we can interview witnesses with some privacy," Redmond said to me.

"We do."

"Let's go inside then. We'll talk to you first, Ms. Roberts."

"I'll be off . . ." Lincoln Goodwill said. "You know where you can contact me if you need me, Chuck."

"Certainly, sir," Williams said.

"I don't think—" Redmond said.

Williams interrupted her. "Mr. Goodwill is here to conduct business. He owns the house next door and is trying to sell it. Seems natural enough he'd be around this morning. Clearly, he had nothing to do with these events."

"That's rubbish!" Rose said. "He's into it up to his eyeballs. I wouldn't be surprised if—"

"You are not helping, Rose," I said. "Edna, my grandmother needs to sit down. Why don't you take her into the dining room?"

Edna threw me a grateful look. She tucked Rose's arm in hers, patted her hand, and said, "Come with me, dear. Let's have a nice cup of tea to settle your nerves."

"I'll give you a nice cup of tea," Rose growled. But she allowed Edna to lead her away.

A man rounded the house at a run, a big black Nikon camera hanging around his neck. "*North Augusta Times*!" he called, pushing his way through the crowd. "Detective Williams, do you have a statement for the press?"

Williams puffed himself up, straightened his shoulders, and lifted his chin. "Not at this time." He put on a serious expression while the photographer took his picture.

In contrast, Redmond moved silently out of range.

Not wanting to have my picture in the papers, either, I followed my grandmother into the house. She and Edna took a seat at a table for two. I gave Rose a small nod as I passed, leading the police into what we grandly called the drawing room.

To my surprise, and obviously to Detective Redmond's, before she could take a seat or ask a single question, Williams ordered her back outside to supervise the gathering of forensic evidence. She left the drawing room in a towering but silent rage, leaving me with Williams and a uniformed officer who didn't seem to know how to talk.

Once she'd gone, and the door had shut behind her, I calmly and efficiently—I hoped—told Detective Williams where I'd been and what I'd been doing this morning and how I'd come to discover Jack Ford at the bottom of the bluffs.

He hadn't asked me a single question about my previous encounters with Ford before telling me I was dismissed and asking the officer to show Bernie in next.

Before going into the dining room to try to play the charming hostess, I'd called Cheryl and Marybeth and asked them to do what they could in the tearoom without me. They were able to make sandwiches, and I had an adequate supply of scones and pastries in the freezer in case of an emergency.

A man dead on our property counts as an emergency.

Edna had brought in the chocolate chip cookies I'd made for the children's tea as well as some of the Buckingham Palace shortbread. When Bernie's interrogation was over, I sent her into the kitchen to make more pots of coffee and tea, and Simon helped her ferry plates and cups back and forth.

A couple of cops wandered into the dining room and wandered out again, clutching fistfuls of cookies.

As I served and chatted, I kept one eye on the hallway. When it was Rose's turn to be questioned in the drawing room, I asked Edna, in earshot of the police, to stand outside the room and help my grandmother when she was finished. What I really meant was for Edna to try to listen at the door and tell me what was going on. Too many people were coming and going for me to be able to stay hidden and eavesdrop.

I hoped Rose didn't say anything that would have her dragged out in handcuffs.

About fifteen minutes later, Edna appeared at the door of the dining room. She gave me a quick nod and flicked her thumb down the hallway, telling me Rose was finished and was returning to her rooms. I nodded in acknowledgment.

I wasn't the B & B owner here; Rose was. I needed to get to my tearoom, and it should be up to Rose to placate her guests. But I didn't want Rose having any more encounters with either the police or Gleeson and Goodwill.

"More tea?" I asked a woman sitting by herself next to

the windows and paying a lot of attention to the comings and goings.

"Thank you. That would be great. Do you know what's happening outside? So exciting, isn't it, having the police poking around?"

"Exciting, yes." I poured the tea.

The police were finished with us sooner than I would have expected.

The guests dispersed, Edna left, Bernie went home, declaring she was *desperate* to get out of her dress, and Simon returned to the gardens. The weekend housekeeper, Mrs. Zagorsky, arrived at eleven, as usual, and was running the vacuum cleaner through the dining room prior to doing up the bedrooms.

Rose remained out of sight.

Williams found me sitting on a reproduction antique chair at the reception desk in the hallway outside the drawing room, ordering supplies on my phone. I'd kept in touch with Cheryl and Marybeth, and they told me they'd gone through a prodigious amount of not only what I'd prepared for today but also my emergency supplies. I'd be working all night, trying to get more baking ready for tomorrow.

"We're done here for now," Williams said. "You can have your house back."

I got to my feet. "Thank you."

"We've cordoned off the section of lawn near the staircase and the stairs themselves. No one's to go there."

"I understand."

I fell into step beside him as he walked through the dining room toward the French doors. "Do you have any idea what might have happened?" I asked.

"If I do, I won't be sharing my insights with you," he said.

"Just asking."

"Tell me about this place. You run it?"

"Not me. I own the tearoom by the main road. My grandmother's in charge of the B & B." Too late, I realized I'd stepped into a trap. Rose had, probably foolishly, continued to try to present herself as frail and slightly dotty. Not someone capable of running her own business. "Uh . . . ," I said. "She has good staff." As if on cue, over our heads the vacuum cleaner roared to life.

Williams left, and I went into the kitchen. I needed to sit down, I needed a cup of coffee, I needed to think about what on earth was going on, and I needed to get to the tearoom and try to salvage the rest of the day. But most of all, I needed to talk to Rose.

My phone buzzed with an incoming text.

Bernie: **Everything okay there? Cops gone?**

Me: **Gone from the house. Still at the cliff and beach.**

Bernie: **Need anything?**

Me: **No. Thanks.**

Bernie: **Okay then. Now to important stuff: tell me about that gardener!!!**

Me: **Nothing to tell. Qualified. Looking for a job.**

Bernie: **You sneaky girl. He's hot, hot, hot. And that accent!!**

Me: **I hadn't noticed. Bye.**

Next, I texted Rose: **Coast is clear. Where are you hiding?**

She answered immediately: **Private room, of course.**

I groaned. Of course.

I left the kitchen via the doors to the hallway and strolled casually past the drawing room. The door was open and no one was inside. Trying not to be too obvious about it, I ensured no one was around. The sound of Mrs. Zagorsky humming tunelessly while she made beds and tidied bathrooms drifted down the wide oak staircase. The downstairs utility closet, used for storing table linens, was tucked under the stairs. I opened the door. Two of the shelves had been removed and were leaning against the wall, and stacks of neatly folded and perfectly ironed linens were piled on the floor. I reached for the lever beneath the uppermost shelf and pulled. The bottom section of the wall slid open on silent hinges. I bent over and crawled in.

The tiny room was comfortably furnished with a small table and a single wingback chair removed from service after a guest dropped a lit cigarette onto the soft seat. The guest had also been removed from service and shown the door. Rose's laptop was open on the table; a tiny lamp illuminated the screen and keyboard.

"You shouldn't leave things out of place when you come in here," I said to her in a quiet whisper.

"Edna has finished for the day and Mrs. Z. has no reason to be in the downstairs linen closet. If one of the guests has the cheek to poke around behind closed doors, I'll tell them I'm hunting for mice."

"I assume you heard everything?"

"Not everything. Unfortunately, I had to wait in the dining room for them to question me, so I didn't hear what you or Bernie had to say. You can fill me in. Do you think Jack Ford was murdered?"

"Rose, I have no idea. But whatever happened to him, I wish it hadn't been here."

The room, being under the staircase, had no windows. It was next to the drawing room, and not only was the adjoining wall excessively thin, but discrete holes had been driven through the lath and plaster, and were concealed on the other side by a picture of an eighteenth century warship in full sail hanging over them.

We had not made the secret room, but we loved knowing it was there.

This house had been used as a B & B before Rose bought it, but the previous owners had not lived in it. She wanted a full suite for herself on the ground floor and hired a contractor to make the necessary modifications. Before going ahead, Rose had carefully studied the architectural plans of the house, and discovered some, shall we say, discrepancies. Such as this carefully placed and hidden room.

Only Rose and I knew about it.

She got to her feet and switched off the lamp. In the darkness, I crawled back into the linen closet and listened at the door. All was quiet, so I opened the door, peeked out, and stepped into the hallway. Rose followed, and I slid the partition back into place, and replaced the shelves and linens.

"That Inspector Williams . . . ," Rose said.

"Detective Williams," I corrected.

"Whatever. He's surprisingly incompetent. Either that or excessively lazy."

"Don't play him for a fool, Rose," I said.

"He is a fool. I suspect that young woman is not. She'll get to the bottom of it."

"What do you know?"

"Me? I know nothing. Nothing at all. No one Inspector Williams questioned claimed to know anything. I find it hard to believe that the late, unlamented Jack Ford was early for his meeting and decided to go for a stroll along my stretch of beach. But stranger things have happened. It has nothing to do with us."

"I won't say I told you so, but I told you to get that gate fixed."

"Ask your young gardener to do that. I must say, he's surprisingly handsome, isn't he?"

"Is he? I hadn't noticed."

"You spend too much time in that tearoom, Lily."

"That tearoom is my livelihood," I said.

"Pshaw. The gardener at Thornecroft ran off with the

cook's assistant. That was my lucky break. I was promoted from kitchen maid to cook's assistant. And as Mrs. Beans was a sloppy old drunk the family kept on out of loyalty—or perhaps she was bribing them—that meant I was, in fact, the head cook at Thornecroft."

I'd heard more than enough stories about the kitchens at Thornecroft over the years. "Yes, Rose. I know all that. It has nothing to do with what's going on here. I have to get to the tearoom."

The front door opened, and a laughing couple in their midtwenties came in, arms wrapped around each other. Rose had earlier told me they were on their honeymoon, but she needn't have bothered. It was written all over their faces and screamed out from their body language.

"Good afternoon, Mrs. Campbell." The woman was presumably addressing Rose, but she kept her eyes on the face of her new husband. "Another beautiful day."

"I hope the police activity hasn't bothered you," I said.

She laughed. "Heavens no. We've been standing as close as we dare, watching. It's like *CSI* come to life! Or a good police procedural novel. I belong to a mystery book club back home in Albany, and I can't wait to tell my friends all about it. We're going to wash up and go over to the tearoom."

They climbed the steps, smiling at each other and staring deeply into the eyes of their beloved. If they didn't pay more attention to where they were putting their feet, I thought, we'd have another accident.

I turned to see Rose studying me.

"What?"

"Young love. There's nothing on earth like it."

"I wouldn't know."

At two o'clock, I was finally able to get away from the house, and I headed for the tearoom. The parking lot was full, and every table on the patio was occupied. I wouldn't have time to bake many more pastries, so we might be able to offer only a cream tea this afternoon. The cookies in the freezer had been obliterated. As well as offering them to B & B guests ordered to remain in the house and to any cops who wandered through, I'd asked Edna to take some down to the forensic technicians and the officers guarding the scene.

Never hurts to be friendly with the local police.

She'd reported back that they were searching the top of the bluffs and the area at the foot of the stairs.

I was opening the gate to the tearoom garden when I heard the sound of sirens approaching. A cruiser took the turn into our driveway on two wheels. It roared past me and came to a screeching halt in front of the house. A uniformed officer was driving, with Detective Williams in the front passenger seat and Detective Redmond in the back. They leapt out and raced up the steps.

Guests enjoying their tea on the patio stood up to see what was going on, and others peered out the doors and windows. Someone pulled out binoculars they no doubt normally used for birding.

I ran. I reached the house as the front door was opening in answer to Williams pounding on it. Rose's face peeked out. She blinked in confusion. "Oh, good afternoon, Inspector. Did you forget something?"

I galloped up the stairs. "What's happening?"

"I have further questions for you, Mrs. Campbell," Williams said.

"Let them in, Rose," I said. The door swung open.

"Tea, Inspector?" my grandmother asked.

"Let's go into the drawing room, shall we?" I glanced at Amy Redmond. Her face was impassive, but her eyes darted around the hallway, taking in the floor, tiled in black-and-white checks, the pale green wallpaper, the reproduction eighteenth-century English portraits, the recent photo of the queen framed and hanging over the reception desk, the neat stacks of Cape Cod tourist brochures laid out next to the vase of fresh flowers on the desk, the staircase with the scarlet runners and oak bannisters, the closed double doors leading into the dining room.

At that moment, Mrs. Zagorsky appeared on the stairs, dragging the vacuum cleaner behind her.

Bump-bump-bump.

She gave the police a curious glance but carried on down the hallway to the ground-level guest rooms without a word.

That wasn't unusual. I don't think I've heard Mrs. Zagorsky say more than five words in all the time I've been here.

I turned to our visitors. "Can I ask what this is about, Detectives?"

Williams ignored me. "Did you kill Jack Ford, Mrs. Campbell?"

Chapter 8

"Pshaw," Rose said. "Stuff and nonsense."

"Please answer the question," Redmond said.

"I did not kill Jack Ford. I might have considered it, but—"

"But nothing," I said. "What are you getting at, Detective?"

"When I got back to the police station," Williams said, "I was informed that Jack Ford filed suit against Rose Campbell only last night. He claimed she was spreading false and malicious rumors about him."

Oh, that. I'd forgotten about that.

"What if I did?" Rose said. "Doesn't mean I then shoved the man off the cliff. And, for your further information, I said nothing false. I presented my case in a calm and reasoned manner."

"Your letter to the newspaper has been taken as evidence," Redmond said. "I've read it. I wouldn't say it was calm and reasoned."

"Why don't we sit down?" I was about to offer my guests tea when I realized that I'd have to leave them alone with Rose while I made it. Not a good idea.

"I'm feeling quite faint." Rose leaned on her leopard-print cane.

I took her arm and led the way into the drawing room. "Don't lay it on too thick," I whispered.

"What was that?" Redmond asked.

"Nothing."

I settled Rose into a chair covered in red and gold damask and propped her cane in front of her. She folded her hands together over the top of it. What we grandly called the drawing room was the common room for the use of our guests, a place for them to relax and read, particularly if it was a rainy day. Blue drapes framed the wide windows overlooking the gardens. The wallpaper was blue flecked with gold leaf. Bookshelves overflowed with volumes, most of them well-used paperbacks, and a selection of board games. A reproduction antique desk was against the far wall. Well-worn brown leather chairs sat on either side of the big fireplace, full of flowers at this time of year, and prints of eighteenth-century British paintings hung on the walls.

Williams took the chair behind the desk. Redmond crossed her arms and leaned against the wall next to the fireplace. I lowered myself onto a leather chair and perched on the edge.

"You didn't like Jack Ford," Williams said to Rose. "Why?"

"Because he was an unlikable man."

"Plenty of unlikable men around," Williams said. "Do you plan to kill them all?"

I shot forward. "Now, see here—"

"He was interested in buying the property next door," Redmond said. "You were opposed to that."

"He wanted to build a golf course and resort monstrosity. I was opposed to that, yes. I value the peace and quiet I have here."

"You thought you'd discourage him by slandering him in the newspaper?" Redmond said.

"We don't need his type around here."

"What type is that?" Redmond asked.

"Crooked businessmen."

"If you had reason to believe he was acting outside the law," Redmond said, "you should have contacted the police."

Rose turned her head so she was looking directly at Detective Williams. "You mean *him*? I've heard things about you, Inspector."

Williams's eyes bulged. He started to stand.

"Rose," I said. "This isn't helping."

"I'm not trying to help," she said.

"Yes, you are. Look, Detective Redmond. My grandmother is somewhat outspoken, as anyone can tell you. She believes in speaking the blunt truth." *Whether that's wise or not*, I thought but didn't add. "She wasn't in favor of rezoning the Goodwill property. She was prepared to fight the motion. But to suggest she killed someone over a golf course . . ."

"This is a nice place," Redmond said. "Must cost a lot to keep it up."

"It pays for itself."

"Wouldn't leave you with a spare half a million dollars if you lost a legal suit, would it?"

"I wouldn't have lost," Rose said.

"Sure of that, were you, Mrs. Campbell?" Williams said.

"Yes," Rose said.

"No," I said. "I mean, it wouldn't have come to that. Rose would have apologized to Mr. Ford."

"I most certainly would not."

"When Detective Williams spoke to you earlier today," Redmond said, "you told him you were in your rooms until you heard the commotion outside when the police arrived."

"That's correct," Rose said.

"Is that still your story?"

"Of course it's still my story. Because it's the truth."

"It was almost nine forty when we arrived."

"So?" Rose said.

"My grandmother often remains in her rooms until breakfast is over," I said.

"Funny way to run a B & B."

"I do the cooking," I told her. "Edna serves breakfast."

"The autopsy will be done later today," Redmond said. "At an estimate, it would seem Mr. Ford died not long before he was discovered. Around eight thirty."

I said nothing. Fortunately, neither did Rose.

"Do you always use a cane to get around, Mrs. Campbell?" Redmond asked.

Rose blinked. I could practically read her mind. The police had to have a reason for asking about a cane. After pretending to be unable to walk without assistance, she could hardly come out now and say she didn't always rely on the support. "When I go outside, it helps on rough ground," she said at last.

"How many canes do you have?"

"One. This one." She clenched her hands, and the knuckles turned white.

"The autopsy will tell us more about the circumstances of death," Williams said, "but the initial examination suggests Mr. Ford didn't trip on the stairs, or even lean on the gate and have it break beneath him. He struck it with sufficient force to indicate he was propelled toward it."

"Which might have happened," Redmond said, "if he'd been surprised by a hit with a solid object. Something like a baseball bat."

Silence stretched through the room.

"Or a cane," Williams added.

"Then you'd better find out who did that," Rose said. "And stop wasting an old lady's time."

Williams stood up. "Rose Campbell, I am—"

"A word please, Detective," Redmond said.

"What?"

"Can I have a word in private for a moment?"

I leapt to my feet. "We'll wait in the hallway. Rose, come with me."

Rose stood up with a speed that belied her claims of old bones.

"I promise, we won't go far." I took Rose's arm and led her into the hallway.

"Watch the door," I whispered to her. "Drop a book on the floor if it's not safe for me to come out." I ducked into the linen closet, shoved the linens out of the way, removed the shelves, pulled the lever, and slipped into the tiny room.

Williams's voice rose and came through the thin wall loud and clear. "Out of line."

"I'm stopping you from making a big mistake." Redmond spoke calmly, but I could hear her clearly. She must be directly facing the wall behind which I crouched.

"This case is open and shut. That old lady whacked Ford with her cane and pitched him down the stairs to stop his golf course. I'm taking her in."

"You haven't even spoken to those men who were supposed to be meeting Ford this morning."

"I know Lincoln Goodwill. His family's—"

"That's it, isn't it? You know him. Old-time North Augusta family. Old-time money."

"Watch yourself, Detective. You're new here. You don't know how things work."

"I don't?" she said. "I think I know how things work well enough. It's the same everywhere. If you want to arrest Rose Campbell, go ahead. But when the press and the chief ask what other suspects we have, I'll have to tell them you didn't bother looking for any."

At that moment, something brushed against my foot and scurried off into the darkness. I leapt into the air, hit my head on the low ceiling, and sucked back a yelp of pain and surprise.

"What was that?" Redmond said.

"Are you always so jumpy?" Williams said. "These old houses are always making noises. They should rip this thing down and put up a nice modern hotel."

"I'll ignore that crack this time. And remind you that Rose Campbell might sound like she's fresh off the boat from England, but she's lived in America for a long time and is a citizen. She has extensive family and a business here. She's not a flight risk. If I'm wrong—"

"Which you are."

"Then you can arrest her at the appropriate time. After you've prepared a case that won't be thrown out of court on the first objection. Now, if we're finished here, I'm going to pay a call on Lincoln Goodwill. You can come if you want. Or not."

The detectives emerged from the drawing room to find Rose sitting behind the reception desk, checking the reservations for next week, and me tidying the linen closet.

We smiled at them.

Redmond glanced between me and my grandmother. I decided it was a mistake to be smiling at her as though she were a guest checking in and wiped the expression away.

"Thank you for your time, ladies," she said. "We'll be in touch. I have to ask you both not to leave town without checking with me . . . or Detective Williams, of course . . . first."

"We've no plans to go anywhere," I said. "It's the busy season here."

"Is that your only cane, Mrs. Campbell?" Redmond asked.

Rose glanced at it. "As I told you. Yes."

Redmond took plastic gloves out of her pocket and put them on. I couldn't help but notice that her nails were chewed down to the quick and a torn hangnail was beginning to heal. "May I take it with us?"

"Why?" I asked.

She replied, "I'll return it when we're done with it."

Done checking, I assumed, for evidence of it being used to send Jack Ford tumbling over a cliff. I glanced at it, while trying not to be seen doing so. It looked okay to me. "Let her have it, Rose."

"How will I get around?"

"We'll go into town and buy another."

"If I must." Rose handed the cane to Redmond.

"Thank you," she said.

"Do stop into the tearoom for tea one day," Rose said. "It will be our treat. Bring your wife, Detective Williams. Oh, I'm sorry. That was tactless of me. I heard she's left you."

He glared at her. I smothered a groan.

We stood at the top of the steps and watched as the police got into their car and drove away, after first putting Rose's leopard-print cane into the trunk.

When I was sure they weren't coming back, I turned to my grandmother. "Are you trying to get yourself arrested?"

"Why would you think that?"

"What was that crack about his marriage for?"

"Everyone knows he and his wife are having marital problems."

"I didn't think you knew him."

"I don't. They were talking about it at bridge last week. It seems that Ann Black is quite good friends with Mrs. Williams. Not good enough friends, apparently, to prevent her from delighting in spreading the gossip. Their marriage has—"

"Rose, I don't care about the state of the detective's marriage. You do know that at this time you are the prime, and perhaps only, suspect in the death of Jack Ford, don't you?"

She genuinely looked confused. "I am? They don't actually believe I whacked him over the head with my cane, do they? Let me assure you they'll find nothing incriminating on it."

"I'm pleased to hear it. Redmond and Williams don't get along very well. To put it mildly. From what I overheard, he's an old-time small-town cop and she isn't. He's focused on you because that will make his job easier, and then he won't have to question people like Lincoln Goodwill."

"Ah, yes. The scion of the Goodwill family. You Americans think you don't have a class system. It might not be as formal as back in England, but it exists nonetheless. The Goodwill family is old North Augusta money. Money and bloodlines. Even if most of their money's long gone."

"Not entirely a class system," I said. "Redmond doesn't respect that."

"Good for her," Rose said. "But let's hope her determination not to let it affect her judgment doesn't end up having the opposite effect. I didn't kill Jack Ford, but I don't want to see an innocent person railroaded into a conviction so she can prove a point. I'm sure the odious Mr. Ford had enough enemies."

Simon ran across the lawn toward us and climbed the steps. "I see the police came back. I thought I'd stay away and let you handle it. Was that the right thing to do?"

"It was," I said. "They had a couple more questions. Nothing important."

"Bad business, this."

"I, for one, find being under suspicion of murder most tiring," Rose said. "I'm going to lie down. I'd better get what sleep I can while I'm not yet confined to a cell. I've heard the beds can be highly uncomfortable."

She went into the house.

"Your grandmother isn't really under suspicion, is she?" Simon asked me.

"Right now, I think the police haven't got a clue as to what happened, so everyone is under suspicion. Other than that, how was your first day on the job?"

"Good. You have challenges for sure, trying to have something resembling an English country garden in this soil, but my uncle did a brilliant job, and he left everything in good condition."

My phone buzzed with a text. "Sorry," I said to Simon, "I have to take this. I'm supposed to be at work."

Cheryl: **I see cops have left. Scones long gone. Few macarons left. We're making sandwiches.**

Me: **Can you stay after closing and help in kitchen?**

Cheryl: **Sorry. No. Choir performance. Marybeth's husband is away, and she has to pick up kids on time.**

Me: **Okay. Be right there.**

Cheryl: **Customers are happy watching police activity.**

Me: **That's not a good thing. On my way.**

I gave my head a shake and put the phone away.

"Problem?" Simon said.

"I've lost almost my entire working day. My staff ran out of scones hours ago and have been through almost everything in the freezer. Tomorrow's Sunday, the busiest day of the week at the busiest time of the year. We have sandwich ingredients on hand, but people don't come to a tearoom just for sandwiches. As it is, we'll be down to nothing but peanut butter soon. I guess I'll be baking all night."

"Do you need a hand?"

"I could use one, but both Cheryl and Marybeth are busy tonight. You don't happen to know a pastry chef with a few hours free, do you?"

"Not a qualified pastry chef, but a reasonably competent baker. That would be me."

"You?"

He laughed. "Me. My mum isn't a professional baker, but she does wedding cakes and catering for weddings for miles around, and I grew up helping her. I've made more than my share of scones over the years. My dad's a gardener. I had my choice of becoming a cook or a gardener. Never so much as considered doing anything else."

"Are your parents still active? You said they're looking after your dogs."

"Semiretired. Mum bakes for her friends' daughters' and granddaughters' weddings, and Dad keeps the church gardens the best in Suffolk." He held up his soil-encrusted hands. The knees of his overalls were covered in dirt, grains of sand were trapped in his hair, and a streak of mud ran down one cheek. He grinned at me. "Why don't I go home and wash up? I can pop into town and do any shopping you need. Be back in about an hour."

"That's nice of you, but are you sure? You were here at six, and you've been working all day."

"I'm sure," he said. "You can help me sometime when I'm behind."

Chapter 9

I threw scone ingredients together as quickly as I could, put them in the oven, and set the timer. When I'd announced to my family I was opening my own tearoom, my sister gave me a timer that crowed like a rooster greeting the dawn when it went off, and I use it exclusively for timing scones. I checked the contents of the fridge and the pantry and sent a text to Simon, telling him what I needed from the shops for a nighttime of baking. Marybeth and Cheryl ran in and out of the kitchen, making tea, assembling sandwiches, carrying trays, and returning with dirty dishes.

"No one's complaining that the full menu isn't available," Cheryl said as she added fragrant leaves to a pot before pouring in water straight off the boil. "Pot to the kettle, not kettle to the pot," I'd taught my staff, as my grandmother had taught me. Meaning that for most (but not all) types of tea, the water had to be as hot as possible when brewing the tea. "They're being very understanding. You should consider adding the children's cookies to the main menu. The chocolate chip ones are really popular."

I grinned at her. "Anna, Duchess of Bedford, would be

appalled." Legend has it that Anna, lady-in-waiting to Queen Victoria, invented afternoon tea when she felt a touch peckish in the late afternoon.

"No one has to tell her," Cheryl said.

"I've no doubt poor Anna has rolled over in her grave more than a few times over the past two hundred years."

"I like to think she'd be proud of how her tradition has carried on and expanded." Cheryl checked that sufficient time had passed for the tea to steep, lifted the ball of tea leaves out, put the teapot on a tray, along with matching cups and saucers. "I saw two women reading the menu by the garden gate yesterday. They shook their heads and started to walk away. I asked if I could help, and they said they'd heard we did high tea, and they were disappointed not to see it on the menu."

"You educated them, I trust."

"Exactly as you taught me. They came in and ate every crumb. Left a big tip, as I recall." Cheryl carried her laden tray through the swinging doors.

Afternoon tea, as invented by Anna, Duchess of Bedford, and served at Tea by the Sea, is not to be confused, as it often is in America, with high tea, which is a working family's or children's evening meal. In the past, afternoon tea was occasionally called "low tea," meaning served at a low table in a drawing room, as opposed to the high table in the kitchen, around which a family would gather to have their "high tea." Just to confuse things more, some places in America refer to afternoon tea as "high tea" when it comes with an additional, more substantial course, such as a soup or salad.

Marybeth ran into the kitchen, interrupting my thoughts about Duchess Anna and the proper serving of tea. "You're not going to like this, Lily."

"Today there's not much I like. What's happened now?"

"The cops are back. They've just pulled up outside the house. They brought a forensic van with them."

"Keep an eye on those scones and take them out when the rooster crows. Then close the tearoom. No more customers. We can't cope any longer."

I ran through the restaurant. Curious guests had once again taken position next to the windows.

I found Cheryl in the patio, laying a fresh place setting. "We're closing early. Finish serving the ones who are here, but no new customers."

I flipped the sign on the gate to CLOSED and ran up the driveway.

Rose was standing on the verandah, holding a piece of paper in her hand. Williams faced her while she read. His arms were crossed over his chest, and his feet planted widely apart. Three people, wearing the white overalls of a forensics team, watched. Mrs. Zagorsky's rusty van was gone.

I ran up the steps. "What on earth do you want now?"

"Pardon the inconvenience," Williams said. "I would have thought you'd want us to get to the bottom of this, Ms. Roberts."

"Of course I do. What have you got there?"

"A warrant to search your and Mrs. Campbell's private residences."

"What? Let me see that." I ripped the paper out of Rose's hand and read quickly.

"I tried to argue that we need to search the whole house, but the judge didn't go along with that. Something about guests' privacy."

"This says you're looking for a black cane?"

"Earlier today, Mrs. Campbell told us she has only one cane. The one with the leopard-print pattern."

"That's right."

"We found a picture in the *North Augusta Times* of her

at a bridge tournament about a month ago. You were accepting a trophy, Mrs. Campbell. And holding a black cane. A solid-looking cane with a heavy brass base. Did you forget to tell me about that one?"

"I am not totally senile," Rose said. "Not yet, anyway. I didn't mention that one, because I no longer have it."

He raised one eyebrow. "Really?"

"Really," Rose said. "You remember, Lily."

"I do. That cane wasn't nearly as solid as it looked. It got a crack in it, and we didn't trust it anymore. We threw it out weeks ago and bought the new one. The one you took away."

"So you say," he said.

"So I say. Because it's the truth. Where's Detective Redmond?"

"Not that I have to tell you, but I will. She's investigating another matter." He waved to the people gathered on the driveway to join us on the verandah. "We'll see to your rooms first, Mrs. Campbell. Why don't we wait in the front room?"

I needed to be with Rose to ensure she didn't insult Detective Williams again or say something he would interpret as incriminating, but I also wanted to supervise the search. Not that I didn't trust the North Augusta Police Department not to plant evidence, but . . .

We went into the house. The few guests back early from the beach or an expedition stood in the hallway, watching.

"I'm checking out," a woman said. "Right now. I can't have my children staying in this house a moment longer." Three children were gathered around her on the stairs, looking as though they wanted nothing more than to stay and watch.

"As you like," I said.

"You can leave whenever you want," Rose said, "but you have to pay for the entire weekend."

"I don't think this is the time—" I said.

"The safety of my children is more important than money." The guest turned with a huff and marched upstairs, dragging three reluctant children behind her.

"Once again, you're the talk of the town, Rose Campbell." Edna came into the house. "I thought you might need me. What can I do?"

I let out a sigh of relief. "Can you show these people to Rose's suite, please? And then can you stay and . . . uh . . . ?"

"Make sure they don't plant evidence?" Edna held out her hand. Rose dug her key out of her pocket and passed it over.

Edna led the way down the hall, and Rose and I went into the drawing room with Williams.

We didn't have to wait long. If all the police were allowed to search for was a cane, they wouldn't have to leaf through pages of books or search small drawers.

"Nothing," a man said from the doorway.

"Your room next, Ms. Roberts," Williams said.

"Edna," I said. "Will you wait with Rose?"

"Happy to."

I led the way through the dining room and out the French doors. We crossed the lawn to my cottage as curious guests watched. I unlocked the door and stood back to let the police in. Éclair is normally a very friendly dog, but perhaps today she sensed my attitude toward these people and set up a round of furious barking, complete with bared teeth.

"Control your animal please," a man said.

I scooped my dog up and carried her to the backyard. I put her down, gave her a quick pat, and shut the door before she could slip past me. She continued barking.

The search of my place took less time than Rose's. Other than under the bed or in the closet, there was no place large enough to hide a four-foot-long cane.

"Satisfied?" I said to Williams when we were once again all gathered in the drawing room.

"For now," he said.

And then they left. When I shut the door behind them, all I wanted to do was lean against it and let out a long sigh. Instead, I forced a smile and turned to the honey-mooning couple standing in the hallway. "Do you have plans to do something special this evening?"

"We have reservations at the restaurant on the pier."

"You'll love it. If the sky stays clear, you'll get a lovely sunset."

Gradually, the guests began to disperse.

"The family in room two-oh-five left," Rose said. "I saw them stuffing their cheap suitcases and unruly children into their car. Make sure you charge them for two nights."

"Me? I don't do the billing."

"I'm far too tired to worry about that now. Most distressing, all this fuss. Edna, you can take me to my room."

"I can, can I?" Edna said.

"Yes, you can. A cup of tea would help me relax."

"It would help me relax, too," Edna said with a glance at me.

I pretended not to have heard that.

The guests had returned to their rooms or gone out for a walk in the gardens, leaving the three of us alone in the foyer. I stepped closer to my grandmother and spoke in a low voice. "I don't like this, Rose. Williams seems to be fixated on you as a suspect."

"As I didn't do anything, I have nothing to worry about," she said.

"I wouldn't be so sure about that," Edna said.

"What do you know?" I asked.

"Chuck Williams has a reputation of not always being one to follow the rules, if you know what I mean. Frank and the paper have had their eye on him for a long time, but he never quite goes over the line."

"What sort of not following the rules?" I asked. "You mean like planting evidence?"

She nodded. "If that's what's necessary to keep his friends out of trouble and land their enemies in it, yes."

"I am hardly anyone's enemy," Rose said.

"But you are," Edna said. "Your opposition to the development plans for next door puts you smack-dab at the top of Lincoln Goodwill's enemy list. He *has* to get that land sold, and he *has* to get a lot more than the house itself is worth, being in the condition it is. The Goodwill family is on their last legs financially and going down fast. Lincoln made some bad investments with the money he inherited from his father, and he's in a lot of trouble. If he can sell the property and reinvest the proceeds, he has a chance of recovering. If not . . ."

I let out a long breath. "Sounds like he might not be averse to greasing a few palms."

"Police palms, you mean," Rose said. "I'll be in my rooms. I've some research to do."

Chapter 10

I made my weary way back to the tearoom. I found it hard to believe Detective Williams would openly try to frame Rose for the murder, but I had to face facts: Edna's husband, in his role as editor in chief of the newspaper, would know more than most people what went on in the police station. He probably knew more about what went on than most of the people who worked there.

I tried to tell myself that Amy Redmond, at least, seemed like an efficient and honest cop. It was obvious she and Williams were butting heads. Surely she'd put a halt to any mischief Williams might get up to? I could only hope.

A lone motorcycle was parked in the tearoom lot, and Simon had taken a seat in the garden, a pile of supermarket bags at his feet. He stood when he saw me approaching. The light, salty breeze ruffled his fair hair. He'd cleaned up very nicely indeed. "Everything okay?"

"Yeah," I said. "For now."

"I got what you need, so let's get to it."

"Let's. Those scones won't bake themselves."

He laughed. "That's what my mum always says."

Deep in my pocket, my phone buzzed to announce an incoming text.

Bernie: **I'm in town, writing in coffee shop. Heard someone say cops are back at your place?**

Me: **Gone now. All okay.**

Bernie: **On my way.**

Me: **Can you stop at the drugstore and buy a cane for Rose?**

Bernie: **Okay.**

The tearoom was dark and quiet. Before leaving, Marybeth and Cheryl had set the tables with clean linens, swept the floor, washed and put away the dishes, and tidied the kitchen.

"What's first on the list?" Simon said.

"Can you make the scones?"

"Yup."

"I'll get you the recipe I use. Make half with raisins and half plain, please. We need several batches. While you're doing that, I'll poach the chicken and start on green tea cupcakes and a chocolate tart. Then macarons. They're always hugely popular."

"You're only a tearoom, right? You don't do breakfast or lunches?"

"All we serve is afternoon tea. I've been open only since early spring, but so far we're busy enough I don't need to consider expanding the menu. I might have to in the off-season, but for now, all our customers get is some variation of afternoon tea as it would be served in the Orangery at Kensington Palace."

Simon took butter out of the fridge and flour down from the shelf. He set about weighing and measuring, while I filled a stockpot with water and set it to boil, unwrapped and seasoned the chicken breasts he'd bought, and measured a quarter cup of Darjeeling leaves, which would be added to the water when it boiled. I then checked my recipe for green tea cupcakes and gathered the necessary ingredients.

"My mum would love this place," Simon said. "It's like a proper English tearoom."

"That's what Rose and I wanted."

He cut butter into the flour and said, "I've not exchanged more than a word or two with your grandmother, but I'd recognize that Yorkshire accent anywhere. How'd she end up here?"

I put butter in the stand mixer and switched it on. "She began life as a kitchen maid in a stately home called Thornecroft Castle. That was back in the fifties, when many of the grand old houses were being demolished or turned into museums, but the Earl of Frockmorton, who owned the place where she worked, wasn't the sort who minded getting his hands dirty. Between the wars, he'd worked hard, had a lot of luck, and made tons of money. Something to do with shipping, Rose thinks. He and his wife loved to entertain . . . the grander the better. Lavish dinner parties, country house weekends, hunting parties. All terribly nineteenth century. To achieve all that, they kept a full staff. Maids, footmen, cook, kitchen workers, gardeners, the lot."

"Rose was a kitchen maid?"

"She started when she was fourteen and worked there for eleven years, eventually rising to become the cook's chief assistant. Lady Frockmorton loved to have guests for afternoon tea. All dreadfully formal and stuffy."

"Pinkies in the air," Simon said.

"Yup. Royal Doulton china, hand-embroidered linens, flowers picked in the garden or greenhouse that morning, everything arranged exactly so, a little bell on the tea tray to summon the maid, the lot. Rose grew up knowing how to prepare and serve afternoon tea. To this day, the whole tradition around it is important to her. My grandfather,

Eric Campbell, was in the American army. He was stationed in England at the end of the fifties, and one day he was in Holgate, not paying attention to where he was going, and he was knocked flying by a young cook's assistant coming out of the butcher on the high street. Feeling bad about it, Rose visited him in the hospital whenever she could get away from work."

"And here you are today," Simon said.

"And here I am today. Poaching chicken for sandwiches." I added the tea leaves to the boiling water and carefully dropped in the breasts.

"I guess your grandfather's passed away?"

"He died four years ago. When he got out of the army, he and Rose moved to Iowa, where he was from. They loved each other to pieces until the day he died."

I thought about the rows of photographs in silver frames laid out on Rose's dresser, the ones she dusted herself every morning. In one of those pictures, the one of Rose and my grandfather standing on the church steps after their simple village wedding, as the rain fell in torrents, the bride might be mistaken for me posing in old-time clothes. My mother takes after her father, Eric, dark and Scottish. My siblings most resemble our father's maternal Italian ancestors. I'm the only one clearly carrying Rose's English genes: fine, straight blond hair, pale skin, small chin, light blue eyes, and a thin frame (lucky me!). Perhaps our shared appearance is part of the reason Rose and I have always been so close. But whereas Rose is very short, the one thing I inherited from my father is my height.

"My mother, Tina, is the oldest of their five children."

"So you're from Iowa? A long way from home."

"No, I was born and raised in Manhattan. My mom moved to New York as soon as she could get out of Iowa, became an actress and singer, and married a guy from the Bronx. That was my father. They divorced years ago, but he and I are still close. When my granddad died, Rose took their life savings and bought this place."

"A big move for a lady of her age."

"She loved my grandfather and the life they'd made together, but she hated Iowa. An Englishwoman, she always told me, needs to be by the sea."

Simon went to the sink and poured himself a glass of water. "I'll drink to that. I sometimes think my blood is made of seawater. When I'm away from it, I can feel the tides pulling at me."

"When my mom and her siblings were little, the family came to Cape Cod a lot on vacation, and Rose loved it here. She always wanted to come back permanently. She kept up with the goings-on in the Cape, and when she saw this house was for sale, she bought it."

"I can see why she'd want to do that, but why such a big place? Why'd she take on all the work and responsibility of a B & B?"

I pointed in the general direction of Victoria-on-Sea. "Because that house looks exactly like the stately home of Earl and Lady Frockmorton. Thornecroft Castle itself is nothing these days but a pile of moss-covered stones, but the family named their house after it when it was built by the first earl in the early days of Queen Victoria."

"Really?"

"Really. I don't fully understand it myself. Rose has had a good life. She had a strong and loving marriage to a good man, and together, they raised healthy and successful children and grandchildren. Most of them, anyway. I guess at heart she's still that little kitchen maid, dreaming she'll someday be lady of the manor."

Simon's big hands folded the dough in silence.

"The problem," I said, "is that she used every penny of her savings, plus what she got for the house in Iowa, to buy it. She can barely afford the upkeep and the taxes, never mind her own living expenses. She needs to earn income from the house. Thus the B & B."

"And you, Lily?" he asked. "What brings you here? You obviously know your way around a bowl of batter."

I saluted him with a wooden spoon. "I'm a culinary school–trained pastry chef. I worked in Manhattan, first at a bakery and then at a one-star Michelin restaurant."

"Impressive," he said.

"Maybe. But that's a high-stress life. Horrible hours, demanding people, customers as well as bosses and coworkers. Even in the world of celebrity chefs, the head chef at our restaurant—you'd recognize his name if I told you—was famous for his temper. I was the brunt of that temper one too many times. So I quit." I didn't bother to mention that that chef had also been my boyfriend. And that he'd come at me with a meat cleaver.

"And so you came here."

"Not right away. Rose wanted me to help her manage the B & B, but I had no interest in doing that. I was out of work, not sure if I wanted to stay in the restaurant business, when I came for a visit over the winter. When I saw this building, standing empty, with its own little garden—"

"You thought, *Tearoom*."

"Immediately. Rose loved the idea, and here we are. To sweeten the pot, she turned the guest cottage over to me."

"You're happy here," he said.

I smiled to myself. "I guess I am. When I have time to stop and think about it. But I'm worried she's trying to hand more and more of the running of the B & B over to me. Even if I wanted to, and I don't, I can't do both."

A rapid knocking sounded at the door, and a voice called, "Anyone here?"

"We're in the kitchen, Bernie," I said.

She came in, waving a pink cane high in the air. "Got it.

Oh, you have help already. Hi. I'm Bernie. We met earlier, but not under the best of conditions."

"Simon. I'd shake hands, but as you can see . . ." His were covered in dough.

Bernie leaned the cane against the counter and put a bottle of wine beside it. "I'm here to help. I figured you wouldn't have gotten much done today with all the police activity happening. What can I do? I'll do anything I can. Which, as you know, means no cooking. Why don't I start by opening this bottle?"

The only wineglasses I have are flutes in which we serve champagne as part of our special royal tea. Bernie took three down, twisted the cap off the bottle, and poured. She handed one flute to Simon, who took it in his sticky hands, and put mine on the counter next to my workstation. Simon took a sip before putting the glass down and turning to reach for a baking sheet.

The moment his back was turned, Bernie jerked her head toward him and wiggled her eyebrows at me. She waved her left hand in the air, as though it were on fire, and mouthed, "A man who can cook!"

I ignored her. "You can start by washing up those dishes. And keep at it. There'll be a lot. I need to not only make enough for tomorrow, but to replenish the freezer and make extra in case the police come back."

"Do you think they will?" Bernie squirted dishwashing liquid into the big square sink. "What did they want earlier?"

"They searched Rose's and my rooms, looking for the murder weapon."

Bernie swung around, her mouth open. "Murder weapon? They think this was murder? I thought he'd tripped and fallen down the stairs."

"They can't possibly think you or your grandmother had something to do with it?" Simon said.

"It would seem so." As I poured cake batter into cupcake papers, I told them Williams had first suggested Rose killed Jack Ford because he was suing her, and then he'd come back to accuse her of using her cane to whack him over the head before tipping him off the bluff. "Which is why," I said, "Rose is presently without a cane. The police took it as evidence. I wish we hadn't thrown away that black cane. It would be better if we could hand it over and they could see there isn't any evidence on it, but she threw it in the trash weeks ago."

"Never mind," Bernie said. "He's fishing. It'll turn out to be an accident, and if not, the cops'll soon move on to other suspects. Ford was in construction, wasn't he? The mob's heavily involved in the construction business, aren't they?"

"I don't know what the mob is involved in," I said.

"Yeah, that's it," Bernie said. "A mob hit."

"If so," Simon said, "the crime might never be solved. The mob has a way of covering their tracks."

"How do you know that?" I asked.

He grinned at me. "Not through personal experience, if that's what you're asking. I read the newspapers."

I thought about the mob. And mob money.

And a cop rumored to be corrupt.

I didn't like the conclusion I came up with.

Chapter 11

"I didn't think much of that older cop," Bernie said. "The woman seemed okay, though. At least she could think things through. He gets an idea in his head, and he sticks to it."

"What makes you think that?" I'd had the same impression, but I'd spent a lot more time with Detective Williams than Bernie had.

"I'm a writer," she said. "It's my business to be an excellent judge of character."

I refrained from commenting on Bernie's past experiences of judging character. This wasn't the right time or place to get into a discussion of her romantic entanglements. "This once, you're probably right."

"Writer?" Simon said. "What do you write?"

Bernie filled him in while I checked that the chicken had cooked properly. It had, and I set it aside to cool while I strained the tea leaves from the poaching liquid. Another batch of scones and the green tea cupcakes were in the ovens, and the kitchen was warming up and filling with the delicious scents of fresh baking. Outside, in the west, the sky was a portrait of gray, orange, and red streaks, and the shadows cast by the bushes lining the road were long. Headlights turned into the B & B driveway as guests returned from dinner.

Bernie threw down her dishcloth. "Look, there's not much I can do here to help, and you obviously have things well in hand."

"The icing for the cupcakes needs to be made," I said. "I was going to ask you to do that while I start a chocolate tart."

"My time would be better spent on the computer. I'm going to find out what I can about Jack Ford and who might have wanted him dead."

"It's not our business, Bernie," I said. "Leave it to the police."

"I'm starting to agree with her, Lily," Simon said thoughtfully. "You're dealing with a small-town police department and a possibly incompetent or even corrupt cop. You . . . we . . . need all the ammunition we can get if the police do decide to charge Rose."

"I don't want to think about it," I said.

"Good thing for you, I do." Bernie picked up the new cane. "I'll take this to Rose on my way."

Simon and I worked well together. He didn't need any instruction once he'd been shown my recipes, and everything he made came out perfect. I appreciated the fact that he didn't chatter away. Once Bernie had left, he got down to the task at hand and let me do the same.

By the time the last of the sun had drained out of the western sky, we had the chicken poached in Darjeeling deboned and shredded, the eggs boiled for tea sandwiches, a mountain of scones, piles of beautiful bright green macarons, green tea cupcakes, and a glistening Earl Grey chocolate tart.

I took off my apron. "A good evening's work. Leave the

dishes for tomorrow. Cheryl and Marybeth will do them when they get in. You've done so much, Simon. I don't know how to thank you."

"Don't worry about it. I was happy to help. I've missed getting my hands properly stuck in a bowl of dough."

I switched out the lights, locked the back door behind us, and walked Simon to his motorcycle.

"Good night," I said.

He unfastened his helmet and twisted it in his hands. I took a breath. He gave me a soft smile, put the black helmet on his head, fastened the straps, shrugged into his leather jacket, and zipped it up. "Good night, Lily. See you tomorrow."

He got on the big machine, revved the engine, and drove away. In the silence of a summer night, I could hear the sound of the engine, getting ever fainter, for a long time.

I walked slowly up the driveway toward the house. Stars twinkled overhead, and the sea murmured softly as it rushed to shore. The roof of the Goodwill house was nothing but a faint outline against the night sky. Lights were on in Rose's rooms, but I didn't bother to stop in and say good night. I was absolutely beat.

I'm accustomed to working long hours late into the night—I worked at a Michelin-starred restaurant, after all. Having also had a job in a busy bakery, I was used to starting work early. But not both on the same day, and I certainly wasn't accustomed to starting my day being questioned by the police.

The following morning, the police tape was still in place around the broken gate but, I was happy to see, no police officers appeared to be around. As I stood at the top of the bluffs, keeping well away from the broken gate, I saw a police launch approaching. It cruised along the shoreline, moving slowly.

I called to Éclair and went to work. I let myself into the kitchen, put the coffee on, and checked the requirements for breakfast.

Two empty rooms. Yesterday we'd been full, and in the busy season we accept only weekend reservations for two nights. Meaning two groups had left early.

I should mention that to the police. Perhaps the killer had booked a stay at Victoria-on-Sea, hoping for the chance to get close to Jack Ford. Maybe he or she had arranged for Ford to meet with them on the bluffs yesterday morning. A memory niggled at the back of my mind. I'd heard something in all the hubbub of the police activity and the guests gathering to watch, but it had fled, and now I couldn't quite put my finger on it.

I got out the mixing bowls. Today I was going to do two coffee cakes. I never make scones for the B & B breakfast. If people could have my scones here, why would they come into the tearoom?

The sausages were sizzling and the cakes were rising nicely in the oven when Edna arrived.

"Morning, Lily," she said. "I don't suppose you've been on the computer yet today?"

Something in her voice made me look up from the tomatoes I was slicing. "No. What's happened?"

"Word's getting around someone was murdered here yesterday."

"Have the police said it was murder?"

"No, and the paper isn't reporting it as such. The paper is also not naming Victoria-on-Sea, just mentioning that the incident happened near the bluffs south of North Augusta. But you know how these things spread on social media."

"Regardless of the truth," I said. "Looks like a couple of guests left last night. I hope this doesn't affect our business."

Tap-tap-tapping from the hallway announced the arrival of Rose and her new pink cane.

"You're up early," I said. Robbie's nose twitched as it caught the scent of sausages. On Sundays we served sausages *and* bacon; as soon as the cakes came out of the oven, the bacon would go in. He leapt onto the counter, next to where I was slicing tomatoes and mushrooms. I scooped him up and put him in my grandmother's lap. He hissed at me before settling down to be petted.

"Didn't sleep a wink," Rose said as her fingers stroked the thick fur. "This horrid business is most upsetting. Have you heard from Bernie this morning?"

"It's quarter to seven, Rose. Bernie's unlikely to call me at this time of day. Why do you want to know?"

"No reason."

I didn't believe her, but if Rose wanted to play coy, I'd let her.

"Two guests left prematurely yesterday, and I've had two cancellations," she said. "One was for the double suite for the entire week, tomorrow to Friday, and the other for two nights."

"That's not good."

"No, it is not. I intend to charge them the full amount. It says right there on our web page that we require forty-eight hours' notice of cancellation."

"They'll fight you," I said.

"Let them." Steel glimmered in her eyes. "As I was not sleeping, I spent some time in the wee hours consulting with the cursed Mr. Twitter."

"I thought you liked Twitter." Edna loaded her tray with butter, jam, fresh orange juice, and milk and cream.

"I love Twitter. When I first came to live in America, I had to wait weeks for a letter to arrive from home with the latest news. But I do not love it when it's spreading rumors about us."

"Is that why those people canceled, do you think?" I asked.

"I know it is. They wrote to tell me this establishment is not a safe place to spend their vacation. Pshaw. When did people become such cowards? In my day—"

"In your day, people didn't like to be around crime scenes, either, I bet. Some people, anyway." I remembered the eager crowd that had gathered at the edge of the bluff yesterday morning. "Others seem to love it." I took out the nicely golden cakes, decided they were ready, turned up the heat on the oven, and popped the bacon in. "Nothing we can do about it, except hope it all blows over."

"We'll see," Rose said.

"What does that mean?"

"I've changed my plans for today. I'm going to attend the duplicate bridge tournament at the community center this morning."

Edna came into the kitchen in time to hear that last statement. "I thought you didn't like duplicate bridge."

"I don't dislike duplicate, but I despise that bunch of old biddy-bodies who are constantly putting their hands in the air and calling for the director." Rose sniffed. "As if I'd be caught cheating."

I rolled my eyes.

Rose noticed. "I said caught cheating, love. If I cheat, I don't get caught."

Edna laughed and put the bowl of fruit salad on her tray.

"Why are you going, then?" I asked.

"No reason. I need to get back to the computer. Let me know when Bernie arrives."

"What does that mean? I'm not expecting Bernie this—"

"Edna, I'll have my tea in my suite this morning."

"That's fine," Edna said. "The pot's set out. Help yourself."

"I don't like the sound of that," I said when the *tap-tap-tap* of Rose's cane faded away.

Breakfast went smoothly, and everyone was served by nine o'clock. I called for Éclair and slipped out of the kitchen, leaving Edna to clean up. I was crossing the lawn, trying not to look at the yellow police tape waving in the wind or the police boat patrolling the shoreline, when I saw Bernie trotting toward me.

"Good morning!" she called.

"Hi. What brings you here so early?"

"I haven't been to bed. Where's Rose?" Bernie wore the same black shorts and red T-shirt she'd had on last night.

"What's going on?"

"I found something. I'll tell you and Rose at the same time."

"What sort of something? Are you and my grandmother conspiring behind my back?"

"If it was behind your back, I wouldn't be telling you about it now, would I? Before we go in, what's the deal with you and Simon? He's a real cutie. And the way he rolled that dough in his hands positively gave me the swoons. I'm assuming that bike parked outside the tearoom last night belongs to him. I love a man who rides a motorcycle almost as much as I love one who can cook."

As if the gardener heard us talking about him, the Weedwacker came to life at the front of the house.

"There is no deal," I said. "He works here. He's my employee."

"You don't own the B & B."

"No, I don't. Rose does. I just work here."

"Therefore, Rose's gardener does not work for you."

"Moot point," I said, "as I'm not looking for a relationship with a handsome motorcycle-riding English gardener with excellent baking skills or anyone else."

"So you admit he's handsome."

"Only if you like the big, gruff, soft-spoken outdoor type."

"Who can cook," Bernie said.

"I'll admit," I said, "that if I *was* looking for a relationship, he might be of interest."

She opened her mouth, and I raised my right hand in the universal stop gesture. "Until summer's over, I'll hardly have time to breathe, never mind date. He's leaving at the end of the season, anyway. He's going back to England. He came to America for a summer job in New York, but that fell through, and he was at loose ends when his uncle Gerry told him about this position."

Bernie wiggled her eyebrows. "A lot can happen in two months."

"A lot cannot. No. This summer is about getting the tearoom established and keeping Rose's B & B open and earning her some much-needed income. I don't have time for anything else."

We'd walked as we talked, and we arrived at Rose's suite. "I don't have time for answering police questions, either, but I might not be able to get out of that one."

"Which"—Bernie rapped loudly on the door—"is why I'm here."

"Door's open!" my grandmother called. We went in to find her sitting in front of the big computer in the corner of her sitting room that she used as the B & B office. She and my grandfather had owned a home-renovation firm in Iowa. For more than forty years, Rose had done the books, hired and fired the staff, placed the orders, and generally kept things operating. She now used all those skills to run Victoria-on-Sea. She hinted, often and loudly, that age was slowing her down and it would soon be time for me to think about taking over. I had absolutely no intention of doing so, and as for Rose slowing down, I'd seen no sign of that happening.

"What did you find?" she asked Bernie without lifting her head.

Bernie pulled up a chair. The only place left for me to sit was on the chintz-covered love seat, so I stood behind Rose and peered over her shoulder. The computer screen showed the bridge schedule for the North Augusta Community Center.

"If I arrive at eleven," Rose said, "that should be perfect."

Rose's sitting room was neatly divided into office—steel desk, ergonomic chair, twenty-five-inch computer monitor, black filing cabinet, large calendar pinned to the corkboard on the wall—and ladies' parlor—flower-patterned chair and love seat, Dresden china shepherdess figurines, hand-painted plates of English country gardens, sterling silver–framed family photographs on delicate piecrust side tables.

"Perfect for what?" I said.

They both ignored me.

"Jack Ford's company is called Ford Properties," Bernie said. "Most unoriginal. It's owned solely, far as I can tell, by him. Some speculation on what will happen to it now, but no one really knows."

"Children?" Rose asked.

"Three. Two sons from his first marriage, a daughter from his second, and none from his third. Which is his current. Current marriage until yesterday, I suppose. None of the children appear to be involved in the company, and both his divorces were bitter and expensive. The current wife is around his age and comes from family money of her own."

Rose held out her hand. "Pictures."

Bernie dug in her bag, pulled out sheets of computer paper, and handed them over. Rose flicked through them.

"I've never seen any of these people." She passed them to me. "Lily?"

"No one I recognize. Are you two going to tell me what's going on?"

"In due course," Rose said. "What did you learn about his business practices?"

"Shady but not openly illegal," Bernie said. "As far as I can find, anyway. I have some feelers out, so I might be able to come up with the dirt."

"Excuse me," I said. "Can we have a time-out here? I'm guessing Bernie spent most of the night looking into Jack Ford and his business. May I ask why?"

"Because," Rose said, "if we are going to find out who killed him—and we'll be proactive by assuming someone did, until we're notified otherwise—we need to know what enemies he had."

"Why are we getting involved?" I asked.

"We talked about it last night, remember?" Bernie said. "Simon and I agreed we can't trust the North Augusta PD not to railroad Rose."

"You involved Simon," Rose said. "Excellent idea."

"I thought you meant we were going to be careful of what we said. Not run a parallel investigation."

"I'm having trouble with the plot of my book. The Cape Cod fishing families idea isn't working out so well. If I think about something totally different, that will allow a separate part of my mind to divide itself off and work independently."

I didn't bother to point out that that didn't seem to have happened over the previous two years, when Bernie worked as an accountant while trying to write her book.

"Shady businessman means shady business contacts," Rose said. "Which means enemies. Keep digging, Bernadette.

What about Roy Gleeson, the councillor? More opportunity for graft and corruption. My money's on him."

"He seems to be clean," Bernie said. "Clean enough, anyway. Councillor is a part-time position, and his real job is a high school teacher. He lives, far as I can tell, on what a high school teacher makes. One point of interest . . . His son, Grayson, is an executive at Ford Properties."

"His son's name is Grayson Gleeson?" I said. "How did he ever survive high school?"

"That is worth knowing," Rose said. "A possibility of conflict of interest perhaps?"

"If the son's directly involved in the Goodwill project, then maybe," Bernie said, "but he lives in Boston and works on the industrial side of the company. Meaning factories and warehouses and the like."

"Keep digging." Rose checked her watch. "It's past nine now. People will be arriving in their offices. You can make some calls."

"I'll try," Bernie said, "but as I told you, most of my contacts are in Manhattan, not in Massachusetts."

"One thing leads to another," Rose said. "And nothing spreads faster than gossip. In that, I assume accountants are no more discreet than any other profession. We learned a few things about Lincoln Goodwill yesterday. He has money problems. Big ones. Yet another case of an heir squandering his inheritance. Rags to riches to rags in three generations, isn't that what they say? Too bad more of them can't be like the fourth Earl of Frockmorton, who saw the writing on the wall and set about learning how to do business. At Thornecroft—"

I pointed to the computer screen. "In the middle of all this, you're going out to play bridge? I hope you've updated the web page to show that we have vacancies for the coming week."

"We've had another vacancy since I spoke to you,"

Rose said. "Another cancellation. Unfortunately, it was for later in the week, so they got in under the forty-eight-hour deadline. Drat."

"You didn't hear from the police again, did you?" I asked.

"No. It's unfortunate the younger detective is a woman. Otherwise, I could set Bernie to working her wiles on him."

Bernie wiggled her eyebrows at me. I stifled a groan. I wasn't sure if Rose was joking or not.

"Then again," my grandmother said, "Detective Williams is a man."

"There are some things I wouldn't do, even for you, Rose," Bernie said. "In answer to Lily's earlier question, while I'm poking around on the Internet, Rose will be heading directly for gossip central. You want to know what's going on in town? Try the bridge club."

I stifled another groan. "As you two seem to have everything under control, I'm going to work."

Chapter 12

At ten to eleven I glanced out the window to see Rose's battered old Ford Focus station wagon bouncing down the driveway. I wasn't entirely happy about her interfering in the police investigation. Not that she, or Bernie, called it interfering. It was one thing to gather gossip, as Bernie and Rose were doing, but I couldn't see them stopping there. If they learned something they thought important, they'd act on it.

And that would be interfering.

I'd tried to bring that up when we'd been in Rose's sitting room earlier, but neither of them would listen to me.

What did I expect? They never did.

Rose's car turned right, heading toward town. A sleek red two-seater BMW convertible passed it and turned into our driveway.

I returned to the task of assembling chicken-poached-in-tea sandwiches. Scones were baking in one oven, and strawberry tarts in the other. We had enough reservations to have a full house today. More than enough; we'd had to turn people away.

I hate doing that. I hate it even more when we turn people away and then the reservations don't bother to show up. It was difficult juggling space on rainy days, but today promised to be another beautiful, sunny day, and we could always squeeze a few more into the patio.

"One children's tea for two," Cheryl said. "And one traditional for four." She put fresh water in one of the air pots and set it to boil, then got down two teapots, selected the appropriate tea for each from the canisters on the shelf, measured the leaves into tea balls, and put the balls in the pots. She placed cups and saucers and side plates on a tray while I arranged the food.

The children's tea was served on a two-tiered stand, the china as fine as any other and their choice of apple juice or iced tea in champagne flutes. The food consisted of peanut butter sandwiches cut into pinwheels, and ham and cheese on squares of alternating white and brown bread that resembled a checkerboard. For the desserts, I laid out miniature cinnamon buns with white icing, chocolate brownie bites, and chocolate chip cookies, and tucked chocolate-dipped strawberries and green grapes around the food.

"A single man's come in," Cheryl said. "That's unusual. He's taken a seat inside and ordered a cream tea."

"Maybe he's on holiday by himself."

"Not bad looking, either. About your age. No wedding ring."

Is everyone trying to fix me up?

The air pot reached the boil, and Cheryl poured water into the teapots. She set a small timer for each, as different teas require different water temperatures and steeping times. When the tea was properly steeped, she lifted the balls out of the pots and carried her laden tray out of the kitchen. The rooster timer crowed, and I checked the scones. I was slipping on oven mitts when Cheryl came back.

"He's asking if he can speak to you."

"Who's asking?"

"The single man."

"I'm kinda busy here." I placed the hot baking sheet on the cooling rack. The second batch of tarts was ready to go in. "He's probably a salesman. Tell him I have enough insurance and I'm satisfied with my regular suppliers."

"Okay."

She was soon back.

"He says it won't take long and it's a personal matter, and he'd appreciate a moment of your time. No hurry. He'll enjoy his tea and scones while he's waiting."

"Did he say that?"

"Yes."

"Let me get these cupcakes iced, and then I'll pop out for a moment. If I sit down, bring me a cup of tea. English breakfast."

"Will do."

I finished piping icing onto the green tea cupcakes I'd made last night. I took a moment to admire them—I don't believe anything in this world is more beautiful than a perfectly decorated cupcake—before taking off my apron. I quickly checked my face in the mirror over the sink for flour or green icing, pulled off my hairnet, shook out my hair, and went into the dining room.

Our day was just beginning, but the place was already satisfyingly full. Outside in the garden, most of the tables were occupied. Cheryl and Marybeth were busy taking orders and serving refreshments.

I spotted the man immediately, sitting quietly in a small alcove, at a table for two under a window, a pot of tea and a plate of scones in front of him. Sunlight streamed through the window, illuminating the handful of silver threads running through his dark hair. As Cheryl had said, we didn't often get men coming in here (like never) on their own. As I watched, he raised his teacup to his lips. Then he lifted his head and caught sight of me watching him. He put the cup down and got to his feet. I crossed the room.

He had exceptionally dark eyes, prominent cheekbones, and a strong jaw, and was dressed in jeans and an untucked blue shirt. He held out his hand. He was quite a bit taller than me, lean and fit and tanned. "Ms. Roberts, I assume. Thank you for agreeing to meet me. I'm Matt Goodwill."

"Oh," I said.

"Please, take a seat."

"I don't mean to sound rude, but I'm very busy. What's this about?"

"As we're neighbors of a sort, I wanted to meet you." He gestured to the chair. "I understand you've met my father already. Please? I'm sure you need a break." He looked around the busy room. "Nice place you've got here. I like it a lot."

I sat down slowly. He took his seat and picked up his cup. It was white with a pattern of pink roses and a thin silver rim. It looked small and fragile in his hand. "I'm not normally a tea drinker, but this is making me think I've been missing something all these years."

I felt myself relaxing. It was nice to sit down. "That's because you've never had a properly made cup of tea."

Marybeth slipped a full cup onto the table next to me.

"I won't beat about the bush," Matt said. "I know there's been some . . . disagreement between your grandmother and my father."

"To put it mildly." I added a touch of milk and half a spoonful of sugar to my tea and stirred.

"My father wants to sell the house."

"We have no objection to him selling it—it is his house, after all. My grandmother's opposed to the property being developed beyond what the current zoning allows." I sipped the tea. English breakfast: sturdy, hot, and delicious, with the slightest touch of sweetness. "Zoning exists for a reason."

"So it does," he said.

"You should be speaking to my grandmother, not to me. She owns Victoria-on-Sea, not me."

"I'm looking forward to meeting her." He smiled at me. "I was hungry, so I came in here first."

At that moment, Bernie walked into the tearoom. She started when she saw me sitting at a table, drinking tea in the middle of the day. Her face broke into a grin when she saw that my teatime companion was a handsome man.

"I wanted you, and your grandmother, to know—" Matt broke off when Bernie arrived at our table.

"Hope I'm not interrupting anything," my friend said.

"You're not," I said. "Bernie Murphy, this is Matt Goodwill."

The teasing sparkle disappeared from her eyes, and her face hardened. Color flooded into her cheeks. "Goodwill? Surely you're not related to the family that wants to build a monstrosity of a golf resort on this lovely, quiet, largely undeveloped stretch of the coast?"

"I have to confess that I am, but—"

"You've got a nerve," Bernie said, "coming in here and acting all friendly and neighborly."

"It's okay. Bernie." I attempted to smooth what was rapidly becoming turbulent waters. "It never hurts to talk things over."

"My sentiments exactly." Instead of taking offense at my friend's rudeness, Matt's eyes twinkled with amusement. "Why don't you join us?"

Bernie harrumphed.

"I was about to explain to Lily that—"

"As long as we're talking, where were you yesterday morning, say, around six o'clock?" Bernie asked.

Matt's eyes opened wide.

"Bernie!" I said.

"I don't mind the question," he said. "If you must know, I was at home in Chatham, enjoying a good night's sleep." He glanced at me. "Although, I have to confess I have no alibi, as I was alone."

I blushed, but Bernie didn't. "So you say," she said.

"So I say." He took a big bite out of his scone. "These are good."

"If you've finished your tea, Lily . . . ," Bernie said.

"I'm not."

"You can finish it in the kitchen." She snatched the cup out of my hand. "I've discovered something important I have to tell you about."

"You can talk in front of me," Matt said.

"We cannot. Let's go, Lily." Bernie practically lifted me to my feet.

"Uh," I said, grabbing at the saucer to take with me. "It was nice meeting you, Matt."

"It was not." Bernie dragged me away.

"Could you possibly have been any ruder?" I asked her once we were safely behind the kitchen doors.

"Yes, I could have been."

"He's a customer, for one thing. He was having tea and scones."

"At worst, he's a potential murderer, and at best, a framer of innocent old ladies."

"At best, he's a friendly neighbor. You have to admit he's rather nice looking."

"I hadn't noticed. Besides, I thought you liked Simon the gardener."

"No, Bernie. You like Simon the gardener for me."

"There's a difference?"

"A considerable difference. What do you need to tell me?"

"Royal tea for four," Marybeth said as she came in. Bernie touched her fingers to her lips and jerked her head toward Marybeth. I refrained from rolling my eyes. While Marybeth prepared the pots of tea and got a bottle of prosecco out of the fridge, I arranged the food trays. Bernie snatched a chicken sandwich off the platter and tossed it into her mouth.

"Hey," I said. "I need that."

"You've got plenty more."

"All of which are required to help provide me with an income."

"Charge it to my account. This one, too." She took another.

Marybeth left with the flutes of sparkling wine. I finished arranging the food.

"Jack Ford—" Bernie stopped talking when Cheryl came in. Cheryl took the canister of Creamy Earl Grey off the shelf, measured leaves into a silver tea ball, popped the ball into the pot, and added hot water. While she waited for the appropriate amount of time, she unloaded the dishwasher. Earl Grey ready, she removed the tea ball and took the pot into the dining room.

"Is . . ." Bernie took up exactly where she'd left off. "Or I should say Jack Ford was . . . as crooked as a three-dollar bill."

Marybeth came back to get the food tray I'd arranged. Once she'd left again, Bernie said, "We can't talk here."

"You can talk in front of Cheryl and Marybeth. If you don't want to, nothing I can do about that. I've already had my break."

"Drinking tea with the enemy," she said.

"Drinking tea with a friendly neighbor. Which, until he's proved himself to be my enemy, is all he is."

"I'll talk quickly. I've had a productive morning digging around on the Internet. Jack Ford had been skirting the edges of the law his entire business life. He never quite went over it, meaning the police couldn't nail him for anything, but he made a lot of enemies around here. He was known for sweet-talking elderly widows into selling their property to him at cut-rate prices and—"

"Two orders of traditional afternoon tea for four and one order of light tea for two," Cheryl said.

Bernie threw up her hands.

"Cheryl," I said, "do you know anything about Jack Ford and his business practices?"

"Nasty piece of work. Not a lot of people in North Augusta are mourning his passing."

"Anyone in particular?" I asked. "Can you think of anyone he recently cheated or offended?"

"Dorothy Johnson would have done him an injury if she could have."

Marybeth came through the swinging doors. "Where's that order of Palace Chai, Mom?" She was referring to one of our supplier's special blended teas, made with Assam tea, Jaipur roses, and green cardamom.

"Coming, coming," Cheryl said. "I can't do everything at once."

My two helpers left the kitchen.

I smiled at Bernie. "Anything else you need to know?"

It was coming up to four o'clock and I was elbow-deep in batter, making vanilla cupcakes for the children's tea, when yet another person, a woman this time, needed to speak to me.

"Tell her I'm busy," I said to Marybeth. "She can make an appointment. I'll be free January the tenth, at two p.m."

"I have no intention of waiting that long." Detective Redmond came into the kitchen.

Marybeth scurried away.

Amy Redmond checked out the small, crowded room. She didn't look all that impressed. When we renovated the building to turn it into the tearoom, in order to save money, we'd left the kitchen pretty much as it was after installing two professional ovens, a big fridge and freezer, and a butcher's block island. Redmond was looking at cracked linoleum flooring, chipped laminate countertops, and cheap plywood cabinets.

"I've always been interested in what goes on behind the scenes in a restaurant," she said. "Peaceful serenity outside, total chaos in the back."

"This is nothing. If you want chaos, you should visit a Michelin-starred restaurant in Manhattan on a Saturday night in December."

"I get enough chaos at crime scenes."

I shook my head. "Doesn't even begin to compare to some of the restaurants I've worked in. What can I do for you, Detective?"

"Tell me about Rose Campbell."

I put down my spatula. "She's my grandmother. My mother's mother. She moved to the Cape three years ago, when she bought the house and turned it into a B & B. She's exactly what she appears to be, an elderly widowed lady."

Marybeth slipped into the kitchen. She peeked at Redmond out of the corner of her eye as she began emptying the dishwasher.

"Perhaps," the detective said, "you'd prefer to talk in private."

I'd have preferred not to talk to her at all. I guessed that wasn't an option. "If you can wait one minute," I said. "I'll put these cupcakes into the oven, and we can go outside."

While I filled muffin tins with batter, Redmond leaned one hip against a counter. Marybeth dodged around her, putting the clean dishes away.

Cheryl came in. "One traditional tea for four."

"Can you take over for a couple of minutes, please?" I said.

Cheryl and Marybeth eyed Detective Redmond.

I put the cupcakes into the oven and set the timer and then led the way out the back door. Redmond followed me, and we stood on a patch of scruffy beach grasses next to a stunted oak tree. I checked the time on my phone. "I have twenty minutes before I have to check the cupcakes."

"Rose Campbell," Redmond said.

"Why are you asking?"

"That doesn't matter."

"I don't know what else to say. She's my grandmother. She owns the B & B. I own the tearoom."

"She had a public altercation with Jack Ford the day before he died."

"I wouldn't call it an altercation. I wouldn't even call it public. She objects to the proposed development of the property next door. She told him so, along with Mr. Goodwill, the owner, and Mr. Gleeson, who is some sort of town politician."

"She was heard to say the project would go ahead over her dead body."

"Just an expression."

"Or someone else's body."

I gave the detective a sickly grin.

She studied my face. I shifted from one foot to another. I checked the time on my phone. One entire minute had passed.

"My grandmother cares about this place," I said. "That's all. She bought it with her life savings after my grandfather died, and this is where she intends to spend what years she has left. Can you understand that?"

"I can understand that perfectly. Which is why I'm wondering what she might have done to preserve it."

"You can't seriously think—"

"Rose Campbell has come to police attention before."

"She has? Oh, that silly little dispute." I laughed lightly. I suspect it came out more like a choked growl.

"She was escorted out of town council for disrupting the meeting on the proposed highway extension."

I'd meant something else, but I decided not to point that out. "My grandmother cares about her neighbors and the environment. That's called civic engagement. It's considered a good thing."

"Was it a good thing when she was arrested back in Iowa?"

"She was arrested?"

"More than once. For public disobedience. She participated in anti-fracking protests and blocked a public roadway."

This was the first I'd heard about anything like that. "You've been checking up on her?"

"Did you doubt I would?"

"I guess not. I suppose you've been checking up on me, as well."

She said nothing.

A seagull landed on a branch of the struggling oak. It cocked its head and watched us.

"I'll admit," I said, "that my grandmother cares about things deeply. She's a passionate woman. She's English, you know."

Redmond cocked her head to one side. She might not have been deliberately imitating the seagull, but it looked that way. "The English are not exactly famous for displays of temper."

"I'm guessing you didn't grow up with an English grandmother. But *temper* is never a word I'd use to describe Rose."

"That is precisely the word Roy Gleeson used. He said she had a temper tantrum and threatened him and Jack Ford."

"You're barking up the wrong tree. Rose is eighty-five years old. Ladies in their ninth decade do not go around murdering people."

"Until they do," Redmond replied.

"Why are you telling me this? If you're expecting me to say something to incriminate Rose, I wouldn't do that even if I knew such a thing. Which, I assure you, I do not."

"I also have a grandmother, whom I love very much. Perhaps I'm suggesting you keep Rose out of trouble. More trouble."

"Everything okay here?" Simon McCracken came around the corner of the building. His hair was tousled by the wind, and his cheeks were tinged red. His overalls were streaked with good Cape Cod dirt, as were his hands.

"Perfectly okay. Thanks for asking," Redmond said.

"Good to hear. Lily?"

"We're fine, thanks. I think we're done, Detective. I have work to do."

"I'll let you get to it, then. Nice chatting to you." She took a few steps. I let out a breath.

I'd relaxed too soon. Redmond turned quickly. "A word to the wise, Lily. If I'm not around, you need to make sure your grandmother doesn't antagonize Chuck Williams. No more than she already has." She walked away.

"You okay?" Simon asked me once the detective was out of earshot.

"Yeah, I'm fine. She had some questions, more questions, about my grandmother's relationship with the deceased. Not that she had a relationship with him."

"I heard some of the conversation. It sounded tense. Hope you don't mind that I decided to intervene."

I gave him a smile. "I don't mind. I don't know what to think of Detective Redmond. One minute she sounds like she's on our side, and the next she's almost accusing Rose of killing that man."

"She's on one side only," Simon said. "Finding out the truth. Which is not what I've heard about the other cop."

"You mean Detective Williams?"

"I called Uncle Gerry last night and asked for the local gossip. Williams has the reputation of being not exactly crooked but lazy. He'll pursue the truth, if that's the easiest route. If not . . ."

"Good to know," I said.

"I suspect going after the Goodwill family, if it comes to that, will not be the easiest route. As Williams sees it, anyway. I don't like that Redmond seemed to be saying she might not be on this case much longer."

I sighed. "What a mess."

The back door opened, and Cheryl called, "We have an order for ginger tea, but the tin seems to be empty. Is there any more?"

"I think so. Check the back of the cabinet. That one's not very popular, so it gets pushed aside."

The door closed, and I turned to Simon. "Better get back at it."

"Me too. Talk to you later, m'lady." He touched his forehead and headed back to his gardens.

I went into the tearoom, pulling out my phone as I walked. I pressed buttons and then tucked the phone between my shoulder and my ear and put on oven mitts.

"What's happening now?" my mother said as I checked the cupcakes.

"Did you know Rose was arrested, more than once, back in Iowa? Over some sort of environmental protests?"

"Yes, I knew. You can be sure Ricky told me all about it." Ricky is Mom's youngest brother. "After Dad died, Mom had a lot more time on her hands. She sometimes used that time in ways the family didn't consider entirely appropriate."

"Like getting arrested at protests."

"Exactly. I assume you found out about it because of the current unpleasantness?"

"If by unpleasantness, you mean a man dying on Rose's

property, yes. The police happened to mention that my grandmother has a criminal record."

"Not really a record, Lil. She was let off with a warning every time."

"Every time? How many times were there?"

"I was hoping this B & B nonsense would at least keep her occupied and out of trouble. That appears not to be happening. You need to keep her under control."

"Me? She's your mother, and I don't see that you were ever able to control her."

"She's older now," Mom said. "Should be easier."

"Yeah, right."

"I have to run. If you need any help, let me know."

My mother hung up before I could tell her I needed her to come to the Cape and try to "control" her mother.

Chapter 13

"A good day," Cheryl said as she took off her apron.

"It was," I replied. We'd been full to overflowing all afternoon, but everything had gone smoothly. Not a single complaint or spilled cup of tea. Smoothly, except for the visit from the police that is.

Cheryl and Marybeth had finished the washing up and set the tearoom back to rights, all ready for tomorrow. I planned to stay for a while and get some more scones and tarts baked.

"Good night," my assistants called as they let themselves out. I heard them exchange greetings with Bernie, and a moment later my friend came through the swinging doors into the kitchen.

"Good," she said. "You're finished. I wanted to let you know where we're going in case something goes wrong."

I weighed the cold butter. Slightly short, so I added a thin slice. "Who's *we*, where are you going, and what might go wrong?"

"Rose is back from the bridge tournament. I told her about Dorothy Johnson, and we're going to pay a call on her."

"Who's Dorothy Johnson?" I threw the butter and shortening into the food processor, added flour combined with salt and a touch of sugar, and switched the machine on.

"The woman recently swindled by Jack Ford. Cheryl told me she's living in a retirement home in North Augusta."

I turned the food processor off. "That's none of your business."

"Sure it is. The man died on our . . . I mean Rose's property. That makes it our . . . I mean Rose's business."

"It does not. It's up to the police to investigate murders. Not you. And certainly not Rose."

"You try telling your grandmother we're not going. She's waiting in the car. If I'm not back in a couple minutes, she'll leave without me. Besides, I don't like that Detective Williams. I think he has Rose in his sights and he's not going to look much further."

I thought about my conversation with Amy Redmond. The police did seem to be paying a lot of attention to my grandmother. I also thought about what Gerry had said to Simon about Williams being lazy and Redmond implying she might not be around much longer.

"Oh, for heaven's sake." I twisted the bowl off its base and put it in the fridge.

"What are you doing?" Bernie asked.

"Unfinished pastry keeps okay in the fridge. I'm coming with you, of course. I don't trust either of you not to get yourselves into a heap of trouble."

At that moment, a car horn sounded. I hung up my apron and ran after Bernie.

Rose was in the driver's seat of her Focus, leaning on the horn in an attempt to hurry Bernie up. I clambered into the back. "I don't think it's a good idea for you to be interfering in the investigation."

My grandmother ignored me. "Let's go. Dinner's served

at that home at six. It's after five thirty now. We want to catch her going into dinner."

"Why?" I asked as we tore down the driveway and took the corner onto the main road on two wheels. I felt my side of the car dipping into the sandy shoulder and quickly fastened my seat belt as the wheels found the pavement. More than once we'd had to call a tow truck to haul the Focus out of the sand.

"The best time to interview suspects is when they've got dinner on their mind. She'll be in a hurry and not minding her tongue."

"How do you know about interviewing suspects?" I asked.

"Really, love. I've seen every episode of *Midsomer Murders*, haven't I? I've also read all of Deborah Crombie's books."

"Don't think I know those ones," Bernie said. "What are they about?"

"Never mind fictional detectives," I said. "Are you sure about this, Rose? Mrs. Johnson might not want to tell you her life story."

"I don't want to hear her life story, love. Just about her and Jack Ford."

"Tell Lily what happened at the bridge tournament," Bernie said.

"Did you learn anything?" I asked.

"This detecting can be a time-consuming process," Rose said.

"You're supposed to stop at a stop sign," I reminded her.

"No one was coming."

"I don't think that matters."

"Rose made what we call in the business 'contacts,'" Bernie said.

I refrained from asking what business that might be. "Contacts?"

"It's extremely difficult to talk at duplicate bridge," Rose said. "If the director herself isn't rudely shushing you, you can be sure some of the thin-lipped players will be. Those are usually the less capable players, I've found."

"Whatever," I said.

We whipped along the busy coast road. The blue waters of Cape Cod Bay sparkled in the distance.

"I managed to make arrangements for tomorrow," Rose said. "We'll be having tea at one o'clock, Lily. Have a table for six ready for us."

"I will if you phone to make a reservation."

North Augusta is a small town, located south of the better-known North Truro. The year-round population isn't more than a thousand, but in the summer it swells to ten times that as the hotels and B & Bs and campgrounds fill up and day visitors stroll the tree-lined streets and pop in and out of cafés and shops.

The Augusta Retirement Home is located on the outskirts of town, so we didn't have to fight the supper-hour traffic to get there. We arrived at ten to six.

Rose screeched to a halt at a taxi stand by the front door.

"You can't park here," I said.

She turned off the engine. "We won't be long."

What could I do but get out of the car?

I held the door for Rose, Bernie handed her the new pink cane, and the three of us climbed the steps.

It was immediately obvious that the Augusta Retirement Home didn't spend a lot of money on upkeep. The flower beds were weed choked, and overgrown bushes intruded onto the pathways. A crack ran from one side of the glass pane in the front door to the other.

I pushed open the door, and we went in. The reception area was dimly lit, probably, I thought, in an attempt to hide the dirty carpet and dusty furniture. Beyond the entranceway, the room widened into what appeared to be a combination common room and dining area. Elderly people were gathering for dinner, some already seated and some heading for their seats.

"Good afternoon," Rose said to the woman behind the desk, who looked about as worn as the carpet. "We're here to see Mrs. Johnson. Dorothy Johnson."

The woman didn't bother to stifle a yawn, and I got a better view than I wanted of stained and chipped teeth. "Are you her guests for dinner?"

"No," I said.

"Yes," Rose said.

"She's probably in the dining room. You can go on in."

"Do you know what Dorothy looks like?" I whispered to Bernie.

"I can't tell her from the Abominable Snowman."

"The thing is, love"—Rose leaned over the desk—"my eyes aren't quite as good as they once were. You know how it is." She tittered in embarrassment. "I might not be able to pick dear Dorothy out in the crowd. And wouldn't that be awkward?"

The receptionist looked at me. I shrugged.

She shoved herself to her feet, accompanied by an enormous sigh, intended to show us how much trouble she was taking. She walked to the entrance to the dining area, slowly lifted one arm, and thrust out a long, sharp red-tipped finger. I thought of the Ghost of Christmas Yet to Come, pointing Ebenezer Scrooge to his doom. "In the blue sweater and glasses, crossing in front of the fireplace. She's heading to the table in the far corner, near the piano."

Rose peered myopically across the room. "Oh, yes. I do think that's her. Thank you so much for your help. Let's go, girls. Dorothy will be so thrilled to see me again after all these years."

The woman in question moved with great care, using the assistance of a walker. As we watched, she reached her table, parked her walker against the wall, and settled herself slowly into her seat.

I couldn't believe Rose's luck. Dorothy was the only one sitting at a table for four. "Snag those chairs," Rose ordered. "Quickly now, before anyone else gets them."

I strode as fast as I dared across the room, dodging people, walkers, canes, and chairs. The room was clean, although the furniture was tired and the decor aged. The most modern thing in the room was the giant TV mounted on a wall, facing a circle of upholstered chairs. The fabric on the chairs was torn, and I saw stains on the seats and the arms I didn't want to investigate. The tables in the dining area were covered in brightly patterned cloths, which went a long way—although not the whole way—to disguising the stains. The few potted artificial trees and plants scattered about needed a good dusting, as did the frames of the mass-produced pictures of various Cape Cod scenes. The whole place, I thought, was simply depressing.

"Mrs. Johnson?" I said.

She looked up, blinking rapidly from beneath thick glasses. "Yes?"

"I'm, uh . . . I'm . . ."

I was saved from trying to decide who I was by the arrival of Rose and Bernie. Rose immediately took the chair next to Dorothy Johnson.

"Hello," Dorothy said. "Are you new here?"

"In a manner of speaking. My name's Rose, and I believe you are Dorothy."

"I am. I hope you're not a vegetarian, Rose."

"I'm not."

"Good. They serve a vegetarian option here, and I've been told it's perfectly dreadful. I hope we're not having what they call steak tonight. Whenever they serve beef, I'm sure the poor cow died of old age."

"Are these seats reserved?" I said. "I wouldn't want to put anyone out."

"No. We sit wherever we like. I rarely have companions at meals." Dorothy glanced around the room. "Miserable bunch."

"Uh . . . okay," I said. I slipped into a chair, and Bernie took the other.

Dorothy gave me a vacant smile. "Is this your daughter, Rose? How nice of her to visit."

I decided that considering the woman's bad eyesight, I'd not take offense at being taken for my mother's age.

Dorothy next smiled at Bernie. "And your daughter brought her daughter. How nice."

Bernie snickered.

"Such a pretty girl, too. Such gorgeous red hair," Dorothy said. Bernie pointedly avoided my eyes. "If you want your visitors to eat, Rose, you need to advise Maria ahead of time so she can ensure the exorbitant cost goes on your bill. Did you do that?"

"They don't need to eat," Rose said. I wasn't disappointed to hear that. Young waitresses, high school students most likely, had appeared with trays of soup. I've seen dishwater that looked more appealing. The bread intended to accompany the soup was nothing but thin slices of white bread from a supermarket package.

A waitress dumped a bowl containing a drizzle of soup in front of Dorothy and another before Rose. She glanced at Bernie and me.

"Not for us, thanks," Bernie said.

Dorothy picked up her spoon, and Rose pushed her soup to one side. "Jack Ford," she said.

Dorothy froze, the spoon halfway to her open mouth.

"You knew him," Rose said. "Did you hear he died?"

"I heard. I would have danced a jig around my apartment if my hip wasn't so bad these days."

"Is that so? He wasn't a friend of yours, then?"

Dorothy's eyes narrowed. "What are you saying?"

"He was no friend of mine, either. I heard he did you wrong."

The watery old eyes blazed fire. "You heard right." Dorothy put down her spoon with a sigh. Tears welled up, putting out the fire. "He wasn't a nice man."

Rose placed her hand on top of Dorothy's. "Do you want to tell me about it, love?"

"I wasn't sure I was ready to sell the house yet. We'd had so many happy years there. But it was getting too much for me. A big house, the garden, snow in winter. He came knocking on my door, saying he was looking for a home in the area and admired mine. It was a lovely neighborhood, and I have to admit my house was looking a bit . . . tired. I didn't have the energy to keep it up, nor the money to pay anyone else to. He was so friendly. So charming. He'd heard, he said, the public school was an excellent one. I didn't know about that—it had been a long time since I was concerned about the school—but I said that was true. He wanted a nice home in a nice neighborhood for his family. I was happy to do without realtors and their exorbitant fees, so I sold mine to him for what he told me was an excellent price."

"What he told you?" Rose said.

Dorothy nodded. "First thing he did was tear it down. My lovely house, gone. My rosebushes tossed on the dump, the big old trees dug up. There's an office building going up there now. He hadn't told me that section of the block had been rezoned. A horrible thing with a parking lot and no trees. Mr. Ford never had any intention of living there. I since learned I could have sold my house for a lot more than I got. But I thought he was nice."

Rose patted her hand.

"I always intended to move to Florida when I sold the house." Dorothy dipped her spoon into her soup bowl and let the thin liquid dribble off it. "Instead, here I am. In this horrible place. It's all I can afford. But now Jack Ford's heading for his grave, so I can say he's worse off than me."

"What about your children?" Rose asked. "Do they help you?"

"They've worries of their own. My daughter has the children, you know. They keep her so busy."

"I'm sure they do." Rose stood up. Bernie and I hurried to do the same. "Thank you for talking to me."

"My son lives in Boston, and he hasn't spoken to me since he found out what the house next door sold for. Almost twice what I got."

"You didn't check with the neighbors?" Bernie asked. "To find out what was going on in the neighborhood?"

"I didn't have anything to do with those people," Dorothy sniffed. "Miserable bunch, the lot of them."

Okay then.

"It was nice meeting you, Rose. I assume you aren't moving into this place?"

"No."

"You're lucky."

"At least you can stay in North Augusta," I said, trying to be cheerful. "Close to your friends."

"My friends! I never could stand any one of them. Why do you think I wanted to move to Florida?" She went back to her soup.

"That was interesting," I said when we were standing outside.

"Interesting," Rose said, "but not informative. We already knew Jack Ford was a sleazy businessman."

"Mrs. Johnson didn't exactly hide her feelings for him,"

I said. "I hope you're not going to tell the police she had a motive."

"Hardly. She might have quite cheerfully killed him, but I can't see her stalking the man across my lawn in the early hours and wrestling with him at the edge of the cliff, can you?"

"No," Bernie and I agreed.

"Poor thing," I said.

"I wouldn't feel too sorry for her," Rose said. "She foolishly wouldn't take the advice of a realtor, because she begrudged them their fees. I sense a bitter old woman who would have been bitter no matter what happened. She wouldn't have been any happier in Florida. We take our attitudes toward people with us wherever we go. It's our choice whether we get on with others or not. This isn't one of the better retirement homes, but I've seen a lot worse."

"Where to now?" Bernie asked.

"Home," I said. "I have baking to do for tomorrow."

"Home," Rose said. "Our inquiries have dried up for today. We will resume tomorrow."

"We will, will we?" I said.

"We will."

Chapter 14

I spent a restless night. Éclair shuffled and sniffed and groaned and thrashed. I tossed and turned, pounded my pillow, tossed and turned some more. The wind was high: outside my windows, waves threw themselves against the shore, branches scraped the glass, and the old cottage squeaked.

Events of yesterday and today had been churning around and around in my mind, refusing to let me settle. Every time I'd been about to drop off, an image of Detective Williams almost accusing Rose of being a killer popped into my mind.

Finally, I threw off the covers and got up. Éclair opened one eye, saw it was still dark, and went back to sleep. I made myself a cup of chamomile tea and sat at the kitchen table to drink it. My iPad lay in front of me. I eyed it. Using electronic devices is the worst way, so they say, of luring oneself to sleep. Nevertheless, I opened it.

I started at the NAPD web site to find out what information was available for Amy Redmond and Chuck Williams. Williams, I read, had been with the department for almost twenty years, his entire police career. Redmond, two weeks.

I expanded my search. Williams was regularly featured in the local paper, making a statement about a break and enter or a traffic accident or handing out awards at service clubs. He always smiled broadly for the camera, even at times when I thought smiling to be a touch inappropriate. He loved being the center of attention, all right.

I left the *North Augusta Times* web site and accessed the community forums. The more I read, the less favorable the attention became. Citizens complained Williams wasn't investigating their concerns properly. A couple of letters to chat boards said he hounded what he considered to be unsuitable elements out of town. He was accused of grandstanding—making a minor situation seem more important than it was in order to make himself look better. About a year ago, an anonymous letter writer accused Williams of causing a traffic accident when he was drunk on duty and behind the wheel of a cruiser. I tried to find more on that story, but it ended abruptly. Not another word was said.

I found several pictures of Williams with Lincoln Goodwill: Goodwill making a donation to the police charity drive, Goodwill at the opening of the new police station a couple of years ago. The police chief's name was Martin Summerdale, and he didn't appear to be one for the limelight. In many of the public photos, he stood slightly to one side, with a pasted-on smile, while Williams took center stage.

As for his career, Williams had no highs and no lows. A plodding small-town cop heading for retirement. As I read, I realized there had been no murders in North Augusta for many years. Meaning Detective Williams was way out of his depth investigating the death of Jack Ford.

Detective Amy Redmond was another story entirely. She came from Boston, where she'd been a cop for ten years. She'd been one of the lead detectives on a high-profile murder case: a sports star had killed his wife's lover and claimed self-defense. Photos in the Boston papers showed Redmond coming out of court after the verdict of not guilty came down. She did not look happy. Her name popped up in other cases, many of them big ones and most of them resulting in a conviction.

I wondered what had brought her to sleepy little North Augusta.

I remembered how she'd edged away when the photographer had arrived at the scene of Jack Ford's death. At the time, I'd assumed she figured she had more important things to do than pose for the camera. Now I wondered if she'd been consciously trying to avoid having her picture taken.

I picked up my cup and realized it was empty. I glanced at the clock. Two thirty. I had to be up in three hours, ready to start another fourteen-hour day. I headed back to bed. Éclair was spread across the bed, snoring happily. For a forty-pound animal, she could take up more than her share of space.

I shoved Éclair over and crawled between the covers, hoping sleep would soon come.

I awoke in a panic, convinced I'd forgotten to do something important. Then it came to me—ensure Rose and her friends had a table at one o'clock. I fumbled for my phone in the dark and called the tearoom, where I left a message on the answering machine. The clock on the phone told me it was three o'clock. When I lay back down, I discovered Éclair had moved and was smack-dab in the middle of my section of the bed. I shoved her over. She resisted, but I was stronger . . . barely. I finally drifted off to sleep, lulled by the steady breathing of my dog and the steady, comforting beat of the waves rushing to shore and breaking on the rocks at the bottom of the bluffs.

* * *

"Do you recognize this item?" Detective Williams held out a photograph.

"It looks like a hiking pole."

"So it does. I asked if you recognize it."

"I've seen quite a few of those around here. People who walk along the cliff path often use them. I don't own one, if that's what you're asking."

"How about your grandmother?"

I tried not to sigh. It was noon, and I was expecting a full house all day, but instead of coming to the tearoom to question me, as Redmond had done, Williams sent a uniformed officer to "escort" me to Rose's house. My phone had gone off as we walked down the driveway, and the officer snarled at me not to answer it. I'd peeked at the screen under cover of turning the sound off: *Rose*.

I was now with Williams in the drawing room, where I feared he was beginning to make himself altogether too comfortable.

"Have you asked her?" I said.

"I'm asking you."

"She doesn't own anything like that. She uses a cane, not hiking poles."

He tried not to look too disappointed. "That's what she says. I've asked around, and no one remembers seeing her with something like this."

"Saturday morning, as I was coming to the house to start breakfast, shortly before six, I saw two women going for a hike. They had poles. They said good morning and went down the stairs. I don't remember if they were exactly like that one, though."

"Were these women guests here?"

"I can't say. I don't usually mix with the guests." I described them as best I could, and Williams jotted the information in his notebook.

I stood up. "If we're finished . . ."

"We're not. This one looks new. I've got officers going to the outdoor equipment stores, showing the picture and asking if anyone remembers anyone buying one like this. If you or your grandmother or your red-headed friend did, I'll find out."

"Well, we didn't, so you won't. Where did you find it?"

"We've been searching the shoreline, looking for whatever might have been used to knock Jack Ford off balance and send him over the cliff. This"—he nodded at the photograph—"was found on the beach, a hundred or so feet farther along, this morning. The sea was rough last night. It must have washed up on the rocks."

"You don't know if it was used on Ford. Someone might have lost it."

"Police work, Ms. Roberts, is all about details. Details and little things. It's often the little things that trip people up." He eyed me, no doubt expecting me to trip up at any moment.

I said nothing.

"You can go," he said.

"Thank you," I said.

Two can play at that game. I headed for the door and then turned sharply around. "You have to come, too. This is private property, and you have no right to be in this room alone."

He sputtered but stood up. "I've left notes for your guests to contact me when they return. We'll be asking them about this hiking pole."

"You do that."

I waited on the verandah while Williams and the officer got into their car and drove away. Then I checked my phone.

A text from Rose: **They have a blue hiking pole. Not mine. Never seen it before. Is it yours?**

I replied: **No.**

* * *

"Rose has arrived," Cheryl said at two minutes to one.

"Punctual, as always. Make sure she gets a nice table."

"You mean not like the un-nice ones we have for ordinary people?"

"Very funny. Try not to spill tea into her lap."

"Let me see if I can remember that. No spilled tea. Check." She carried a three-tiered stand into the dining room, still chuckling.

I gave Rose's friends time to arrive and be served, and then I washed my hands and took off my apron and went to greet them. They'd been seated at the big round table in the center of the main room. The ladies were all close to my grandmother's age, nicely dressed in bright summer dresses or colorful blouses over pressed trousers. Their hair was neatly cut gray or carefully styled dyed blond; their jewelry subdued but tasteful. Various perfumes, some applied with an excessively heavy hand, battled with the scents rising from the teapots.

"There you are," Rose said with delight. She'd dressed for the occasion in an ankle-length, full-skirted, sleeveless dress in every possible shade of purple pulled over a yellow T-shirt. "Girls, this is my granddaughter Lily, the founder of the feast, as Charles Dickens would say."

The women all muttered some form of "Nice to meet you."

"This is absolutely delightful," a woman with a tidy bob of pure white hair said. "You must be so proud of this marvelous place."

"Thank you. I am."

She lifted her glass in a salute. They'd been served the royal tea, which included a glass of sparkling wine each. I'd asked Marybeth to set the table with a full set of matching white china with an edge of navy blue and gold trim, and to use blue linen napkins.

"Do you do any catering?" one of the perfectly styled blondes asked. "It's my turn to host the euchre club next week, and I'd love to be able to serve something like this."

"Sorry, no. I can barely keep up with business in the tearoom as it is."

"This chocolate tart's amazing," another woman said. "I've never had anything quite like it. Do you share your recipes?"

I smiled at her. "I can tell you it's made with Earl Grey tea, but no more."

"If people can make it at home," Rose said, "why would they come here?"

"Nice meeting you, ladies," I said. "Enjoy your tea." I took a step back and tripped over a cane propped against one of the chairs. I stumbled and fell backward, crashing into Marybeth, who dropped the tray she was carrying with a sharp cry.

I did a smart little dance, trying to keep to my feet, while the tray and its load crashed to the floor. Some of the teacups and plates smashed, spraying fine china in all directions. People jumped, and a couple of women cried out in surprise.

"Oh, my gosh," I said to a red-faced Marybeth. "I am so sorry. It was entirely my fault. Get the broom." Fortunately, the dishes had been used, so we hadn't lost any food.

Two of Rose's friends started to stand up. "Please," I said, "continue with your tea. We'll have this all cleared up in a jiffy."

While Marybeth ran for a broom, I began gathering the intact china and the bigger of the broken pieces. In all my years working in fancy restaurants and Manhattan bakeries, I'd never broken so much as a plate. This pleasant little tearoom had put me off my guard. Good thing Marybeth's tray hadn't contained hot food or water just off the boil.

"Where were we?" Rose said to her friends. "Oh, yes. We were talking about our esteemed mayor. Please continue, Alice."

"Far be it from me to spread idle gossip, but . . . ," the woman who'd asked me about catering said, "like everyone who's having an affair, she thinks she's being *sooo* discreet. Meanwhile, everyone in town knows all about it."

"Everyone but her husband," another woman said.

"As far as I'm aware, he doesn't know. Then again, maybe he does. The police haven't solved the murder yet, have they, Rose?"

"It doesn't appear so," my grandmother said.

I reached between her feet and grabbed the handle of a cup. It was a nice cup, too—one of my favorites. Then again, they were all my favorites at one time or another. I love nothing more than visiting antique shows in search of heirloom china at bargain-basement prices. Rose lifted the edge of the tablecloth and peered under the table at me.

"Do you need us to move, love?"

"No. I've got it."

"If you're implying that Al Powers killed Jack Ford, you've got it wrong." My ears pricked up. Marybeth arrived with a broom and dustpan and began sweeping. I stayed where I was—under the table.

"Al doesn't care one whit what Carla gets up to. I can tell you—and keep this just between us—that he's been seen in Provincetown in the company of a woman much, much younger than he is."

The women at the table tittered.

Carla Powers. That was the name of the mayor of North Augusta. She'd been here for the grand opening of the tearoom. She made some sort of speech, although I hadn't heard most of it, being in the back, trying to save a pan of in-danger-of-burning brownies.

Above my head, the table creaked as a woman leaned forward. "If not Al," she said in a low voice, "maybe Carla did it herself."

Several women gasped.

"Why do you say that?" Rose asked.

"Jack Ford was a scoundrel. Please, he'd never have left Janice. Her brother's one of the best divorce lawyers in Massachusetts. Janice would have taken him for everything he had. And then some."

"You sound as though you know of what you speak, Judy."

"I will admit that between my second and third marriages, Jack suggested we'd make a nice couple," Judy said, a touch of pride in her voice. "I took his measure fast enough."

"I'm sure you did," someone said.

Marybeth finished sweeping up broken china. She bent over and looked at me crouching under the table. I put my fingers to my lips and gave her a wink. She shrugged, straightened up, and walked away. Rose had moved her legs to one side. She knew I was listening, and she wanted me to stay.

"Yes, I did," Judy snapped back. "Poor Carla isn't quite so . . . observant about men."

"As you are, with your years of experience."

"If you want to put it that way," Judy said. "Whereas I could tell immediately what sort of man Jack was, some women need a bit longer."

"You can't possibly be suggesting Carla killed Jack Ford," Rose said.

Judy crossed her legs. I grunted as the sharp toe of her stiletto-heeled shoe hit my shoulder.

"What was that?"

"Lily's sweeping up the last of the broken dishes. She's so very thorough," Rose said. "Pay her no mind."

An upside-down gray head peered at me. "Are you okay there, Lily? Do you need us to move?"

"No, I'm fine. Got the last of it, thanks." I crawled out from under the table. I waved the cup handle as evidence. "Carry on."

I went back to my kitchen as Judy said, "I'm not suggesting anything. I'm merely pointing out that . . ."

Half an hour later, Rose came into the kitchen in a swirl of purple. "We're leaving, love, and my friends wanted me to thank you for the lovely tea."

"My pleasure." I lowered my voice. "Did you get what you wanted?"

"Wanted?"

"By way of the North Augusta gossip grapevine."

The edges of her mouth curled up. "I might have. I'll report to Bernie as soon as I get home. It seems as though—"

The doors flew open. "Big rush," Marybeth said. "Several cars are pulling up outside. I think the three o'clock reservations are early."

"You might give some thought to catering," Rose said.

"I most certainly will not," I said.

"It would bring in some income over the slow winter months."

"I'm not . . . ," but I was speaking to my grandmother's back.

Oh, dear. Once Rose got an idea in her head, it could be very hard to dislodge it.

Rose didn't return, and so I had to wait until the end of the day before finding out the rest of the gossip about Mayor Carla Powers.

The last of our patrons lingered over their tea and finally left at five thirty. Marybeth and Cheryl cleaned the kitchen and dining room, hung up their aprons, bid me a good evening, and left. No rest for the weary: I needed to get several batches of scones made for tomorrow. Despite all the baking Simon had done for me on Saturday evening, I'd almost run out today.

That would have been a disaster. Can't run a tearoom without scones.

I was putting the first batch into the oven when I heard the roar of a motorcycle coming down our road. Moments later, a knock sounded on the back door.

I opened it to see a grinning Simon. He'd changed out of his overalls into jeans and a denim jacket over a clean T-shirt and scrubbed the evidence of our gardens off his hands and face. He carried his helmet in one hand and supported a flat white box with the other. "I figured you'd still be working. I can smell baking scones a mile away. I brought dinner."

"Dinner?"

"I hope you like pizza. All Americans like pizza, don't they?"

"I don't know about all of them, but I certainly do."

He came in, carried on the scent of fried onions, spicy sausage, and risen dough. He put the box on the butcher's block, while I took two clean plates out of the dishwasher and tore several sheets of paper towels off the roll.

"You look like you need to be off your feet for a while," he said. "Be right back." He went into the dining room while I lifted the lid on the box. I breathed deeply.

I do love pizza. The more toppings, the better, and this one was loaded.

Simon came back, dragging two chairs, and waved to me to sit.

"I didn't know what you like on your pizza," he said, "so I got pretty much everything."

"I like pretty much everything." I grabbed a slice and lifted it to my mouth, trailing thick strands of melting cheese. I was suddenly ravenous.

He helped himself to a piece. "You seemed to be busy today. Every time I passed, your parking lot was almost full."

"The tearoom's proving to be a huge success, and I'm pleased, but I have to confess I'm worried about the off-season. It can be pretty quiet here."

"This isn't a tourist spot in the winter?"

"Not really. The town tries, but we don't have much in the way of winter sports. There are nicer places in New England for those who want to ski or spend time in the winter woods."

"You could put a nice ski hill running down the bluffs."

I laughed. "Ending with an icy cold dip. The bay doesn't freeze over." I'd been trying not to think about how I'd get through winter, when the tourists went home and the locals were more likely to stay in, huddled around their fireplaces. Catering might be an option, although one I dreaded.

I changed the subject. "How are you finding our garden?"

"It's great. Challenging, to be sure, but I'm enjoying it. I've worked in big gardens and had a boss, if not a direct supervisor. It's nice to have a free hand."

The rooster next to the oven announced it was time for the scones to come out, and I hurried to see to them.

Simon popped the last of the crust of his third slice of pizza into his mouth. "You're busy. I'll let you get back to it. Do you need a hand?"

"I'm going to make one more batch and then call it a day. Thanks for this." I gestured to the empty box. "It was very thoughtful of you. I work with food all day, and yet sometimes I forget to eat."

"I remember that from when Mum was catering and I was her helper. She'd slap my hands and say the food was for our customers, not me. Imagine telling a teenage boy he couldn't eat."

I laughed and walked him to the door. I opened it while he took his helmet off the counter. He stepped outside, and then he turned and looked at me. For the briefest moment, I thought he might kiss me.

But he didn't. He put his helmet on his head and walked into the deepening twilight.

I needed to talk to Rose, but before I did that, my dog needed a bathroom break. I gave Éclair a minute to sniff around our little yard and then called her to come and opened the gate. A few guests were sitting on the garden benches, enjoying the long, lingering twilight of a Cape Cod summer's evening. They greeted me politely and fussed over Éclair, who loved nothing better than to be fussed over. Yellow police tape still flapped at the gate to the steps leading down to the beach. I tried not to look in that direction and called Éclair to come. We went into the house, and I knocked lightly on Rose's door.

The door opened, and her head popped out. "Lily, do come in. We were just talking about you."

"We?"

"I have a guest," she said.

I looked over her shoulder to see Matt Goodwill rising to his feet from an armchair. A cut-glass tumbler rested on the table next to him. "I was telling your grandmother how much I liked your tearoom."

Éclair rushed into the room and headed straight for Matt, yipping in excitement. He bent over, way over, and gave her a rub on the top of her curly head. "Hey there, little fellow. Aren't you a cutie."

"Little lady," I said. "She's a girl."

Robert the Bruce crouched on the top of the bookshelf. He hissed. Robbie liked to be the one being fussed over.

Éclair and Robert the Bruce aren't exactly friends, but they tolerate each other, while displaying signs of total contempt.

Rose settled herself into her favorite chair, her nightly gin and tonic at hand.

"I stand corrected." Matt picked up his glass and downed the last of the amber liquid. "Time I was on my way. Remember what I said, Rose. I'm glad we understand each other."

"Thank you for stopping by," she said.

"Please, don't get up. I can show myself out." He gave her a warm smile. Rose colored prettily.

When the door had closed behind him, I turned to my grandmother. "What do you understand each other about?"

"He's a nice young man, isn't he?" Robbie climbed off the shelf and crawled into Rose's lap. She stroked him. He gave Éclair a smirk and then stuck his little black nose into the glass in Rose's other hand.

"I don't think it's a good idea for your cat to be drinking gin," I said.

"No point in stopping him now. Would you like one?"

"No thanks. I won't stay long. What did Matt Goodwill want?"

She sipped her drink. "He and his father don't see eye to eye on the future of the property. Matt wants to keep it in the family. Lincoln, as we know, wants to sell it. Matt's trying to put the money together to buy it, but time's running out."

"I assume Lincoln owns it."

"He does."

"Then it doesn't matter what his son wants, does it?"

"No. But one can hope the son has some influence over the father."

"The way my mother has influence over you?"

"Perhaps not the best example," Rose said.

"What's happening with the property now Jack Ford's out of the picture?"

"The rezoning motion will come before council the week after next. That's the first step in selling it, if Lincoln's going to get the price he wants."

"Roy Gleeson's the one bringing the motion forward, or so I heard. Is the mayor in favor?"

Rose raised one eyebrow. "Ah yes, Her Honor might be involved in this in more ways than one."

"Which brings us to why I'm here. I assume you had the bridge group to tea to interrogate them about Jack Ford. From what I heard, you learned something important."

"I learned a great deal," she said. "That he had enemies because of his business practices, we know. We did not know he was rumored to be having an affair with Her Honor and that both parties are married." She shook her head. "Tsk, tsk. Secrets lead to betrayal, and they can also lead to blackmail. You need to speak to Mrs. Powers."

"Me?"

"Bernie and I have come up with a plan of attack. Bernie checked the mayor's public schedule, and nothing's mentioned for this evening. Tomorrow afternoon, however, she will be throwing out the first ball at some baseball tournament. Bernie's planning to attend. You can go with her."

"Yeah, right. Never mind that I have a business to run, Rose. Do you expect that when the ball is in the air at this tournament, we'll corner her and ask if she killed her illicit lover?"

She peered at me over the top of her glass. "I trust you can be more discreet."

"Rose, I have absolutely no idea—"

"I'd go myself, but I've seen the baseball arena in passing . . ."

"Diamond."

"Did someone give you a diamond? Why don't I know about this?"

"Baseball isn't played in an arena. An arena's an indoor space. Baseball's played outside, and the configuration is called a diamond. Because that's the shape it's in."

"Regardless of what it's called, I've seen that field where they play baseball. The seating is dangerous for a person of my years."

"You don't have to sit in the bleachers. People sometimes bring folding chairs and set them up on the grass."

"I don't own folding chairs. Do you?"

"Why are we talking about seating arrangements and baseball diamonds, anyway? The mayor's hardly going to confess to a couple of total strangers that she murdered Jack Ford."

"I had yet another visit from Detective Williams," Rose said.

"What did he want this time?"

"I suspect he's trying to trick me or catch me in a lie. The same questions, over and over. All to the same point . . . How far would I go to stop the development next door?"

All of a sudden, my strong, tough, willful grandmother, whom I love so very much, looked small and frail. "He's out to get me, Lily. And I'm very frightened."

Robert the Bruce touched Rose's cheek with a paw, and Éclair rubbed herself against her legs. I felt tears in my eyes.

Yes, I could see Williams doing that. He might even be on the take, paid by the killer to find another suspect.

Who better to pay off the cops than the mayor?

"If you think it's important, then I'll go to the game with Bernie," I said. "But I think you've overlooked another suspect."

"Who might that be?"

"Mrs. Ford. If she knew her husband was cheating on

her, and the wife usually does, she'd have a powerful motive. Maybe he was planning to leave her for the mayor. All the more reason to do away with him before that could happen."

Rose smiled at me. "I knew I could count on you, Lily. Be ready in ten minutes. We're making a condolence call."

Chapter 15

"Jack Ford's address isn't on 411.com," I said into the phone. "Can you find out where he lived?"

"I already know it," Bernie said. "Why do you want it?"

I pulled a clean pair of capris out of my closet with one hand and held the phone to my ear with the other. "Rose wants to make a condolence call on Mrs. Ford."

"Why would she do that? She barely knew Mr. Ford, and their only meeting wasn't exactly friendly."

"Who knows why Rose wants to do what Rose wants to do?"

"You can't fool me. You're investigating. I'll pick you up."

I danced around the room, trying to put on my pants while talking into the phone. "Bernie, we can't all go."

"Sure we can. I'll pick you up."

"I don't—"

"If I don't drive, how are you going to get there? You don't know the address." She hung up.

I sighed. Éclair watched me, her head cocked to one side. "Between Bernie and Rose," I said to her, "I haven't got a chance."

I finished changing, splashed water on my face and gave

my hair a quick brush, told Éclair to guard the cottage, and went outside.

I found Rose sitting on one of the white wicker chairs on the wide verandah that runs the length of the house. The sun was sinking in a pink and gray sky, casting long shadows across the gardens toward us. A middle-aged couple stood next to Rose, chatting. Her hands were clasped together, resting on top of her new cane.

"Beautiful home," they said as I walked up.

"Thank you," Rose said. "It's because I love it so much, I enjoy having the chance to let others appreciate it, as well." That was a total and complete lie. Rose hated having to turn her home into a B & B.

"Do you have any idea when we can use the stairs to the beach again?" the man said. "It's a long way to the next easy access point."

"The police will be removing the tape tomorrow."

"That's great. Thanks."

"Good night," the woman said.

"I'm looking forward to another one of those fabulous breakfasts tomorrow," the man chuckled. "Makes it mighty hard to go back to a bowl of cold cereal at home."

The woman poked him playfully in the ribs. "You are so hard done by." They walked away, their light laughter drifting on the wind.

"Bernie's picking us up," I told my grandmother.

"Good."

"I forgot to ask. Any more cancellations?"

"No. The news cycle moves on to the next lurid item, and outside of North Augusta, no one's paying us any more attention. As soon as the rooms were marked available on the web site, they were scooped up. I do love modern technology. Almost as much as I love the simple fact that if people wanted to cancel with us, they'd be hard-pressed to find anything else available on such short notice. Although technology does have its drawbacks. The server that hosts our page and the one for the tearoom, was down for a few hours this afternoon.

"Whilst we're waiting, love, call the police and tell them to take that ridiculous tape down."

"You mean they didn't say they'd do it tomorrow?"

"They need a nudge. Make the call."

"Me? Why don't you do it?"

"You're much more persuasive."

That was not true, but I did as I'd been told. I dug Detective Redmond's card out of my bag and made the call. She answered almost immediately. I thought I heard the sound of water running and dishes clattering in the background.

"I'm sorry if I'm bothering you at home," I said. "It's Lily Roberts."

"You aren't bothering me, Lily. What can I do for you?"

"My grandmother's wondering when the crime-scene tape can come down."

I turned my back on Rose, who was telling me I was not to ask but to tell.

"I think we have all we need. I'll check with Detective Williams, and if he gives the go-ahead, I'll send someone around tomorrow to take care of it."

"Thank you. If you don't mind my asking, how's the investigation going? I'm sure you have plenty of suspects."

"Thing is, Lily, I do mind you asking." Redmond hung up.

"Thanks for your help," I said.

Bernie's car bounced down the driveway.

"At your service, madams," she said when we were buckling up.

"This is what we're going to do," Rose said. "While I'm expressing my heartfelt condolences to the recent widow, Bernie will be watching her for signs that she's hiding something, and Lily will be surreptitiously checking out our environment."

"Like searching for bloodstains on the carpet?" I said. "He didn't die in his house, remember."

"Look for evidence," Rose said, "that their marriage might have been in some distress."

"You mean divorce papers laid out on the coffee table for anyone to see?"

"Something like that."

I rolled my eyes. I was in the backseat, so neither of them could see me, but I did it, anyway. Despite her age, my grandmother rarely showed the slightest vulnerability—all that English reserve probably—and she rarely got sentimental. I knew she loved me very much, and I loved her to pieces, but we never said so to each other. Her recent flash of openness, when she revealed how frightened she was at the direction Williams's inquiries were taking, had twisted my heart, and so I'd agreed to pay a call on Mrs. Ford. That might not, I thought now, have been such a good idea. I hadn't actually meant right now. As in tonight.

A couple of miles from Victoria-on-Sea, a road turns off the coast road, veering inland for the North Augusta business district, but Bernie didn't turn along with it. She kept to the winding road running alongside the bay. Lanes broke off, leading to ocean-side houses on big lots. The vegetation was rough, salt sprayed, and windswept, marked by a few patches of tamed gardens, hedges of tall, swaying pampas grass, and imported trees. We hadn't gone far before Bernie slowed and turned onto a private road. Several driveways led off it, but she drove on until we came to the end. The sun was dipping below the horizon of the bay in a spectacular display of red, pink, and deep gray. Triple garage doors were closed, and no cars were in the driveway. A motion-detector light came on at the side of the house.

"We should have called ahead," I said.

"We don't want to give her advance notice," Rose said.

"We do want her to be home. It's nine o'clock. Late for a condolence call."

"Need I remind you, Lily," Rose said, "this isn't really a condolence call. It's a police investigation."

"Need I remind you, Rose, we aren't the police."

"As I believe Sherlock Holmes said, 'I shall be my own police.' "

I rolled my eyes once again. Rose and Bernie got out of the car, and I scrambled to do likewise.

In for a penny, in for a pound, as my grandmother often says.

The house in front of us was large and multistoried, with a fabulous view over the bay. Unlike Victoria-on-Sea, it was fully modern, all glass and concrete and sharp edges. Lights burned over the door and inside the house. We climbed the wide stone steps between giant black iron urns overflowing with red and white geraniums and sprays of fountain grasses.

Bernie rang the bell. The door opened almost immediately.

The woman who stood there was in her fifties, dressed in a faded red T-shirt and jeans that bagged at the knees and seat. Her brown hair, heavily streaked with gray, was scraped back into a rough ponytail. She wore no makeup, and it looked as though she'd cut her bangs herself, probably with nail scissors. The skin on her face was soft and plump, and deep circles lay under her eyes. Her eyes and nose were not red, and she showed no signs of recent crying. "Yes?" she said.

I was about to ask if Mrs. Ford was at home, but Bernie spoke first. "Good evening, Mrs. Ford. I hope you don't mind the late call. I'm Bernadette, and this is Rose. We've come to pay our condolences."

What was I? Chopped liver? I forced out a smile.

"I'm sorry," Janice Ford said. "Do I know you?"

Rose leaned her cane against Bernie's leg and reached out with both of her hands. Instinctively, Mrs. Ford took them in hers. "I'm so sorry about your loss," Rose said. "We have not met, my dear, but I came to correct that oversight. I hope I can call you Janice?"

"Uh, yeah." The Widow Ford's eyes flicked between Bernie and me. "Okay, I guess."

"Janice. Your husband and I were business acquaintances."

"That's nice, but I have to tell you, I wasn't involved in my husband's business affairs."

This was getting awkward. Janice Ford didn't seem at all inclined to invite us in, and there was no reason she should.

Trust Rose to take care of that. She swayed slightly, pulled her hands away from Janice Ford's, and lightly but rapidly patted the approximate vicinity of her heart. Bernie thrust out a hand and took her elbow. She handed Rose her cane and said, "Here you go. Be careful now."

"Uh, would you like to come in?" Janice said.

"Thank you, dear. That would be very nice. Just for a few minutes." Rose stepped over the threshold; Bernie and I followed. The floor of the large foyer was covered in terra-cotta-colored ceramic tiles, and a huge crystal chandelier hung from the ceiling.

Janice led the way down the hallway. To my right, I got a glimpse of the living room. The red leather couches, glass tables, and modern art on white walls showed excellent taste, but to my mind, the room had a soulless quality, as though the decor had been plucked directly from a designer's catalog.

Janice turned left, and we followed her into a much smaller room. Bernie helped Rose, and I trailed along behind.

A wingback chair in a far corner showed signs of use.

The fabric was faded in places, and dirt was ground into the edges of the armrests. A cheap plywood bookcase packed with a mixture of hardcover and paperback books stood next to it, and a reading lamp shone over the chair. One wall was filled with a gas fireplace, unlit in late spring. A glass of wine and a book rested on the side table.

This, I guessed, was the library. Nice to have a house big enough to have a library, no matter how small.

"Please." Janice gestured to an aging beige sofa against the far wall. "Have a seat." She didn't offer us anything to drink.

Rose sat slowly, still clinging to her cane. Bernie settled next to her. They smiled at Janice. Janice took the wing-back chair and smiled back at them. There was nowhere left for me to sit, so I leaned against the wall and wondered if I'd somehow disappeared.

"You were in business with Jack, you said?" Janice asked.

"Of a sort," Rose said. "Regarding the Goodwill property."

Janice snorted. "Not that eyesore. I'm sick and tired of hearing about it. The place should have been sold off long ago and the property divided into lots. A nice little subdivision would fit on that land."

Rose visibly shuddered.

"That Lincoln Goodwill's too proud for his own good," Janice continued. "He clung to that property far longer than he should have because it's been in his family for a hundred years or so. Now he has to get rid of it, and he can't find anyone dumb enough to pay what he's asking. Are you the interested buyer, Rose?"

"No," Rose said.

"I didn't think so. You look like a woman with common sense. Some of the neighbors are vehemently opposed to rezoning the property. Are you one of those neighbors, Rose?"

My grandmother smiled. "I confess that I am."

"You're the owner of the B & B next door. The property where Jack died."

Rose nodded.

"As your husband died on Rose's property," Bernie said, "she wanted to express her condolences to you in person."

"Did you kill him?" Janice asked.

For once Rose looked startled. "Good heavens! What a question. No, I did not kill him."

"Then you don't need to express your condolences to me. I know he was planning to sue you over some silly idea that you slandered him. He always was a fool."

Janice certainly could be blunt when she wanted to be.

"I told him a knockdown public fight with an elderly widowed lady never looked good. But Jack never much cared what I had to say. He did, however, care what my lawyers had to say, and I intended to have them put a stop to it. Doesn't matter now, does it?"

"Uh, no," Bernie said.

"Can I offer you a glass of wine?" Janice asked.

"You may," Rose said.

Bernie declined, as she was driving.

I wasn't even asked if I wanted one, but I said, "Thanks," anyway.

"I'll be right back." Janice left the room.

Bernie and I glanced at each other. Rose pointed to me and then waved her finger around, no doubt telling me to be observant.

I didn't have much time to observe anything. Janice must have run to the kitchen, because she was back in seconds, bearing an open wine bottle and two glasses. She handed glasses to Rose and me and poured. She wasn't exactly generous. I considered the amount I got to be more of a dribble, and Rose's was the same. Janice topped up her own glass and took her seat. She lifted her drink.

"To Jack Ford. Gone to his reward at last."

I almost spat out my wine. That would have been a waste. It was very good.

"An interesting sentiment," Rose said.

"But an honest one. I believe in being honest at all times, don't you, Rose?"

"Absolutely," my grandmother said. If not for the glass of wine in one hand, she would have had her fingers crossed behind her back.

"Jack and I lived together in this house, but otherwise, we didn't have much of a life together." Janice held out her hands, encompassing her chair, the reading lamp, the bookcase, and the side table. "I have my own space, and I let him have the run of the rest of the house. I don't spend much time here anymore. I have an apartment in Boston, which I much prefer, where I was all of last week. I came here Saturday morning, after the police called me with the news. I haven't yet decided if I'm going to sell the house. Would you like to buy it?"

"No," I said.

"As for Jack, I allowed him to play at being a property developer, and that kept him from annoying me."

"You 'allowed' him?" I could hear the air quotes in Rose's voice.

"When my father died, he left me rather a lot of money. Shortly after that, Jack and I met. His business was failing, and his children, wisely, had no interest in being involved. Dutiful wife that I wanted to be, I invested a substantial amount of my own money in the company. Jack assured me that with an infusion of new cash, he'd be able to turn things around and make his fortune." She chuckled. "As if. I never make the same mistake twice. Giving him money was a mistake, and marrying him was a mistake."

"He didn't have a reputation as a respectable businessman," I said. "He skirted the law."

"Because he wasn't smart enough to work within it."

"He cheated a lot of people."

"As I said, I wasn't involved in the details of his business practices. Some people are too greedy for their own good. Like that Roy Gleeson, hoping to get on Jack's good side if he pushed through the zoning change. Or the mayor herself, silly woman."

In for a penny. "Are you aware it's rumored your husband was having an affair with Mayor Carla Powers?" I asked.

For the first time, Janice looked straight at me. "You're blunt. I like that." She tossed back most of the contents of her glass. "Jack was always the subject of rumors. He liked it that way. Made him sound mysterious and interesting. Important. He was a fool. Jack was happy if people were talking about him. I'd have thought he had better taste than Carla Powers, though. I guess he was getting old." She laughed at the expression on my face. "Have I shocked you? Poor dear. I assume you're more comfortable in your tearoom. I hear it's quite charming. I should pop in one day."

I put down my glass. "We've taken enough of your time. Thank you."

"Why didn't you divorce him?" Rose asked.

Janice shrugged. "Too much bother."

"Whew," I said as we drove back to Victoria-on-Sea.

"Whew is right," Rose said. "What a thoroughly unpleasant woman."

I leaned forward and rested my arms on the back of the front seats, one on each side. "Gave me chills the way she brushed off people like Dorothy Johnson, as though it was their fault Jack cheated them."

"Nasty as she is," Bernie said, "and as much as she enjoys being nasty, do you think she killed Jack?"

"No," I said. "In her words, why would she bother? She has money of her own, so no reason to stay with him if she didn't want to. If she wanted to be rid of him, all she had to do was divorce him."

"I disagree," Rose said. "We have no reason to believe anything she said was true. Maybe she did resent him for having affairs."

"More likely she hated knowing everyone knew about it," Bernie said.

"Agreed," Rose said.

"Divorces can get nasty and expensive," Bernie said. "I wouldn't put it past Janice Ford to decide that offing a troublesome husband was the cheapest and easiest way out. I'll see what I can find out about her personal finances. Her father might not have left her as comfortably off as she claims."

"Or," Rose said, "she put all her inheritance into Jack's business and saw it disappear. That would make her bitter. Perhaps she decided desperate measures were necessary to save what little money's left."

"I found it interesting," Bernie said, "that she knew who both of you are."

"She keeps herself informed of what goes on in North Augusta, for all she pretends not to care," I said, leaning back in my seat and looking out the window. It was fully dark now. Lights shone from inside houses and above porches, and Bernie's headlights lit up the road ahead. A rising moon hung in the eastern sky. I yawned. Five thirty came mighty early, and I hadn't had much sleep last night. "I wonder if she really was in Boston in the early hours of Saturday morning. I don't suppose the detectives will tell us."

"Did you notice what book she was reading?" Rose asked.

"What's that got to do with anything?"

"You were supposed to be checking out the surroundings, Lily."

"So I missed it. What of it?"

"It was *Careless Love* by Peter Robinson. An English detective series. I noticed a good number of crime novels on her bookcase, most by British authors and many of them what are called police procedurals. Clearly, she has the same taste in reading as I do."

"You can start a book club," I said. "I don't see what her reading habits have to do with anything."

"If Janice Ford did murder her husband, she would know the prime suspect is always the spouse of the deceased."

"Don't tell me that," Bernie said. "I'm still hoping to get married someday."

"Fortunately," Rose said, "not all married couples end up hating each other. If she did bump off her troublesome husband, Janice would have made sure she had a cast-iron alibi for the time."

"She might have paid someone to do it," Bernie said. "She's not short of funds."

I stared out the window. The cheerful, welcoming lights of Victoria-on-Sea came into view, and Bernie slowed the car.

"Speaking of books, how's yours coming, love?" Rose asked Bernie.

"I don't suppose you know when the telegraph was invented, do you?" my friend replied.

"I'm not that old," Rose said. "Sometime in the nineteenth century, but I don't know the exact date."

"It's details like that I'm getting stuck on," Bernie said. "I'm beginning to think I should write a more contemporary novel."

"You've been trying to write some version of this book for two years," I said. "You can't give up on it now. You have to get it done. Look up the invention of the telegraph. Mr. Google is your friend."

"All those picky details take time. I want to write. I want to feel my characters speaking to me! I want to hear what they have to say! I want to explore their surroundings!"

She pulled to a stop at the steps to the B & B. "I'll get on the computer tonight and see what I can find about Janice Ford. Maybe we'll be lucky and she'll have a rap sheet as long as Rose's cane."

We said good night. I walked Rose to her suite and then headed for my bed. It had been a long day, but before turning in, I had to take Éclair for a short walk.

I let myself into the cottage, exchanged effusive greetings with the dog, and got down her leash. She did her happy dance; she knows what the leash means. She's well enough trained to come when I call, so I didn't need to fasten the leash to her collar, but I always carry it in case we encounter a wandering dog or a guest who's frightened of dogs.

The lights lining the verandah of the B & B shone on patches of garden. Simon seemed to be doing a good job. I pushed thoughts of him aside. As I'd told Bernie, he was going back to England in the fall. Éclair and I strolled up the driveway as far as the road. Moonlight filled the tearoom's patio, and the teacups hanging from the tree swayed and murmured softly in the warm wind. They reminded me I was far too busy to even consider embarking on a summer romance.

When we reached the road, I said, "Time to turn back. I'm bushed."

We retraced our steps, but before going into the cottage, we walked to the edge of the bluffs looking over the moonlit bay. A few guests were scattered about, enjoying a glass of wine on one of the benches or taking the air. Éclair sniffed at the grass around my feet.

"Lovely evening," a woman said to me. She was in her midfifties, short and slightly plump, wearing an attractive navy blue dress with white trim and white sandals. I guessed she'd been someplace nice for dinner.

"It is," I replied.

"Can I pat your dog? He's so cute. What's his name?"

"Éclair, after the pastry, and she's female."

The woman crouched down and clicked her tongue rapidly. Éclair nuzzled her nose into the offered hand.

"I don't have any treats for you. Next time I'll try to remember to bring something." She gave Éclair a final firm pat and stood up. "I'll be sorry to leave tomorrow. It's been a marvelous visit." She giggled. "We're on our honeymoon."

"Congratulations," I said. "Perhaps you'll come again."

"Definitely. I love the Cape, and this place is perfect."

I remembered seeing her on Saturday morning at the edge of the bluff, watching the police activity. "I hope what happened on Saturday didn't upset you too much."

She shivered and wrapped her arms around herself. "You mean all the police activity? Oh, no. It was very exciting. Like being in a TV show."

I thought that a bit insensitive, but I suppose to someone who didn't know the people involved and wasn't close to the events that brought about a man's death, the death would feel remote. Like watching TV or reading one of Rose's beloved mystery novels.

"Good night," she said as she turned and walked away.

"Good night." I didn't go in immediately. I stood where I was, enjoying the caress of the soft breeze off the water on my face, the scent of salt in the air, and the rustling of the dog at my feet. An airplane flew overhead, heading east toward Europe.

I thought about our visit to Janice Ford. She'd been surprisingly honest with us. If, that is, she was being honest and not spinning a story in an attempt to shock us. Regardless, it was possible she hadn't presented that side of herself to the police. I'd have to tell them what we learned, even if they didn't want to hear from me.

That could wait until tomorrow. Right now, my bed was calling, and I didn't want to take the chance Amy Redmond would want to talk to me in person, rather than over the phone.

Chapter 16

"What do you mean, we have no berries? How is that even possible? It's berry season in New England."

"Nancy called to tell me her son's been ill, so he didn't get out to the bushes," Cheryl said. "I don't think that's true. I bet she got a better offer."

I groaned. The aforementioned Nancy ran a berry farm. She was my main supplier for seasonal berries. The berries we used so many of in our scones, cakes, and tarts at this time of year.

"Maybe you can make lemon squares today?" Marybeth suggested.

"The menu says fresh Cape Cod berry tarts."

"We can scratch that out?"

"Not an option. It's berry season, and our customers want berries in their baked goods. I want berries in our baked goods. I'll take a run to the supermarket. I can only hope no one sees me buying cellophane-wrapped strawberries. Maybe I'll go in disguise." I glanced at the clock on the kitchen wall. Ten thirty, half an hour to opening. "I should be back by eleven, but if I'm delayed, you can open without me. We have enough food prepared to last through the initial rush. I've made a good start on the sandwiches, and you can finish them." I took off my apron. "I've faced worse emergencies in my time. Cheryl, can you call Nancy and tell her I need a firm commitment that the requisite number of berries will be here on time tomorrow?"

"Will do," Cheryl said. "If she says she can't be sure, she'll be struck off my Thanksgiving dinner guest list." Nancy was Cheryl's cousin.

Manhattan native that I am, I don't own a car and never have. Rose and I share hers. I called and told her I needed it for a short while, and then I ran to the B & B to get the second set of keys from the kitchen, and headed into town. The supermarket's located on the far end of the North Augusta main street. Traffic was heavy, but it moved steadily, and I made good time. I ran into the market, swept up almost all their strawberries—enough to last me through today and provide some excess in case Nancy decided to have her Thanksgiving dinner elsewhere this year. If I had too many, I could always use them in muffins for the B & B or freeze them. I was pleased to see a sign over the berry rack announcing local produce. My menu wouldn't be a lie. The tiny fruits were bright red, plump, and glistening with juice—each one a perfect tiny jewel.

I paid for my purchases and was back in Rose's car in record time. I ripped open one of the packages, scooped up a single berry and tossed it into my mouth. I reveled in the marvelous sweet-tart flavor as I headed for the tearoom.

The main street of North Augusta is lined by huge oaks, some over a hundred years old, which provide a delightfully cool leafy canopy. North Augusta is a quiet town of good restaurants, trendy coffee shops, charming stores, and art galleries featuring local artists and crafters. Crowds of tourists browsed the shops, sipped coffee on outdoor patios, or read menus posted on restaurant doors.

The SUV ahead of me had a kayak strapped to the roof and two bikes mounted on the back. It made it through the town's only traffic light in time, leaving me facing the red. I didn't mind. I was making good time and should be back not long after the tearoom opened for the day.

A stream of people stepped off the sidewalk and crossed in front of me, heading for the other side of the street. Tourists, pink nosed from the sun, dragging ice-cream-licking children; shop clerks in casual summer wear; the occasional businessperson in a suit walking briskly, intent on their errand.

The walk signal changed from white to flashing red. A woman passed in front of my car, hurrying to make the safety of the sidewalk before the cars started moving again.

I blinked in recognition and surprise. That this person was on Main Street, North Augusta, at eleven on a Tuesday morning was nothing to be surprised about. But the way she walked was. She stepped onto the sidewalk, then hurried across the cross street and went into the coffee shop on the corner.

The car behind me beeped, telling me the light had changed and I was holding up traffic. I drove through the intersection. Every parking space was taken as far as I could see, so I pulled up beside a fire hydrant. Feeling very guilty indeed, I hopped out of my car. Hopefully, I'd be back before I got towed or, worse, the firefighters needed to use the hydrant.

I didn't wait for the light but dashed across the street, dodging honking cars. I leapt onto the sidewalk, breathing heavily. Pedestrians gave me curious looks.

I ignored them and peered into the window of the coffee shop. The place was full, and there was a line at the counter. My quarry had joined the queue.

I ducked inside. It was a thoroughly modern coffee bar

with hissing espresso machines, granite countertops, glass-fronted display cases, polished wide-planked wooden floors, friendly young baristas, and patrons typing away on their various devices. And a lot of people waiting to be served. I fell in at the back of the line, which slowly edged forward.

"A large caramel latte," Dorothy Johnson said when it was her turn to be served. Her voice was strong, strong enough to reach me at the other side of the busy room. I didn't see her walker, and she hadn't been using so much as a cane when she crossed the street.

The young man beside her grabbed his drink off the counter, turned suddenly, and bumped into her. He clutched his cup as Dorothy leapt nimbly out of the way.

"Can't you watch where you're going?" she snapped.

"Chill, lady," he said. "No harm done."

"No thanks to you," she replied.

He shrugged and walked away.

"Large caramel latte," the barista called, putting a cup on the counter. Dorothy picked it up. She took a sip and then put a lid on the cup and walked out of the coffee shop. I ducked behind the person in front of me, but Dorothy didn't so much as give the other patrons a sideways glance.

I followed her, trying to make myself small and unnoticeable, but it didn't matter. Dorothy paid no attention to what was happening behind her. She marched down the center of the sidewalk, making no move to get out of anyone's way. Everyone else, clearly, was expected to move aside for her. She walked for a block and then stopped next to a Toyota RAV4 parked in a space clearly marked for the handicapped. She pulled keys out of her pocket and flicked the fob. The car's headlights flashed in acknowledgment, and Dorothy got into the car. It started up immediately, and she pulled into traffic. The license plate had a handicapped sticker, and I caught a glimpse of a walker in the back.

Dorothy wasn't as frail and feeble as she appeared at the retirement home. She was pretending to be so in order to take advantage of the kindness of the good people of the State of Massachusetts and park illegally. The rat!

If she could dodge coffee-bearing young men and walk briskly down the street, what else might she be capable of?

Knocking a man off a cliff?

I thought about that for a few minutes. We'd dismissed Dorothy as a suspect because she was frail and had trouble walking. In that, obviously, we'd been mistaken. I wondered if she ever used hiking poles.

Fortunately, I wasn't too deep in thought that I failed to see the parking enforcement officer heading in my direction. I turned and ran. I found the car where I'd left it, with no ticket flapping on the windshield.

I drove back to Tea by the Sea, deep in thought.

Chapter 17

I made good use of the strawberries in the berry tarts, which make up an important part of our dessert plate and the sweet selection of the traditional afternoon tea.

By quarter to three, another batch of scones was in the oven, cupcakes were cooling prior to being iced, the icing was made, and tea sandwiches were resting in the fridge under damp cloths. I was putting the tops on the last of the day's macarons and looking forward to a short break. I had my eye on a couple of those sandwiches and was taking some time to choose what cup and plate I wanted for my tea. My grandmother had taught me that cup and side plate don't always have to match, but they do have to have a similarity in theme or appearance. Black and white would do for today, I thought. I was taking down a white cup and saucer with a pattern of intricate black filigree and a plate painted to resemble piano keys when Bernie came into the kitchen.

"Ready to go?" she said.

"Go? Go where? It's the middle of the day."

"To the baseball game. Rose told you about that. It starts at three. We can corner the mayor once she's thrown out the first pitch."

"I'm busy. You'll have to go without me."

"I can't go without you. I need a wingman. Suppose she runs for it and we have to chase her?"

"Then you're better off without me. I haven't been to the gym since I moved to North Augusta."

"Lily! Rose says you promised."

"Bernie! Rose promised for me. That's not the same."

"Yes, it is. You can take your lunch with you and eat in the car."

I'd been able to hold my own—to flourish even—in the tough world of the New York City restaurant business. But somehow, in pleasant little North Augusta, in the face of Bernie and Rose, I crumbled like a perfect slice of shortcrust pastry. "Okay. If we're quick about it. Cheryl and Marybeth can manage for a while." I took off my apron and dropped a couple of the egg sandwiches into a plastic baggie. "You owe me one hour of work this evening."

"Can't. I have to get back to my book. I've broken the logjam of worrying about historical accuracy and need to work on it."

"If you're writing a historical novel, Bernie, you need to worry about historical accuracy."

"I can fix those details later. Right now I need to concentrate on character development."

"Sounds to me like you're making the bread without first taking into account what filling is going to go inside the sandwich."

"You do that?"

"Of course I do. I wouldn't make a pumpernickel loaf and then decide to have strawberry jelly with it."

"Sounds good to me."

"Which is why you are not the chef."

Cheryl came into the kitchen. "One order of cream tea for three and a dessert plate for one."

"I have to go out for a few minutes," I said to her.

"Everything's pretty much ready for the rest of the day. Are you okay on your own for a while? I have my phone if you need anything."

"We'll be fine," she said. "I'll get Marybeth to finish frosting those cupcakes."

"Thanks. The icing's made and under that cloth."

Bernie and I left by the back door and walked around the tearoom to the parking lot and her car. In the distance, Simon was hard at work with the secateurs, deadheading the perennials. He gave us a wave. I waved back. True to her word, Detective Redmond had sent someone first thing this morning to take down the police tape. The moment that was done, Simon put up a new gate and reinforced the steps and the fence.

"Anything happening on that front?" Bernie asked.

"What front?"

"The Simon front. He looks so good, doesn't he, in those baggy overalls and the big boots? His hair tossed by the wind, his cheeks ruddy with fresh sea air."

"Are you telling me you like Simon?"

"I like Simon fine. But not in *that* way. I'm merely pointing out to you that you could do a lot worse."

"Anyone worse is not in the cards, as I'm not looking for a relationship right now, Bernie." I usually told Bernie everything, and I trusted that she did the same with me, but I hadn't told her about Simon's and my impromptu pizza supper last night. She had intensely disliked Tim, my previous boyfriend—he of the meat cleaver. She'd never said, "I told you so," but she hadn't needed to. I could read it on her face.

A scattering of cars were parked at the ball field. The local team was in a tournament, playing host to the team from Sandwich. The North Augusta players wore yellow T-shirts, and the Sandwich ones were in red. The girls were around ten years old, all bouncing ponytails, smiling sun-kissed faces, scuffed sneakers, boundless energy and enthusiasm. Parents found seats in park bleachers or unfolded chairs on the grass.

The mayor was standing off to one side with two women in business clothes, a man in jeans and a Red Sox ball cap, and two women, whom I took to be the coaches.

As we crossed the park toward them, Bernie nudged me. "Her Honor doesn't look too good."

I agreed. Mayor Powers's eyes were tinged red, and underneath the carefully applied makeup, her face was puffy. "She's been crying," I said.

"Looks like it."

"What do you intend to do? You can't just walk up to her and ask about her relationship with Jack Ford."

"Sure I can. But give me some credit here, Lily. A more oblique approach will work better."

The coaches went to join their teams. The girls were sitting on the benches, and at an unseen signal, they jumped up and ran onto the field. They formed two neat rows along the baselines, and the mayor and the man with the cap joined them.

The man spoke first, introducing himself as the league organizer and welcoming the visitors to our town. He then asked the mayor to open the tournament.

Carla Powers spoke about the joy of youth sports. She mentioned her time playing ball in this very park when she was the same age as these girls. I'd heard her speak at the opening of my tearoom—from the kitchen, where I'd been trying to save my brownies—and thought her a good speaker. Today her heart didn't seem to be in it.

Bernie trotted around the bleachers. I followed. We went up to the two women in business clothes.

"Hi," Bernie said. "Nice day for it."

"It is," they replied.

"I'm Bernadette Murphy, and this is my friend Lily Roberts. We're new to North Augusta."

"Pleased to meet you. I'm Mia, and this is Jenny. We work at town hall." Mia was in her twenties, tall and thin, with long shiny brown hair, perfect makeup, and manicured hands. She wore a dark skirt suit and ironed white blouse, along with patent leather pumps with one-inch heels. Jenny, on the other hand, was a lot older, somewhat rough around the edges, looking like she could no longer be bothered to make much of an effort. Her pants didn't fit too well, and she had sturdy Birkenstocks on her feet.

"Do you have daughters on the team?" Jenny asked.

"We don't," Bernie said, "but we're big supporters of girls' athletics." Bernie—the Warrior Princess—certainly looked the part.

I turned to look at the mayor, who was still talking. Out on the field, the rows of players were getting restless. Girls began shifting from one foot to the other. I saw one nudging another. "It's nice of the mayor to take time out of her schedule to welcome the players."

"Don't read too much into it," Jenny said. "Carla would come to the opening of an envelope."

Mia glared at her. "You can't say that. She loves community sports. She made a real effort to come out today." Her phone rang, and she checked the number. "Sorry. I have to get this." She stepped away from us.

"Why was it an effort?" Bernie asked Jenny.

Jenny glanced at Mia, who'd turned her back to us and was stabbing the air with a finger. Jenny leaned toward us. We leaned toward her. She lowered her voice. "Something happened that's upset her dreadfully. A good . . . uh, friend of hers died over the weekend."

"I'm sorry to hear that," I said.

"She can't talk to anyone about it and has to pretend she doesn't much care. She's not doing a good job of that."

"Why does she have to pretend?" Bernie asked.

Jenny broke into a smile. "Here she comes."

Carla Powers left the field to scattered applause from the parents. The girls ran in all directions, taking their places.

"Just get it done," I heard Mia snap into her phone. "I want no more of your excuses." She put her phone away and slapped on a smile as she walked back to us.

"Good afternoon," Bernie and I said when Carla joined our little circle.

Mia introduced us. I reminded the mayor that we'd met at Tea by the Sea, and she asked me how business was.

"Great," I told her.

"I'm afraid we have to be going," Mia said. "Your Honor, you have an appointment with the budget controller in fifteen minutes."

Carla gave me a "What can you do?" smile. "Nice talking to you, Lily. I must pop into the tearoom again. I hear such great things about it." She started to walk away.

We were supposed to be asking Carla what she knew about the death of Jack Ford, but I had absolutely no idea how to go about doing that. Bernie, however, did.

"While we're here," my friend said, "Lily and her grandmother are wondering if you have any idea what's going to happen to the Goodwill property out near the bluffs. Jack Ford was interested in buying it, wasn't he? Now that he's dead, is the rezoning going to go ahead?"

Carla Powers burst into tears. Mia and Jenny exchanged worried glances.

"Gosh," Bernie said. "I'm sorry. Is something the matter?"

Carla snuffled. "Jack. We were not exactly friends, but I knew him as a citizen and a prominent member of the community. I'm naturally upset about his death."

"Naturally."

"We need to be going, Carla," Mia said.

Carla turned to me, her eyes wild. She grabbed my arm. "He died at Victoria-on-Sea, isn't that right? Your grandmother's place. What happened? Did you see him that day? I hope . . . he wasn't alone, was he? When he died?"

"I'm sorry. I don't know what happened." I didn't mention that I'd been the one to find him. Or that if anyone had been with him, that person had probably killed him.

"They say he fell over the cliff. I don't believe that for a second," Carla said. "He was a strong, fit man. He wasn't at all clumsy."

Mia pried Carla's hand off my arm. "Time to go!"

Carla shook her off. Now that she'd started to cry, she couldn't stop. Tears flowed freely down her cheeks, and she made no attempt to wipe them away. "I found out when I heard it on the radio. No one thought to come and tell me."

"Maybe they didn't know," Bernie said in a low, kind, sympathetic voice, "how close you two were. You were close, weren't you?"

"We were in love! On Friday I told my husband I was leaving him for Jack, but no one else knew. Not yet."

"Carla!" Mia said. "We have to go." She threw a panicked look at Jenny. Rather than make a move to help, Jenny smirked.

"I can't imagine how hard that must be for you," Bernie murmured sympathetically.

"We were going to get married," Carla wailed. "To be together forever."

Mia threw up her hands and took a step back. She pulled her phone out of her pocket and punched buttons.

"The police are saying they suspect foul play," Carla said. "I told them that's nonsense. No one would kill Jack. Everyone liked and admired him."

Bernie and I said nothing.

"I can't get her to stop," Mia said into her phone.

"You were there." Carla clutched my arm again. She had a mighty powerful grip. "Did you see anyone acting suspiciously? Anyone threatening Jack?"

"No, I didn't. Accidents do happen."

"Not to a man like Jack. It might have had something to do with the Goodwill property. There's some opposition to the rezoning proposal."

"Really?" Bernie said. "Imagine that."

"You don't think Lincoln Goodwill had something to do with it, do you? I never did trust that man."

Mia shoved her phone up against Carla's ear. I could hear a man shouting on the other end. Carla took a deep breath. She shook her head, and her eyes focused. "Sorry, sorry," she mumbled into the phone.

Carla pulled a tissue out of her pocket and blew her nose. "I'm so sorry. You don't need to hear my story." She emitted a strangled chuckle. "You won't, I hope, be repeating this conversation to anyone?" She gave us a plaintive look.

"Just between us girls," Bernie said.

"What do you think's going to happen with the rezoning proposal now?" I asked.

"It's coming up for debate at council next week," Jenny said. "Just because one developer is *dead*"—she emphasized the last word as she gave Carla a sideways peek—"doesn't mean another won't be interested. Lincoln Goodwill's pushing for it. He needs to sell that property, and he wants top dollar for it."

Now Mia and Carla were tripping all over themselves in their haste to get away.

Jenny gave us a grin and said, "Nice one." She followed them, making no attempt to catch up.

Out on the field, a girl, ponytail flying, long thin legs and arms pumping, rounded third base and headed for home plate. On the bleachers, one group of parents rose to their feet, cheering.

"I think we also hit a home run," Bernie said.

"Was that weird or what? Why would she tell us, people she doesn't even know, all that personal stuff?"

"Because she's been holding it inside and it's bursting to come out. All we had to do was nudge open the floodgates. This detecting stuff is pretty easy, I must say. I suspect our mayor has political ambitions beyond our little town. Mia seems to be invested in keeping her out of trouble, and that man on the phone told her to shut up mighty fast."

"Having an affair with a married man wouldn't help her political prospects," I said.

"No, it wouldn't. Divorce and remarriage isn't any sort of scandal these days, but illicit affairs still are. I wonder if Jack had any intention of going through with it, or if he was just stringing her along."

"Wouldn't be the first time."

"If Jack was going to marry Carla, he'd have to divorce the current wife first. Janice Ford didn't seem to know anything about that."

"Or she didn't consider it to be any of our business."

"What did you think of Jenny?" Bernie asked.

"I'd say she's not too fond of her boss, and so close to retirement, she figures she doesn't have to pretend anymore. Can we go now? I have to get back to work."

As we drove out of town, I thought about what we'd learned. Carla Powers had been genuinely distraught at Jack's death. I didn't know her, but I doubted she was that good an actor. It was possible, however, that she'd been responsible for his death and now regretted it.

I wondered if the police knew she was planning to leave her husband for Jack Ford. That information opened the door to a whole bunch of suspects: Mr. Powers and Mrs. Ford, as well as Carla herself.

The police might not know. They might not have questioned her, not if they weren't aware she was involved with Jack. We only knew about it from bridge club gossip, and now from Carla herself.

"Are you thinking what I'm thinking?" Bernie asked.

"If you're thinking Carla Powers might have killed Jack Ford, I am."

"Or maybe Mr. Powers. We don't know anything about him. You need to talk to the police about this."

"Me? Why me?"

"Because you're involved. I'm nothing but a helpful observer."

"I am not involved."

She turned into the driveway. "Sure you are. You . . . Oh, look who's here."

Three vehicles were parked in front of the Goodwill house.

"Let's have a chat," Bernie said.

"I don't want—"

She drove past the tearoom. Every seat in the patio was taken, and Marybeth stood at a table for six, writing their order on her notepad.

"I have to be at work, Bernie."

"Won't be a minute." She pulled to a halt behind Roy Gleeson's SUV.

Three men stood near the broken front porch. They turned to watch us approach. They didn't look at all welcoming, but that wasn't necessarily because they didn't want to talk to us. Easy to tell by their body language they'd been arguing among themselves.

"Good afternoon, ladies," Lincoln Goodwill said. "I'm sorry, but this isn't a good time."

"Don't be rude, Dad. It's always a good time to be

friendly." Matt gave us big smiles. I smiled in return. Bernie stuck her elbow in my ribs. I tried to ignore her.

"What are you doing here?" she asked.

"I don't see that that's any of your business," Roy Gleeson said.

"Just being neighborly," she said.

"We're discussing plans for the property," Matt said. "I'm thinking it won't be too expensive to restore the house, not if the owner did a lot of the work himself, and did it over time, as funds allowed."

"Not going to happen," Lincoln said. "I'm sorry, ladies, but I have to ask you to be reasonable. I don't want any trouble, but this is my property, and I have a right to do with it what I like. You can tell your grandmother that."

"She didn't send us," Bernie said. "We're perfectly capable of opposing an environmentally detrimental project all on our own."

"Hardly environmentally detrimental. We're talking about a good hotel designed to be respectful of the surroundings."

"My father and I have a difference of opinion." Matt grinned at Bernie. She tossed her mane of red hair and harrumphed.

"So the rezoning will be going ahead," I said.

"That will be decided by town council," Roy said. "As they see fit."

"Egged on by you," Bernie said.

He spread out his hands. "Not at all. I put the proposal forward, but now I'm stepping back from it. I have no skin in this game. I'm happy to let the town councillors decide whatever they think best." He turned to the Goodwills. "Speaking of which, I have to be off."

"I need your support, Roy."

"I told you, Lincoln, I'm listening to all opinions, and I expect the other councillors to do the same. Jack knew that." He nodded to us and took a step toward his SUV before hesitating and turning back. "Can you move your car please?"

"Which way is Mayor Powers likely to vote?" I asked.

"She hasn't shared her thinking with me," he said.

"But . . ."

The edges of his mouth turned up. "But . . . she and Jack Ford were close. Very close, I'd say. She would have done whatever he wanted her to do. Although that's a moot point now, isn't it? Move your car please, miss."

Bernie stood her ground.

I gave her a nudge and said, "Let's go, Bernie."

"Mrs. Campbell is going to fight you," Bernie said. "Are you prepared to be seen going up against an elderly widowed lady who only wants to spend what few years she has left in peace and quiet?"

Lincoln sputtered.

Matt laughed. "Answer the lady, Dad."

"I don't want any trouble," Lincoln said.

"Tell her to present her case in front of the town council," Roy said. "The meeting's next Tuesday at seven p.m., and the public is welcome to speak. We do listen to the people's concerns, you know. She might even change a few minds."

Lincoln bristled. "What are you saying, Roy? Whose side are you on?"

"I told you, Lincoln. I'm on the side of the people of North Augusta, as always."

"I'm a citizen of North Augusta. My family's been here since—"

"That's the problem, Dad," Matt interrupted. "No one cares how long our family's lived here. Times have changed. For the better in a lot of ways. Except for afternoon tea. Nothing like the old ways for that. I might pop in later, Lily. How long are you open?"

"Until five."

"They're completely full for the rest of the day," Bernie said.

"We are not," I said.

"In that case," he said, "would you like to be my guest for tea, Ms. Murphy? I'm sure you have the connections to get us a good table."

"Will you move your car!" Roy yelled. "I'm late as it is."

"Okay, okay. Don't get all excited." Bernie turned and stomped away.

"Does this mean you're not having tea with me?" Matt called after her.

I chased after my friend and jumped into the car. Bernie revved the engine and backed up in a spray of sand and gravel. She executed a tight three-point turn, drove much too fast for the distance to the tearoom, and screeched to a halt beside the gate.

"Calm down," I said. "There's no point in antagonizing them."

"Antagonizing them? They antagonized me. So patronizing. Will I have tea, indeed? Don't you start getting friendly with Matt Goodwill."

Roy Gleeson's SUV roared past. He barely slowed before turning onto the main road.

"I'm not getting friendly with him," I said, "but why shouldn't I? He seems nice."

"I don't trust him. That good cop, bad cop routine he has going with his father? Ha. You don't think he wants to see the property sold for the big bucks? He'll inherit eventually, remember."

"You don't know anything about their family situation, and neither do I. Maybe he has ten brothers and sisters all in line to inherit ahead of him, or his father plans to leave everything to a shelter for homeless cats. Lincoln might have a much younger wife, who will outlive Matt. Maybe—"

"Enough, Lily. I get the point. I'm telling you, he's not

to be trusted. Now, are you going to work or not? I need to report to Rose on what we learned."

"Don't get her riled up. She's as bad as you are."

"I'll take that as a compliment," Bernie said as I got out of the car.

She backed up again, did another three-point turn, and headed down the driveway for the B & B. I watched her go and then glanced over to the Goodwill property.

Lincoln's finger was waving in front of his son's face, while Matt gestured toward the house and out to sea. The sound of raised voices drifted toward me on the wind, although I couldn't make out what they were saying. Matt threw up his hands and then abruptly turned and walked toward his car with strong, angry steps.

I ducked my head, opened the gate, and went to work.

Chapter 18

By six o'clock, I couldn't put off calling the police any longer. The tearoom was closed, everything neat and tidy and ready for another day. Scones and sweet treats were baked, eggs boiled, chicken salad in the fridge, supplies checked. Nancy, the berry farmer, had promised to have a delivery to us first thing in the morning.

I poured boiling water over leaves of Creamy Earl Grey into a teapot and pulled out my phone while waiting for the tea to steep.

She answered immediately. "Amy Redmond."

"Hi, Detective. It's Lily Roberts here. I hope I'm not disturbing you."

"You're not," she said.

"I . . . uh . . . I learned a few things I thought you might want to know. If you don't know them already, I mean. About the death of Jack Ford."

"I'm not on that case any longer, Ms. Roberts. Detective Williams decided my . . . expertise could be better used elsewhere."

"Oh. Uh, okay. I guess I should phone him, then."

"As it happens, my other case isn't all that urgent. How

about if we talk in person? I'm not far from your place now. Are you at home?"

"I'm still in the tearoom."

"I can be there in ten minutes."

"I'll put the kettle on," I said.

Amy Redmond knocked on the front door of Tea by the Sea in seven and a half minutes. I let her in.

"I've made tea. The coffeepot's switched off, and the leftover coffee thrown away, but I can start a small pot if you'd prefer that."

"Tea will be fine."

"We can talk out here." I indicated the dining room. "I don't have any chairs in the kitchen."

I'd laid out a teapot and two place settings. Perhaps because I wanted to be surrounded by something pleasant when I talked to the police about death, I used my personal set of Royal Doulton. I'd taken some of tomorrow's baking out of the pantry and arranged a proper setting for afternoon tea with scones, pistachio macarons, and slices of chocolate tart, and had put small bowls of strawberry jam and clotted cream on the table. Today's flower arrangement, red roses in a thin glass vase, was still fresh.

Amy Redmond studied the table. She tried not to smile. "Is this a bribe, Ms. Roberts?"

"Call me Lily. I was preparing my own tea when I called you, so I thought you might want to join me. You can consider it a bribe, if you want."

She sat down. "This looks lovely. Do you know, I don't think I've ever had a proper afternoon tea."

"Time to start, then." I lifted the teapot and poured. "I didn't know what you liked, so I've made my favorite. This is a Creamy Earl Grey."

She took a deep breath, clearly enjoying the rich, fragrant scent. "Isn't tea just tea? Usually black, but green in a Chinese restaurant? Served with ice in parts to the south."

"Tea is a highly varied beverage," I said, "although it all has its origins in the plant *Camellia sinensis*. I'd educate you on what goes into making and serving the different varieties, but we'd be here all night, and that's not why I called. But I will tell you that Creamy Earl Grey is based on the traditional Earl Grey, with an added hint of caramel for a boost.

"This place is a labor of love for you, isn't it?"

I smiled at her.

Redmond helped herself to a scone. She cut it in half and spread it with butter, then added a spoonful of jam and a dollop of clotted cream. I put a macaron on my plate and put a splash of milk and a half spoon of sugar in my own tea. I was glad I'd thought to serve tea. This felt a lot more comfortable than a police interrogation should.

"So," Redmond said, around a mouthful of scone, "what did you want to tell me?"

"Do you know a local woman by the name of Dorothy Johnson?"

"That name has come up in our inquiries. She and Mr. Ford had a public dispute over the sale of her property to him. She claimed he cheated her, but as far as we can see, he did nothing illegal. He paid her less than her property was worth, but the onus is on the seller to ensure they get a good price, unless they're mentally incapable of taking responsibility for what they're doing, and there was never any suggestion Mrs. Johnson was in such a state. Why do you ask?"

"You said she's mentally competent. What about her physical condition?"

"Again, Lily, you need to tell me what you're getting at."

I sighed. "Okay. My grandmother and I paid a call on Dorothy."

"Why did you do that?"

"My grandmother isn't happy at being the suspect in a

murder investigation. She thinks she can get to the bottom of things herself. She's like that."

"So I gathered."

"We heard through the North Augusta grapevine about Mr. Ford's business practices in general and his dealings with Dorothy Johnson in particular. So we checked up on her."

"And . . ."

"And . . . she appeared to be a feeble little old lady. Strong willed and bluntly spoken but quite frail."

Redmond nodded and drank some of her tea. Her eyes widened. "Wow, this is good. You say she appeared to be. That was my impression also. Do you know something to the contrary?"

"I saw her in town this morning, running across the street, standing in line for coffee, jumping out of the way of a man who accidentally bumped into her. No walker, even though she has a handicap license plate and she gets around her residence with the aid of a walker. I'd be willing to bet good money she plays up being disabled for the sympathy factor and to get in front of lines. Also helps when the police come to call. Seeing as to how she's perfectly mobile, she might even enjoy the occasional walk along the oceanfront, maybe with the assistance of hiking poles."

"Do you make all the food served here yourself?"

That was an abrupt change of topic. Had she even heard me? Might as well answer the question. "I do, and everything's made completely from scratch. Nothing purchased and nothing out of a package. More than once, people have complained when they saw the prices. We never apologize. Good food, well prepared with excellent ingredients, much of it sourced locally, costs money. Not to mention fresh flowers on the table and real china and silver and linen at every place. Afternoon tea isn't an everyday thing, not even in the UK and certainly not in America. It's a treat, an indulgence, and I believe it needs to be presented accordingly."

Scone finished, Detective Redmond helped herself to a macaron and sipped her tea.

I decided to plow on. "I also just happened . . ."

Redmond peered at me over the top of her cup.

"Just happened to run into Carla Powers today. The mayor?"

"I know who Carla is. Between running this busy restaurant and spying on Dorothy Johnson, you also talked to the mayor?"

"I took a break from the tearoom. I have good staff."

"So it would seem. Okay, I'll bite. What did you learn from the mayor?"

"She was having an affair with Jack Ford."

That, I could tell, came as a surprise to her. For the first time, Redmond's composure cracked. Then the mask fell back into place, and she said, "Is that so? She actually told you that?"

"Believe it or not, she did. On Friday she informed her husband she was leaving him for Jack Ford."

Redmond's hand hovered between another macaron and a slice of chocolate tart. She settled on the tart.

"Which means," I said, "Mr. Powers and Mrs. Ford, if she knew about this, can be considered suspects. As can Carla herself. It's possible, isn't it, that she told her husband she wanted a divorce and then Jack said he wasn't serious, after all? Humiliation can be a powerful motive."

"How do you know that?"

"I've had bad relationships, and I'm sure you have, too. I didn't actually kill the guy, but I might have wanted to."

"Anything else you think I need to know?"

"There is Jack Ford's marriage. It's rather odd, wouldn't you say?"

"I've seen odder." She smiled at me. "I've been in an odder one."

"Oh. Okay. Janice Ford says she was in Boston when her husband died. Were you able to find out if that's true?"

"I'm not going to tell you the results of a police inquiry, Lily."

Oh, well. It was worth a try.

"You and your grandmother have been busy. I can't say I'm surprised. Your grandmother's a strong-minded woman."

"You don't know the half of it," I said.

She pushed her chair back. "Thank you for the tea. I enjoyed it enormously. I'll be back, as a paying guest, I mean." Her face twisted. "I have a lot of free time on my hands right now."

"What case are you working on? I didn't hear about another murder in North Augusta."

She stood up. "Not a murder. A vacation home was broken into last night."

"Was much taken?"

"Some bottles of alcohol, but according to Detective Williams, we have to take it very seriously. Nip this sort of thing in the bud, he says."

"You're working on that rather than a murder?"

"Detective Williams likes to allocate resources effectively. Meaning he likes to work his cases his own way. That should be the chief's job, but I'm beginning to suspect the chief does whatever Detective Williams suggests."

"Should I have been telling him what I've learned, then?"

"You can talk to me. I'll pass your information on to Detective Williams." She looked me straight in the eye. "Thank you, Lily. The police don't always appreciate civilian interference, but on occasion it can be useful."

I walked her to the front door, stepped outside, and

locked up after us. All the food I'd laid out had been eaten, and I could leave the dishes until tomorrow.

"Good evening," Detective Redmond said. "Are you looking for me?"

Simon McCracken and Matt Goodwill were seated at a patio table. They stood up and shook their heads.

"Nope," Matt said.

"Just having a chat," Simon said.

"Nice evening," Matt said.

"Sure is," Simon said.

"Right." Redmond turned back to me. "Call me if you learn anything more, Lily. I'll see that your information is acted upon." She walked to her car and drove away.

Simon and Matt let out a collective sigh.

"What's all that about, then?" Simon said.

"What did she want?" Matt said.

"What are you two doing here?" I asked.

"I saw her drive up," Simon said. "I was getting ready to leave for the day, but I thought I'd stick around in case you needed help."

"I came back to check out a few things at the house," Matt said. "I also wondered what was going on. She was in there for a long time."

"We were having tea and talking over the Jack Ford case."

Two pairs of eyebrows rose.

"They don't think you or Rose had anything to do with it, do they?" Simon said.

"Or Bernie?" Matt added.

"I don't know what the police are thinking. Detective Redmond isn't exactly chatty. But I hope they get to the bottom of it soon. You knew Jack Ford, Matt. Can you think of anyone who might have wanted to get rid of him?"

"I didn't know him. I'd heard of him in passing over the

years, but we'd never met. We hadn't exactly moved in the same circles. These days I don't even move in the same circles as my parents do. I live in Chatham and came up here when Dad called to tell me about Ford's death."

"Are your siblings also wanting to keep the house in the family?" I asked.

"I have one sister. She lives in California and couldn't care less one way or the other what happens to the house. I'll be off now." He lifted a hand in farewell and sauntered away.

"Thanks for looking out for me, Simon," I said. "As you can see, all is well."

"Catch you tomorrow, Lily. Have a nice evening." He put his helmet on and fastened the straps.

I watched him hop on his motorcycle and roar away. Matt Goodwill's BMW convertible came up the rutted and pitted driveway and turned onto the road after Simon.

I walked across the lawn to Victoria-on-Sea, deep in thought. Nice to have two handsome men checking in to make sure I was okay.

But, I had to ask myself, was that what they were doing? Matt in particular. Was he trying to help or wanting to keep tabs on what was happening with the police? He'd said he didn't know Jack Ford. Doesn't mean he didn't. Doesn't mean he's not protecting his father, either. He'd said he was in Chatham on Saturday morning. Doesn't mean he was.

And what about Simon? He'd been on the property at six Saturday morning. He'd said he was at the front of the house, working in the garden, when Ford went over the bluff.

Doesn't mean he was.

I shook my head. This investigating was getting to me. Next, I'd be wondering where Robert the Bruce had been at the time of the murder. I was no detective. I needed to leave the detecting to those who were.

I stopped next to the neatly trimmed boxwood hedge that enclosed the rose garden. I'd told Amy Redmond all I'd learned. What had she said? *Sometimes the police find civilian assistance useful?*

Had Detective Redmond been telling me to keep investigating? Did she not trust Chuck Williams to do the job properly?

Why had Redmond, an experienced major crimes detective, been taken off a murder case to investigate the theft of a couple of bottles of booze, anyway?

Because Williams didn't want her to find out the truth?

If so, why might that be?

Chapter 19

The problem, I thought as I cracked farm-fresh eggs into a pan of sizzling butter, was that I had too many suspects. Not many people had liked Jack Ford, and even those who had, such as Carla Powers, might have had reason to want him dead.

"She'll be glad to hear it," Edna called over her shoulder as she came into the kitchen, balancing a tray piled high with dirty dishes.

Glad to hear it. Where had I heard that recently?

"What are we glad to hear?" I asked.

"Our guests like your cooking. A man told me he'll be back next year just for the breakfasts."

"Always nice to be appreciated. Tell Rose that, will you? Maybe she'll give me a raise."

Edna roared with laughter.

"Looks like we're going to have a full house for the weekend," I said, "now that our murder has dropped off the front pages of the nonlocal media."

"Have the police told you it's murder?" she asked.

"Not in so many words, but they're investigating as though it is."

"That's normal, Lily. The man died under mysterious circumstances. The police always consider the worst-case scenario until they have reason to believe otherwise. Jack fell through the gate and down the bluff. No one saw it happen. It might have been an accident. He might have done it on purpose. Maybe he was mad at something and he gave the gate a good kick. It broke, and his momentum threw him over the edge."

I cheered up a fraction. "I hope that's it. I hate to think someone deliberately killed a man right outside our door. Do you think that's what happened?"

"Not on your life. Someone did him in, all right."

I deflated.

"I have one order of the vegetarian breakfast, two full English, and one for muffins and juice. Two rooms are checking out today, so we'll have a smaller group tomorrow, before the weekend rush." Edna cut a slice of the vegetable frittata and arranged it on a plate. She then added some salad greens, a handful of heirloom cherry tomatoes, and a sprinkling of sunflower seeds and lightly drizzled balsamic vinegar on top, while I served up two plates of hot food. She carried it all into the dining room.

I switched the stove off with a sigh. That was the last of it. For today, anyway. We'd do the same thing all over again tomorrow.

Tap-tap-tap in the hallway, and the door opened. Robbie darted in, followed by my grandmother. "Good morning, love. Did you sleep well?"

"Yes," I lied. When I got home after closing the tearoom, I'd called Bernie and told her what I'd learned—precious little—from Amy Redmond.

"It's interesting she's been taken off the case," Bernie had said.

"Isn't it?"

"That might have a perfectly logical explanation. Maybe she's not a good cop and Williams is trying to keep her out of his way."

"Do you think that's it?"

"No. More likely she objected to his methods or his attitude and he sent her off to do something else. Sounds like she wants you on her side, Lily. Good work."

"She doesn't want me on her side," I said. "She wants to find out the truth about what happened to Jack Ford."

"As you, meaning we, do, too. We are each other's side. Unlike Detective Williams, who I suspect is not on our side."

"Meaning?"

"Meaning he's not on Rose's side. Do you know he got a warrant for her bank records?"

"No. How do you know that?"

"I have my sources. When Rose moved from Iowa to Massachusetts, she transferred her accounts to a bank where a college friend of mine is an executive."

"I can't imagine Williams found anything incriminating in Rose's bank account."

"Probably to the contrary, which would be why he hasn't confronted her over anything he found. It would be to Rose's financial advantage—the tearoom's, too—if a fancy resort went up next door. You'd get the overflow. After the noise and mess of construction is over, anyway."

"I suspect Williams, like too many people, can't look beyond a monetary advantage. Rose is opposed to the development because she bought Victoria-on-Sea precisely because it is quiet and remote. For Cape Cod, anyway. Thornecroft Castle doesn't have any neighbors for miles in all directions. It didn't in her day, anyway. She's never been back."

"Williams will have to look elsewhere for his suspect."

"And we, with almost no effort, have found several."

"When I die," Bernie said, "I hope the list of people who wanted me dead won't be too long."

We said good night. I took Éclair for a walk and then watched a bit of TV and read for a while before turning out the light. I lay awake for a long time, thinking about all that had happened with the Jack Ford case and getting increasingly angry about it.

I wasn't a detective. I was a pastry chef. I didn't want to be a detective. I wanted to make the very best afternoon tea in all of New England.

This morning I was occupied making the very best breakfast in all of New England.

"We have guests leaving today," I said to my grandmother. "You might want to go out and say good-bye."

"If I must," Rose said.

"You must."

She passed Edna on her way into the dining room. "I'll have my tea when I return, Edna."

"Pot's on the shelf," Edna replied. "And milk's in the fridge. Help yourself." She put the dirty dishes on the counter. "Not even a crumb left for the birds."

"Glad to hear it," I said. Then I remembered where I'd heard that phrase recently: Saturday morning, as B & B guests had gathered on the edge of the bluffs to watch the police activity.

I took off my apron and washed my hands and went into the dining room. The morning sun streamed through the large windows and the open French doors. A few guests remained, chatting over the last of their tea or coffee, planning their day.

"I do hope we'll be seeing you again next year," Rose was saying to a table for two.

"Guaranteed," the man said.

Rose crossed the room to a table by the windows. The carpet in this room was thick, and her cane didn't make a sound. "Good morning. Please don't get up. Don't let me disturb you. I wanted to check that everything has been as you expected."

She should have been on the stage, my grandmother. No doubt all that training at Thornecroft Castle taught her to act the perfect hostess regardless of her feelings.

"Just great." The woman who replied was the one I'd chatted to Monday evening. I didn't know how long they'd been staying here—I didn't usually come into the dining room—but she'd been at the top of the bluffs Saturday morning, watching the police activity. When someone said the dead man was Jack Ford, she'd replied, "Glad to hear it."

Now that I was remembering that, I also remembered I'd seen her on another occasion: on Friday, a short plump woman running through the garden, her long skirt flowing behind her, heading for the Goodwill property when Jack Ford's car was the only one there.

Coincidence? Unlikely.

She smiled at the man sitting opposite her. He placed his hand on hers and returned the smile. "We're on our honeymoon," she said with a giggle.

"Congratulations," Rose said. "Where are you off to now?" She managed to sound as though she was genuinely interested.

"We have four nights in Hyannis," the woman said. "Then it's back to work on Monday. I am not looking forward to it, not one little bit."

"Enjoy the rest of your vacation, love." Rose headed back to the kitchen.

"Everything all right, Lily?" she asked me.

"Perfectly fine." We went into the kitchen together. "The last people you talked to. What room are they in?"

"Why do you want to know?"

"No reason."

She took a seat at the table, where Robbie was waiting.

"As Edna doesn't seem to be taking the time to make my tea, I'll tell you while you make me a cuppa." Robbie rubbed against her arm. "Bring a splash of cream for Robbie, please."

Edna, at the moment elbow-deep in soapsuds, turned her head and widened her eyes at me. I didn't laugh as I plugged the kettle in and dropped tea bags into a pot. We didn't bother with a selection of select teas and loose leaves in the B & B.

"Our late-in-life honeymooning couple are in room two-oh-two," Rose said. "Leaving this morning."

I put things away in the fridge and the pantry while waiting for the kettle to boil. As soon as it did, I poured hot water into the teapot and put the pot in front of Rose. Then I poured cream into a small saucer for the spoiled cat.

"I'm off. See you tomorrow, Edna. Have a nice day, Rose." I called to Éclair, and she yawned, stretched every inch of her body, and got to her feet.

My grandmother poured her tea. Robbie dove into his cream without bothering to say thank you.

I put Éclair in the cottage and then came back to the main house. I entered via the French doors to the dining room. The room was empty; the guests were getting on with their day. I went into the hall and climbed the steps to the second floor. All the doors were closed, and soft murmurs came from behind some of them. I knocked on 202.

"Who is it?" a woman called.

"Lily. Rose's granddaughter."

The door opened, and the woman's head popped out. "Hi. Can I help you?"

"I'd like a minute of your time, if you don't mind?"

She opened the door and waved me in. An empty suitcase lay open on the unmade bed, clothes and toiletry bags piled beside it. Pillows were tossed on the floor, and a damp towel was draped over a chair. A twenty-dollar bill, which I hoped was the tip for the housekeeping staff, lay on the night table.

This room was at the back of the house, with a beautiful view over the bay. The drapes were open, and in the distance white sails drifted across the calm waters and powerful speedboats raced past. A whale-watching boat, crammed with eager tourists, headed for the open waters of the Atlantic Ocean.

"Brian's gone for a walk while I get the packing done. We've enjoyed our stay here very much, and I'll put a review up on some web pages."

"Thanks. We'd appreciate that, but that's not why I'm here." I took a deep breath. I wasn't accustomed to asking people about their personal lives, and I had no idea how to go about it. Might as well just get it over with. "Tell me about Jack Ford."

Her eyes widened, and then shutters slammed over them. "I don't know anyone by that name. Sorry." She almost bit off the words.

"The man who died at the bottom of the bluffs on Saturday morning. You were there at the scene. I saw you."

"I came outside when I heard the commotion, as did a lot of people. Terrible tragedy. I don't like to be rude, but we're running a bit late."

"I heard you say something that made me think you knew him. That's all."

She studied my face. "You're mistaken."

"You said—"

"I told you I have no idea who you're talking about. I'll admit I came out to see what was going on, but I went back inside immediately. It was none of our business, and unlike some people, I'm not so rude as to intrude on people's personal privacy." She swept the money off the night table and thrust it into her pocket. "I'm afraid I won't be recommending this place, after all. Not if the *staff* are this nosy." She crossed the room in a few angry steps and stood by the open door.

"I'm not being nosy." I stepped into the hallway. "I apologize for having to ask you, but a man died on our property, and the police are asking questions about my grandmother, and—"

"All the more reason not to come here again next year, if you and your grandmother have police records."

"We don't—"

The door slammed in my face.

This detecting stuff wasn't so difficult, after all. She hadn't told me anything, but I had learned something. It was possible I'd misunderstood what she meant by "Glad to hear it." She might have been talking about something completely different, and I'd thought she'd been reacting to Jack Ford's name.

An easy mistake to make. One at which she'd have had no reason to get so angry with me.

The strength of her anger told me I was on the right track. Now that I was thinking about it, I remembered more of what happened that morning. She hadn't taken a quick, curious look and then returned to her own business. She'd pushed through the crowd of onlookers, almost eagerly, and peered over the railing. The look I'd seen on her face had been one of pure triumph.

As soon as they checked out, I'd have to sneak into the room and leave a twenty-dollar bill. It wouldn't be fair to do the housekeeper out of her tip because I'd inadvertently offended a guest.

I'd have to tell Amy Redmond what I'd learned. The police would then come to the B & B and interview our guest. She'd know I'd ratted on her and be absolutely furious. She'd probably hit the Internet and spread bad reviews about Victoria-on-Sea far and wide.

I sighed. Nothing I could do about that. I didn't even know the woman's name.

I found Rose sitting in her favorite damask-covered wingback chair in the drawing room. A tray with her teapot, cup and saucer, and a plate with the remains of a slice of toast was on the side table. Robbie stood on the wide ledge of the big bay window, staring wistfully outside. The bird feeders had been refilled this morning, and chickadees and finches fluttered about or sat on perches, enjoying their breakfast.

Rose came here every morning between nine thirty and eleven, waiting to help guests check out. She'd be back between three and five for check-in. Outside of those times, the phone on the reception desk rang through to her cell phone.

"What's the name of the couple in two-oh-two?" I asked.

"Why do you want to know?"

"I'll tell you later. Right now I need their name."

"She's Susan Walsh. Whether he's Mr. Walsh or not, I don't know. She made the reservation. They are on their honeymoon." My grandmother smiled at me. "Which goes to show, love, that it's never too late."

I ignored that crack, shut the drawing-room door, pulled out my phone, and punched buttons. My grandmother gave me a questioning look. Robbie licked butter off her toast.

"Hi, Detective," I said. "It's Lily Roberts here. I've learned something about the Ford case you might be interested in."

"What?" Redmond said. Obviously, not a woman who engaged in small talk.

"We have a guest by the name of Susan Walsh. She was here on Saturday morning at the top of the cliff after I found the body. I'm positive I heard her say, 'Glad to hear it,' when Ford's name was mentioned."

"You think that means something?"

"I do. I spoke to her just now, and she got very aggressive. She claimed not to know what I was talking about. Although she would, wouldn't she, if she was responsible?"

"People react in strange ways, Lily," she said. "Don't leap to make assumptions. We interviewed all your guests at the time, but no one stood out as being of interest."

"I think she met with Jack on Friday, although I can't be sure."

"Okay. It sounds as though we need to speak to her again, but it will have to be Detective Williams, not me."

"They're about to leave," I said. "To check out." No doubt Susan Walsh would be in a real rush. A rush to get away from me. I hadn't handled the situation at all well. "She's packing now."

"In that case," Redmond said, "I'll come. Detective Williams is in court this morning. I can't ask you to stop them, Lily, so don't try to. I trust you have her contact information?"

"Rose will have it. Everyone has to show her a credit card when they check in."

"I'll be there as soon as I can. Within the half hour."

I hung up and turned back to my grandmother.

"That was an interesting conversation," she said.

"It's almost ten o'clock. Checkout time is eleven. Let's hope the police get here in time, but if not, can you try to delay the Walshes?"

"Of course. I'll wrestle Mr. Walsh, if that's his name, to the ground and tie him to the desk with the drapery rope, and while Robbie stands guard over him, I'll put Mrs. Walsh in a choke hold and secure her hands with my scarf while I reach for my revolver. Don't be ridiculous, Lily! I'm not holding anyone captive in my house."

I was prevented from replying that I'd been talking about engaging Susan in casual conversation by the sound of footsteps pounding down the stairs, followed by the rhythmic *thump-thump-thump* of a suitcase on wheels. I peeked out. Fortunately, it was not the Walshes, but a family of four.

Rose left her tea and went into the hallway to take a seat behind the reception desk, and handed the woman the bill. "I hope you enjoyed your stay."

"We did," the mother said as she ran her eyes over the bill and signed it. The father carried on out the door, dragging the cases behind him.

"Were you here when that guy died?" their son asked me.

"No," I said.

"Lame. We got here too late for the main action, but I saw the CSI guys poking around the stairs. Cool. They wouldn't let me near, though."

"You are such a ghoul." His sister tossed her long glossy hair and spoke to me. "Never mind him. He's always *sooo* juvenile."

As if to prove her point, he stuck his tongue out at her. She, full of teenage sophistication, rolled her eyes and emitted a world-weary sigh.

The family left, passing Susan Walsh's husband Brian, returning from his walk. He nodded politely to Rose and headed for the stairs.

"Have a nice walk?" I asked quickly.

"Yes, thanks."

"Did you discover any new paths? I don't get much of a chance to get out myself. Too busy at the tearoom. I'm thinking of doing up a map showing the best walking routes and such. Something we can give to guests when they check in."

"I took the steps down to the beach and walked along there for a while."

"Which direction?"

"North, I think. I'm not sure. Maybe south. Is that way south?" He pointed.

"The tide's coming in, isn't it? Does the high tide block access much farther along?" I threw a desperate glance at my grandmother. *I could use some help here.*

"It's low tide right now. Nice for exploring the tidal pools." He walked past the reception desk, heading for the stairs.

Rose began to stand. She let out a sharp gasp and fell to one side as her bad leg gave way, and her cane crashed to the floor. Her hand reached out and scrambled for purchase at the edge of the desk. She began to slide.

I yelled and leapt forward, but Brian was ahead of me. He grabbed Rose around the waist and steadied her, and then he lowered her carefully into the chair, as though she were made of fine porcelain.

"Are you okay, Rose?" I said.

"I . . . I'm fine. A dizzy spell came over me, I fear." She looked at Brian, her eyes wide with gratitude. "Thank you so much, young man." He was fifty at least. "At my age, a fall can be so very dangerous."

"Can I get you anything?" he said. "A glass of water?"

"A sip of tea sets everything to rights, I always say."

Brian threw me a look.

Rose clutched his arm. "My tea's in the drawing room. Can you help me there, please, love? This chair is very uncomfortable." She started to stand. What could Brian do but take her arm? She smiled up at him.

I picked her cane off the floor.

Slowly, ever so slowly, Rose, supported by Brian, walked into the drawing room. While Brian hovered, she slowly, ever so slowly, settled into her chair. Robbie watched from the window seat. He yawned and returned to observing the birds.

Once seated, Rose patted her chest. "That did give me a terrible fright. I'm not quite as young as I used to be. My tea's finished, Lily. Do be a dear girl and get me another cup." Brian glanced toward the door, and Rose jerked her head at me. I picked up the pot. It was almost full.

"If you're okay, Mrs. Campbell," Brian said, "I'll go upstairs and help Susan with our cases."

"Please stay until Lily gets back." Rose's voice quavered ever so slightly. "I . . . I feel a bit faint."

"I . . . ," he said.

"Be right back," I said. "Did you know Brian and Susan are on their honeymoon? Isn't that nice?" I ran for the kitchen. Edna had left for the day, leaving the old kitchen spick and span. I didn't bother making more tea. The clock on the wall told me it was after ten. I called the tearoom, and Cheryl answered.

"It's me," I said. "I'm going to be late again, but not by much. What's the reservation book look like?"

"Slow until one. Then we're almost full for the rest of the day."

"Okay. There's plenty of food to get started. I made the chicken salad for the sandwiches last night and boiled the eggs. I'll try to get there as soon as I can. Did the strawberries arrive?"

"Yes. And Simon brought us a gorgeous arrangement of flowers. Is everything okay, Lily?"

"As okay as can be," I said. "If you need anything, call me."

I carried the teapot back to the drawing room.

"And three grandchildren," Rose was saying when I entered. "They still live in Iowa. I loved my life in Iowa, but I missed the sea so very much."

Brian threw me a grateful look and started to stand.

"It's because I'm English, of course. We English love our sea. My late husband's family was from Scotland. We always gave our cats the names of Scottish heroes. My previous cat was called Flora MacDonald. With a name like Walsh, your ancestors must be from the UK. Do you know where they originated?"

"No. I don't. Sorry." He stood up. "Susan will be wondering where I am."

"I'm sure she's fine," Rose said. "Would you like a cup of tea? Lily, fetch Brian a cup."

"No!" he almost shouted. He cleared his throat. "I mean, no, thank you. We need to be on our way." He walked out of the drawing room as fast as politely possible and took the stairs three at a time.

"Good heavens, but that was exhausting," Rose said. "The poor man. Do you think we bought ourselves enough time?"

I glanced out the window to see Amy Redmond's car pull up. "Looks like it. Why don't you sit at the reception desk in case any of our guests need to speak to you? You can invite the police to interview Susan here in the drawing room. Much more formal than in a bedroom. I'll sort the linens while that's happening."

"Excellent idea." Rose got to her feet in one smooth movement.

"Don't ever scare me like that again," I said.

She grinned at me. Robbie leapt off the windowsill and followed her out.

I showed Amy Redmond into the drawing room and then ran upstairs to tell Susan Walsh she had a visitor. Brian looked confused, while Susan threw daggers at me.

"Sorry," I said, "but we have a duty to help the police, wouldn't you agree?"

"Help the police with what?" Brian said. "You mean

about that guy who died on Saturday? We don't know anything about that. Susan?"

Susan let out a long breath. "If I must. You wait here, honey. I won't be long."

"What's going on?" he said, but she didn't answer.

I led the way downstairs, and Susan reluctantly followed. Rose sat behind the reception desk, flicking through the bookings for the rest of the month. Susan and I went into the drawing room.

Amy Redmond stood at the window, looking out over the gardens. She turned as we came in. "Thanks, Ms. Roberts. You can leave us now. We shouldn't be long. I have a couple of questions, Mrs. Walsh. If you don't mind." Her tone of voice clearly indicated that she didn't much care whether Susan minded or not. I shut the door behind me.

No one other than Rose was in the hallway, and no one was moving around upstairs. I gave Rose a wink and slipped into the linen closet. I shoved tablecloths, placemats, and napkins aside, moved the loose shelves, pulled the lever, and ducked into the secret room.

"We won't be staying at this place again, I can tell you that, Detective," Susan was saying. "Bunch of interfering busybodies, if you ask me."

"As it happens," Redmond said, "I *am* asking you. What did you mean by 'Glad to hear it' when you heard the news that Jack Ford had died?"

There was a long pause. I could imagine Redmond leaning back in her chair, letting the silence drag out.

"I don't remember saying that," Susan said at last.

"Did you know Mr. Ford?"

"I know lots of people. Doesn't mean anything."

More silence.

"Okay, I knew him," Susan said. "I'd done some work for him back in Boston. I was surprised to see him here. I didn't kill him, though."

"What sort of work?"

"I'm a systems analyst. That means I design computer systems. I had my own consulting business for a while. It didn't work out. I did a job for him. He cheated me."

"Cheated you? How?"

"I completed the job as contracted for, and he refused to pay the final invoice. He said the work was substandard. It wasn't. It was a big job, and he cheated me out of a lot of money."

"Did you try to get what you were owed?"

"I tried, but there wasn't a lot I could do. He had lawyers and shell companies, and I was one woman just trying to earn a living."

"When did this happen?"

"Eighteen months ago. I've moved on. It was a blow, but I recovered. I decided to give up being my own boss and get a proper job. I work for a bank now. A lot less stress. Let the Jack Fords of the world try to cheat a bank."

"Was your husband involved in this business of yours?"

"No, and don't you start trying to claim he was out to get revenge or something. I met Brian at my new job. We're on our honeymoon."

"Congratulations," Redmond said dryly.

"Thank you. Now, if there's nothing else . . ."

"Were you aware Mr. Ford lived in North Augusta?"

"I was not. And before you ask, I didn't come on this vacation planning to run into him, have an argument with him, or murder him. It was pure chance that we came here, and a total shock when I realized he was the dead man."

"You were interviewed on Saturday at the scene. Why didn't you tell us you knew him?"

"I didn't think it was relevant. It isn't relevant. You knew his name."

"You gave us your contact information on Saturday. Is that still correct?"

"Yes," Susan snapped. "I'm not in the habit of lying to the police."

"Just of omitting pertinent information."

"I didn't . . ."

"Thank you for your time." I heard a floorboard creak as Susan headed for the door. "One more question. Is Walsh your married name?"

"Yes."

"What name did you have previously?"

"Stringer. Susan Stringer."

"Your company name was?"

"Stringer and Associates."

Footsteps in the hall and then on the stairs as Susan ran back to her room. I heard Rose go into the drawing room.

"Can I get you a cup of tea or coffee, Detective? I always enjoy this time of day. Lovely and peaceful after the guests have checked out or headed off for another day of their vacation." She was telling me the coast was clear and giving me time to get out of the secret room.

I was in the hall in time to meet Redmond coming out of the drawing room. "Did you learn anything?" I asked.

"Thanks for the tip, Lily. Mrs. Walsh is free to go. She is not a suspect at this time." She nodded politely to Rose, and I walked her to the door.

I'd seen Susan Stringer Walsh heading across the B & B property in the direction of Jack Ford's car on Friday. She hadn't told Redmond that; she'd implied that the first time she'd seen him had been after he died. I couldn't see how I could tell Redmond without revealing I'd overheard their entire conversation.

I decided it didn't matter. Susan was now on the police radar, and if there was something to find, they'd find it.

"What did she have to say for herself?" Rose asked me when we were alone again.

"Ford cheated her in business, but she got over it. She was surprised to see him here. That's about it."

I heard banging suitcases, loud footsteps, and Brian Walsh's voice saying, "She had to have had some reason to want to talk to you."

Susan thundered down the stairs. When she reached the bottom, she glared at me. "Good-bye. We will not be returning. You'll be lucky if I don't lay a complaint with the North Augusta Tourist Bureau." She marched out the door, head high.

"Sorry," Brian said. "I don't know what got into her. I thought she loved it here. I do."

Rose handed him his bill. "If you can sign here and return the key."

Chapter 20

It was after eleven before I finally got to the tearoom. Cheryl and Marybeth seemed to have everything under control, so I set to work in the kitchen, mixing and rolling and stirring and cutting and baking and decorating.

"I need one gluten-free option for the cream tea," Marybeth said.

"Scones are in the freezer," I replied.

"We're getting busy out there. The patio's almost full."

"Keeps us employed." I sprinkled chopped fresh green herbs on the egg sandwiches and took a moment to admire them. "A work of art, if I do say so myself."

"If you don't, I will." Bernie came into the kitchen.

"Hey," I said. "What brings you here?"

"I met with Rose for our daily check-in."

"You check in daily with my grandmother?"

"About the case."

"Oh, right. The case. Hand me that big spoon, will you?"

She did so. "Rose told me you discovered that one of the guests had a history with Jack Ford. Well done. You're getting good at this, Lily."

"I am not," I said.

"Let's go over what we've learned." She leaned against the counter and pulled an iPad out of her shoulder bag. "We can talk while you work. I'll make notes."

"You're in the way."

"No I'm not," she said as Cheryl attempted to dodge past her to get to the tea canisters. Bernie moved to the left. Cheryl moved to the right. Bernie went right. Cheryl went left.

"Oh, for heaven's sake," I said.

"Stop!" Cheryl said. "Don't try to get out of my way. I'll get out of yours." She squeezed past Bernie and took down the tin labeled OOLONG.

"Oooolong," Bernie said. "That sounds so romantic. I'll try a cup of that please, Cheryl."

Cheryl's eyes flicked toward me.

"Might as well," I said. "Make a second pot, and you can pour me a cup, too, while you're at it." Sandwiches finished, I got down a big mixing bowl and started on today's batch of pistachio macarons. I sifted almond flour and the pistachio flour I'd made myself by grinding up the nuts with the right amount of sugar.

Cheryl scooped leaves of the delicate tea out of the tin, measured them into a tea ball, and dropped the ball into a plain white pot with gold trim. She added water from the airpot before assembling the gluten-free plate.

Bernie opened the iPad. "I can see you're working—"

"You are observant." I cracked eggs as I talked, and separated the whites from the yokes, put the whites in my mixer, and set it to beat. When they were foamy, I added cream of tartar, sugar, and a splash of green food coloring, and continued to beat them.

"Sarcasm does not become you," Bernie said over the noise of the mixer. "Rose told me you were late getting here this morning, so I know better than to ask you to take a break. We'll have to talk here. You won't repeat anything we say, will you, Cheryl?"

"My lips are sealed," Cheryl replied.

"One order of royal tea for six," Marybeth said.

"Try to use matching cups and plates for the entire table," I said. "We want the royal tea to look special."

Marybeth pulled a bottle of prosecco out of the fridge.

"I'll have a glass of that rather than the tea," Bernie said.

"You will not." I sifted the flour mixture into the whipped egg whites and gently folded it in, testing the consistency as I worked. Macarons can be tricky, but after all these years, I have an eye for when they're perfectly done.

"Let's consider our suspects," Bernie said. "I've started a list."

"A list," Marybeth said. "Sounds serious."

"I *am* serious," Bernie said. "Lincoln Goodwill and his son, Matt."

"Matt wasn't in North Augusta on Saturday." I filled a pastry bag with the egg-white mixture and piped small, perfect rounds onto a parchment-lined baking sheet.

"So he says. First rule of detecting, Lily. You don't believe what the suspects have to say for themselves. Next, Carla Powers. Mr. Powers. Janice Ford. Dorothy Johnson. And lastly, Roy Gleeson."

"Wouldn't put it past that Janice Ford," Cheryl said.

"Why?" Bernie asked.

"She's a strange one. She left North Augusta and moved to Boston."

"That doesn't make her a potential killer," I said.

"Does in my book." Cheryl carried a teapot into the dining room. The aroma of fragrant tea drifted behind her. She left the second pot on the counter.

"Give that one three minutes to steep," I said to Bernie, "and then pour us each a cup."

"Three minutes? Not two? Not four?"

"A proper cup of tea needs to be prepared properly. Three minutes." Macarons piped, I tapped the baking sheets on the counter.

"What are you doing that for?" Bernie asked.

"Have to get the bubbles out, otherwise the shells will crack. They need to dry before going in the oven." I put them aside and took out a saucepan and started on the cream filling by heating water and sugar on the stove.

"Mom doesn't know why anyone in their right mind would ever leave North Augusta," Marybeth said.

"What about you?" I asked. "You ever think about moving away?"

She sighed heavily. "Yeah. I always planned to move to a big city one day. New York maybe, or Los Angeles. I've never been to California. But, well, I married Jimmy, and he has his job here, and his mom's not doing too well, and the kids have school and their friends." She took the prosecco and six champagne flutes into the dining room.

Bernie and I exchanged a look.

"Back at it," Bernie said. "Then there's your B & B guest, Susan Walsh. Rose told me what happened this morning with her. Have I missed anyone?"

"The proverbial person or persons unknown. I've been thinking. Jack Ford had a lot of enemies. There are probably a whole bunch of people like Susan out there who he cheated in one way or another."

"Rose and I did some checking again this morning. He's been sued several times for failing to pay his contractors or staff. He's as slippery as an eel. Always manages to wiggle out of it or delay so much the complainant can't afford to keep the legal action going."

"The killer doesn't have to be someone we've spoken to," I said. "Maybe they saw Jack walking alone by the bluffs and took a chance. Maybe they'd been following him, hoping for their chance, and took it. If that's the case, they probably left town right after it was done."

"We don't know why he was at the stairs that morning," Bernie said. "He was supposed to be meeting Lincoln Goodwill and Roy Gleeson at the Goodwill place. He arrived early. We don't know why he did that. He had no reason to come onto your property."

"You need to find out why he was there." Cheryl came back into the kitchen. She poured two cups out of the small pot and handed Bernie and me a cup each. "Here you go. You don't add anything to oolong."

Bernie took a sip. "Oh my gosh. This is so great. I think it's my new favorite tea."

"Every tea is your new favorite tea when you're drinking it." I started to beat some egg yolks while keeping one eye on the contents of the saucepan, waiting until the syrup reached the exact right temperature before mixing it with the yolks and adding butter. The pistachio cream filling would perfectly match the bright green shells.

"You say that as though there's something wrong with it," Bernie said.

Cheryl began to arrange the royal tea food selections on one of our largest three-tiered stands.

"Don't even think about it," I said to Bernie.

"Think about what?"

"I see you eyeing those tarts."

"Perish the thought. Speaking of thoughts, Cheryl had a good one."

"I did?"

"You did. We need to find out precisely what Jack Ford was doing at the top of the steps on Saturday morning."

"Bernie," I said, "we'll never be able to do that."

"I wonder if he kept a diary."

"Dear Diary, going to meet X this morning. I know he wants me dead, but I am not afraid."

"I meant a business diary. Not a journal."

"Even if he had one, no one's going to show it to you."

"I guess not. His phone records should show if he got an early morning call, but I have no way of accessing those. This is all very frustrating."

"We have to let it go," I said. "Amy Redmond is keeping herself on top of things, albeit unofficially. I have a good feeling about her. I think she's a good cop. She'll get to the bottom of it."

"I worry Williams is out to railroad Rose."

"He can't prove anything, because Rose didn't do anything, and the idea that she's capable of killing a man is nothing but ridiculous." Time to change the subject. "How's your book coming?"

Bernie sighed. "Well enough, I guess. When I get time to work on it. I was in the middle of what's going to be a really great scene when Rose called me with this morning's update. Rose . . . Did I tell you I've decided to call my main character Rose?"

"Not Esmeralda? Glad to hear it."

"Actually, I have two main characters. I've decided on a dual story line. Rose is the upper-class woman living in Boston. The lower-class one, Tessa, lives on Cape Cod. They'll meet when Rose comes to the Cape on vacation. Right now, Rose is chafing under her father's strict thumb, and in this scene she slips out of the house to go to a meeting of a women's suffrage group he's forbidden her to associate with."

Marybeth came into the kitchen with a load of dirty dishes. One lone chicken salad sandwich remained on the tray. "Sounds good," she said. "I'll buy that. Let me know when it comes out."

"If it ever comes out." I admired my cream filling. "You have a book to write, Bernie. I have a restaurant to run. We're not detectives. We've done what we can. It's time to leave it to the professionals."

"I suppose you're right." Bernie pointed to the leftover

sandwich. “Can I have that?” She didn’t wait for an answer before popping it in her mouth. “Yummy. Let’s do something fun tonight.”

“Fun?” I said. “I like fun.”

“Fun.” Marybeth piled dishes in the dishwasher. “I remember fun. Vaguely.”

“How about a movie?” Bernie said. “With something to eat first. I’ll pick you up at seven.”

I smiled at her. “I’d like that.”

And I did. The movie wasn’t very good, but it was nice to be out of the kitchen for an evening, spending time with my best friend, and not thinking about either cooking or murder.

Bernie dropped me off at the B & B shortly before eleven. Thick clouds had moved in, covering any trace of moon and stars. The light over the front door was on, as it always is, and a few lamps glowed behind curtains in the guest rooms. Rose’s suite was dark. I took Éclair for a short walk around the property, using the mini-flashlight attached to my key chain to guide our way. We didn’t see anyone, and I enjoyed the peace and solitude, the only sounds the waves rushing to shore and crashing against the rocks and the crunch of my feet on the gravel of the driveway.

Walk finished, I got ready for bed and crawled between the welcoming sheets. I read a couple of pages of my book before turning out the light and making myself comfortable. I’d enjoyed the night out with Bernie. I needed to . . .

The harsh ringing of my phone woke me. I fumbled for it. My bedroom was wrapped in darkness. Next to me, Éclair rolled over with a grunt.

“Hello?” I glanced at the clock. Quarter past three.

“Lily, someone’s outside.” My grandmother’s voice was low and shaking.

"Rose? Is that you? What's happening? Are you okay?"

"Someone's outside my window."

"It's one of the guests who can't sleep. Maybe an early riser." I was still three-quarters asleep. What sort of person rose at three o'clock when they're on vacation, I didn't know.

"They're"—her voice broke—"trying to get in."

That woke me up fast enough. I threw the covers off and leapt out of bed. "Stay where you are. I'm coming. I'm hanging up now. Call nine-one-one."

"Lily! Be careful. Oh my goodness . . ."

I shoved my bare feet into running shoes, grabbed the key chain off the table by the door, and ran out of the cottage without bothering to tie the laces. I yelled to Éclair to follow. She wasn't exactly an attack dog, but she was a dog. She might be able to find some trace of our intruder. *If* we had an intruder. She leapt off the bed, as wide awake as I was.

Rose wasn't a fanciful woman. She never panicked, and that sturdy English resolve rarely cracked. If she was frightened, it was because she believed she had reason to be.

"Go to Rose," I shouted to Éclair. I don't know if she understood me, but she didn't bother checking under bushes for the latest in squirrel activity. She ran straight toward the big house, her ears back, her short legs working as fast as they could.

I chased after her, my phone in one hand, the flashlight attached to my key chain in the other. It didn't give much light, but enough that I could see where I was going—and see no one was in my path. As I ran, I searched for anything I could use as a weapon if I needed one. A multipronged rake or a solid shovel would do nicely, but Simon was a neat gardener. He always put his tools away after using them.

I rounded the house. All was quiet except for the soft

murmur of the sea and a single car passing on the main road. Lights were on in Rose's suite, but the guest rooms on this side of the house were dark. I could see no sign of anyone on the property. Éclair ran for the front door, and I called her back.

Standing on the grass, I shone my light into the bushes bordering the verandah. They were thick but well trimmed, reaching no higher than my hips. I was confident no one larger than a squirrel could be concealed in there. Éclair sniffed the ground. Her ears didn't come up, she didn't bark, and the hair on her back didn't rise.

I climbed the steps onto the verandah and called in a low voice, "Rose, I'm outside. Are you okay?"

The edge of the curtain folded back, and my grandmother's pale face appeared at the window. She gave me a thumbs-up. I waved.

Before unlocking the front door, I shone my flashlight over it. I could see no signs of tampering or other damage. I called to Éclair, she joined me, and we went inside. I shut the door behind us, firmly twisted the lock, and checked it was indeed secure.

I walked slowly down the hall, my feeble human senses alert. Éclair trotted happily ahead of me; her strong doggy senses clearly noticed nothing out of place.

Rose's suite is at the end of the long ground-floor hallway. No light spilled out from any of the guest rooms, and all was quiet. Except for room 103, the snoring coming from which would wake the dead.

I tapped at Rose's door, and she cracked it open immediately. Her gray hair stood on end, her face was pale, and her eyes wide. My heart turned over. "Are you okay?"

"Okay." She opened the door fully and stepped back. She carried the new pink cane, but her hand was not resting lightly on the top. She gripped it in her fist, prepared to use it as a weapon if needed. She saw me looking at it and gave me a wry smile. "The only thing that came to hand." She wore a long white cotton nightgown trimmed with lace, and an orange shawl was tossed over her thin shoulders.

"No one's outside. No one I saw, anyway, and Éclair didn't sense anything. Are you sure . . . ?"

"I'm sure," she said. "I don't sleep all that well these days. I was awake, reading in bed. I heard footsteps outside and something scratching at the window. No trees are next to that window, and the scratching was rhythmic. A one-two-three-stop-one-two-three pattern. It stopped when I called out, and then started again. Robbie heard it, too. He scratched at the window in response."

The cat watched me from the top of a bookshelf, his tail flicking back and forth, back and forth.

Rose's nightgown had a small pocket at the top. From inside that pocket, a voice squeaked.

"Almost forgot about her." Rose pulled her phone out. "My granddaughter has arrived. She says nothing appears to be amiss."

At that moment, I heard sirens coming down the driveway.

"You wait here," I told my grandmother. "I'll talk to the police."

"No. I'm coming with you. I have to tell them what I heard. Otherwise, they'll think I'm an easily frightened old lady." She gave me a crooked grin. "They'll think that, anyway. Oh, well, can't be helped."

She spoke into the phone. "The police are here. I'm hanging up now. Thank you."

Knowing the police wouldn't want the assistance of a small but helpful dog, I shut the door on Éclair. She wouldn't be happy being confined with Robert the Bruce, but that couldn't be helped.

As we walked down the hallway, heads popped out of guest rooms.

"I hear sirens. What's happening?"

"Is everything all right?"

"Do you need us to leave our room?"

I told the guests the alarm had gone off and the police were responding routinely. Nothing to concern themselves about.

"Good thing the guest list has almost completely turned over since the weekend," Rose said. "We don't need a reputation as the sort of establishment where police activity is the norm."

I hurried to answer the hammering on the front door.

Two uniformed officers stood there. They shone flashlights around the foyer and into my face.

"Thanks for coming. I'm Lily Roberts. My grandmother called nine-one-one because she heard someone outside her window."

Rose wiggled her fingers in a wave.

"I'm Officer Kowalski, and this is Officer LeBlanc. Let's have a look, then, shall we?" one of the cops said. He was an older guy, bald, round bellied, red nosed. "I've called Detective Williams. You had a death here recently, right?"

"Yes," I said. "Wait here please, Rose."

She nodded.

I went outside, and walked with the cops to the far end of the house. I was highly conscious of being dressed only in my summer pajamas, which featured tiny pink bottles of champagne sprinkled over the black fabric of the pants and a pithy saying on the top.

"This is a big place," LeBlanc said. "It's a B & B, right?"

"Yes."

"You have guests staying here now?"

"We do, but before you ask, my grandmother is not fanciful or easily frightened. She didn't just hear someone who couldn't sleep walking in the garden. She definitely heard someone at her window."

I pointed to Rose's windows. One is at the front of the house, opening onto the end of the verandah, and the other's on the side, above a flower bed. I'd not thought to ask her at which one she'd heard the scratching.

The officers had far more powerful flashlights than my little key chain one. They focused them on the floor of the verandah and on the ground beneath the windows. Officer LeBlanc crouched beneath Rose's window. I leaned over him.

I sucked in a breath.

A carefully maintained bed of purple and white impatiens runs along the side of the house. Tonight, directly under Rose's bedroom window, a patch of the delicate flowers was crushed, blooms trodden on, stems broken, the ground trampled.

"Looks like someone stood here," LeBlanc said. "And not long ago."

"Whatcha got?" a voice said, and I jumped. Detective Williams had arrived.

LeBlanc pushed himself to his feet with a grunt. "Lady reported a possible intruder. Seems like someone was at her window."

"These are my grandmother's rooms," I said. "She heard a noise and was sure someone was at the window, so she called nine-one-one and me. It looks as though she was right."

Williams leaned over the flower bed. "How do you know this happened tonight? Might have been some kids playing earlier."

"The damage is fresh," I said. "The foliage will begin to grow back and close up almost immediately."

He grunted. "Sure you weren't poking around yourself?"

If anyone else had asked me that, I wouldn't have bothered to grace the insulting question with an answer. Seeing as how he was the police and he'd already accused my grandmother of murder, I stood a bit straighter, lifted my chin, and said, "I had absolutely no reason to poke around, as you put it. My grandmother phoned me to say someone was outside her room, and I came immediately. I ran past here and called out to let her know it was me. I went into the house without treading on the plants."

"You can go back inside, Ms. Roberts," he said.

"I don't mind watching for a while."

"Go back inside."

"Okay."

I walked away as slowly as was humanly possible while actually remaining on two feet. I heard Officer LeBlanc say, "K-nine?"

I went through the entire house, checking to ensure that the doors and ground-floor windows in the public areas were locked and secure. Nothing I could do about the guest rooms. I didn't want to wake the guests and have them milling around, asking questions.

And probably wanting tea.

But I did make tea for Rose and me, and while it steeped, I let Robbie and Éclair out. Back in the kitchen, I put two leftover muffins onto plates, arranged tea things, and carried the tray into the drawing room.

The drawing room sits at the front of the house with a view over the gardens, down the driveway, past the tea-room, to the road. Rose and I drank our tea and ate our muffins in silence as we watched the activity outside the windows. Robbie curled up on Rose's lap, and Éclair took her place at my feet.

The police seemed to be taking our concerns seriously and didn't simply get in their cars and drive away. Flash-lights moved across the lawn, and people talked, not bothering to keep their voices down.

A tousled head popped into the drawing room. "Hello? What's going on?" It was a woman, her feet bare, her gray hair twisted into a braid that ran down her back, and pillow lines on her cheek. She clutched a blue terry-cloth robe tightly around her.

I jumped to my feet. "I'm so sorry. We believe an intruder was on the premises, and the police are checking things out."

"They're right outside my window. Are we safe? Can we move rooms?"

"You couldn't be safer, now could you?" Rose said. "With the police under your window."

"I guess not," she said. "Good night, then."

"Good night."

Once the woman had gone back to her bed, Rose said, "The other garden-facing room on the ground floor is empty tonight."

"Good thing," I replied.

I went to the window to watch the activity. A van drove up, and the driver helped a vest-wearing German shepherd out of the back. Éclair leapt onto the window seat and began barking. I put my hand on the top of her head and gave her a scratch behind the ears.

"You're better off in here," I told her. "That guy looks like he takes no nonsense from anyone."

We watched the dog sniff the ground, his nose moving as he cast around for a scent.

I turned at the sound of more footsteps in the hallway, and Williams came into the drawing room.

He looked at me. He looked at Rose. He looked at the tea tray.

"Can I offer you a cup of tea, Detective?" I said. "No coffee tonight. Sorry."

"Sure. That would be nice."

I left. I didn't want to. I wanted to stay and hear what Rose had to say. To stop the conversation if Williams tried to imply my grandmother was either imagining things or exaggerating for effect.

But I'd been raised to offer guests refreshments, and the guest had accepted, and the pot was empty.

What else could I do?

The water had barely reached a full boil before I poured it into a mug, dunked a tea bag in the water, stirred it around a couple of times, took a guess he had a sweet tooth, and dumped in a spoonful of sugar and some milk. While the water had been boiling, I'd taken out one of yesterday morning's leftover muffins and slapped it on a plate.

I lifted the tray and walked as quickly as I could back to the drawing room.

I needn't have worried. Rose had simply told Williams, without any drama, what happened, and he'd listened without interrupting.

Robbie sat in Rose's lap, glaring at the detective. Éclair was still standing on the window seat, her attention fixed on the police dog. I wondered if she was thinking there's nothing like a male in a uniform.

Rose smiled at me when I came in. "After I called Lily, I phoned nine-one-one. I then shouted as loudly as I could manage that the police were on their way. I heard no more after that, until Lily told me she was outside. I assume we frightened my intruder off."

I put the tray on the table next to Williams's chair. He grunted thanks, then asked, "Several minutes passed before you got here and the police arrived?"

"Yes," I said.

"You called Ms. Roberts on her cell phone?" he asked Rose.

"She only has the one number."

"Meaning you don't know if she was in her own room when you called."

"Hey!" I said. "What are you implying, Detective?"

He took a big bite of the muffin and chewed. "Mmm, good. I'm not implying anything. Just asking questions."

"Well, you can just stop asking that sort of question." Rose's voice was sharp, and Robbie hissed at Williams. "We told you what happened. We have no reason to make anything up."

Williams looked at me. I bristled. I didn't like that look.

"We found part of a footprint in the flower bed under your window. Looks like an ordinary running shoe." He glanced at my sneaker-clad feet. "Belonging to a woman . . . or a medium-sized man. Do you do the gardening yourself, Ms. Roberts?"

"I do not. As I'm sure you know, I'm busy enough. Our gardener is tall, and he doesn't wear sneakers at work. I didn't step into the flower bed tonight, or at any other time. What did the dog find?"

Éclair's ears twitched.

"He found a recently laid scent trail leading directly to the front door, Ms. Roberts."

"You think one of our guests . . . ? Oh. You think he followed me."

"Most likely. We can't tell the dog to concentrate on one scent and ignore any others. He follows the one most recently laid down. The handler redirected him, and the dog tracked the scent to the parking lot, where he lost it. Did you see a car?"

"I heard something on the road. I didn't think anything of it. There's never much traffic at this time of night, but there's usually some."

"It hasn't rained for a few days, and you have cars coming and going all day. We can't identify any tire tracks specifically laid down tonight." He popped the last of the muffin into his mouth and stood up. "We're done here. Call us if anything else happens tonight."

"What a good idea," Rose said. "I never would have thought of that myself."

Once again, Robbie hissed at the detective. Rose stroked his back and smiled at Williams.

He did not smile in return.

"This has to be related to the death of Jack Ford," I said.

"What makes you think that?"

"Someone deliberately attempted to frighten my grandmother, and that has never happened before. They made no attempt to get into the house. I checked the doors and couldn't find any evidence of such, and I assume your people did also."

He said nothing.

"If someone had planned on stealing from us, there are plenty of windows they could have chosen to gain entry. The window of an occupied bedroom isn't the best option. No one has ever tried to break in here before. No one has ever died on our property before. Therefore, the two incidents are likely to be related. This was a warning."

"What sort of a warning?" Rose asked.

"Don't let your imagination run away with you, Ms. Roberts," Williams said. "People do plenty of things you and I might not understand. Old ladies have the reputation of having lots of good jewelry lying around."

Rose harrumphed. "I agree with Lily. Fortunately for me, but unfortunately for our intruder, I don't frighten easily." I believed her. Even dressed in her nightgown and shawl, like a character out of Dickens (all that was missing was the stub of a candle flickering in a brass candlestick), my grandmother looked surprisingly formidable.

"Why do you think someone would want to send you a warning, Mrs. Campbell?" Williams asked. "It wouldn't be because you and Ms. Roberts here are interfering with a murder investigation, would it?"

"We're not interfering with anything," Rose said.

"That's not what I hear from Detective Redmond. You've told her some interesting things concerning the activities of Jack Ford. As it happens, I was going to pay you a call this morning, anyway, to tell you to mind your own business. I might as well do that now, seeing as I'm here. Mind your own business."

"If you're not considering all the possible suspects," Rose said, "then it might be up to concerned citizens to do so."

"Rose, let's not . . ." I stopped talking when I realized Williams had said the word. "So it *is* a murder investigation?"

"It'll be in the papers tomorrow. This is now an official murder inquiry. Jack Ford was struck on his left shoulder by a blunt instrument. The blow would not have killed him, but it was sufficient to knock him off his feet. The ground's disturbed at the top of the stairs in a way that indicates he fell against the gate. Particles of wood from that gate were embedded in his jacket and pants, indicating the gate broke under his weight, and he fell through it, down the steps, and hit his head on the ground at the bottom."

Rose and I were silent for several seconds. Rose continued to stroke Robbie. Éclair scratched at the window. I wondered if she was asking the bigger dog to come inside and play.

"How dreadful," Rose said.

"A blunt instrument," Williams said, "such as a cane."

Rose snorted. "Not that again."

"You can stop by the police station anytime and pick up your cane," he said. "We found no residue on it."

"If by residue, you mean from contact with Jack Ford, I'm glad to hear it."

"Doesn't mean you don't have another cane." He eyed the one at her side.

She lifted it up and pounded it on the floor. "Bought last Saturday afternoon. I have the receipt if you want to see it."

"I'm sure that won't be necessary."

"Has anyone reported seeing me using another cane in the days leading up to the unfortunate event?" Rose said. "I'm sure you asked."

He shrugged and looked away, not wanting to give her the satisfaction of hearing him say no. Outside, the dog jumped into the van. Officers got into cruisers and drove away, the glow of their rear lights moving through the dark.

"More likely," I said, "to have been a hiking pole. Have you found anyone who can identify the one you found in the water?"

He didn't answer my question, but I hadn't expected him to. "We're finished here, for now."

I walked him to his car. When we reached it, he turned and faced me. "I'm telling you to stay out of this, Ms. Roberts. You can tell your grandmother that also. Stop running to Amy Redmond with your fanciful stories and conspiracy theories. She's as bad as you two."

I dipped my head, trying to appear suitably chastised.

"Good night." Williams got into his car and drove away. I watched his lights turn onto the road without him making a turn signal and disappear into the darkness.

First thing tomorrow, I'd call Detective Redmond. I couldn't see that what happened here tonight—wherever that might be—had anything to do with the Ford case. But, on the other hand, I couldn't see how it couldn't.

I went inside and walked Rose to her suite while Robbie and Éclair galloped on ahead. Without trying to be too obvious about it, I checked behind the drapes and under the tables.

"No ghoulies or ghosties or things that go bump in the night," she said.

Okay, so I had been obvious about it.

"Just checking."

"Thank you for coming out, love."

"As if I wouldn't." I gave her a kiss on the cheek. "Good night."

"Good night, love. Try to get some sleep."

I found it the next morning, half tucked among the flowers in a terra-cotta pot full of geraniums at the top of the steps leading to the kitchen.

I hadn't checked the *outside* of the doors last night, and because Rose's window where the intruder had been was at the front of the house, the police had done nothing more than a cursory check of the back.

Thinking some people needed to be more conscientious about picking up their trash, I pulled a scrap of paper out of the flowers.

I unlocked the door, and Éclair and I went into the kitchen. I put my foot on the pedal of the trash can and was about to toss the paper in, but something about it caught my eye, and I glanced at it. My breath stopped.

Mind your own business. Or this won't be my last visit to your grandmother.

Chapter 21

"Good morning."

I let out a screech, leapt about a foot into the air, and dropped the paper containing the ominous note. Éclair barked.

"Hey! I'm sorry. Didn't mean to scare you." Simon stood in the doorway, his hands in the air. "I was hoping to scrounge up a cuppa before starting work."

My heart slowly settled into place. Simon noticed I'd dropped something, and took a step forward, intending to pick it up. "Leave it!" I said.

"What? Is something the matter? You're as white as a ghost."

I grabbed a plastic sandwich bag out of a drawer and used it to cover my shaking fingers. Éclair sniffed at the note, and I pushed her to one side. Slowly and carefully, I picked up the scrap of paper and laid it on the table. "Don't touch it," I said.

Simon folded his hands behind his back and leaned over to read it. The words were printed on a sheet of ordinary computer paper that had been ripped in half, with black ink in a standard word processing font. Beneath the words was a cheerful yellow smiley-face emoticon. The sort I'd seen a thousand times.

"What does this mean, last visit? Did something happen?"

"Someone tried to frighten Rose last night. They stood at her window, knocking on the glass. She called me, but by the time I arrived, they'd run off."

"You're sure she wasn't imagining it?"

I gave him a look.

"Okay," he said. "You're sure. Even if you weren't, this note sorta proves it, doesn't it?"

"Yes. Clearly, last night was intended to be a warning."

"Warning about what?"

"It can only be related to the Jack Ford murder. Rose and I have been asking some questions." I laughed. "Looks like we're on the right track."

"You don't sound okay. I'll put the kettle on."

"A true Englishman," I said.

He grinned at me. "And proud of it. But first, you need to sit down." Excitement over, Éclair made herself comfortable under the table as Simon pulled a chair out for me.

I sat. He ran water to fill the kettle and plugged it in. Then he took a big Brown Betty and the tea canister off the shelf and tossed two tea bags into the pot.

I studied the note, taking care not to touch it.

Simon stood behind me. His put his hands on my shoulders. I let them rest there, enjoying their warmth, their strength. "I noticed a section of the flower bed alongside the front path marked off by police tape," he said. "I came in to ask you about that."

"That's where the unknown person stood at Rose's window. We called nine-one-one, and the police came quickly. They brought a dog, but he didn't find anything. Looks like they missed something." I pointed to the note. I was pleased to see my hand had stopped shaking.

"You have to call the police again. Tell them to come back."

"Yes," I said.

"Want me to do it?"

"No, I have to."

I considered calling Amy Redmond, but Williams had been pretty blunt last night about letting me know he wasn't pleased I'd been in touch with her. Besides, if I had to wake someone up at quarter after six, it might as well be him.

I called the police station and told them I needed to speak to Detective Williams. They told me they'd pass on the message.

"The police will take the note away when they get here," Simon said. "You should take a picture, so you have a record of it."

"Why do I want a record of it? I don't want to ever think about it again."

"You never know when it might come in handy."

"I suppose you're right." I used my phone to take several pictures, including a couple of close-ups of the details of the print and the smiley face. That grinning yellow face gave me chills right down to my bones.

"Too bad this wasn't produced on a manual typewriter," Simon said. "Those things had individual characteristics. A printer is just a printer."

"That would make it easy, considering there can't be more than a handful of people in all of Cape Cod still using manual typewriters. If that."

A knock on the door. Simon and I exchanged a glance. I hadn't locked the door behind me, and Edna would never knock.

I gave Simon a nod, and he threw open the door.

"Hi," Matt Goodwill said. "I saw the lights and came over to check if everything's okay here."

"Come on in," I called, and he did.

"You can't see the kitchen lights from your property," I said, "and the light over the door is left on all night."

He grinned. "You got me there. Let's say I came over to see if you're okay."

"Why do you need to know if Lily is okay?" Simon asked.

"I heard you had some trouble here last night. Something about an attempted break-in?"

"Word travels fast," I said. "And early."

"My father keeps himself apprised of what goes on around here. I'm always an early riser, so he knew I'd be up, and he gave me a call."

"I assume by keeping himself apprised, he got a call from Detective Williams," I said.

"He didn't tell me how he heard. And I didn't ask." Matt glanced around the kitchen, paying no particular attention to the piece of paper on the table. "Looks as though no harm was done."

"It wasn't," I said. "Just a bump in the night. Happens in an old house full of guests. The tea's ready, but I'm going to make coffee for myself. Would you like one?"

He smiled. "Thanks. Coffee would be nice."

While Simon poured himself a cup of tea, Edna arrived. She started when she saw a kitchen full of visitors. "Goodness, everyone's up and about early this morning. How are you, Matthew?"

"Very well, thank you."

I tried to be unobtrusive about slipping my hand into the plastic sandwich bag and then folding it around the half sheet of computer paper. I wasn't unobtrusive enough. Matt's eyebrows rose.

I slid the bag under the sugar container and got to work. First, I ground coffee beans and put them in the coffee maker to brew, and then I began taking out bowls and measuring cups and spoons to start the morning's baking.

"Can I help with anything?" Matt asked me.

"Heavens no!" Edna said. "The last thing she needs is a couple of amateur cooks getting in the way. You can, however, get that tray down from the shelf and pour the milk and cream into those containers. Take them out to the dining room and put them on the table next to the cereal." As she talked, Edna began taking fruit out of the fridge and laying it on the cutting board.

When the coffee was ready, I poured three cups. Simon said, "I'll get off to work, then. I'll bring the mug back when I'm finished. Cheers."

"Matthew," Edna said. "Slice that fruit. Ensure the pieces are relatively uniform in size. It goes into that glass bowl over there."

Matt sat at the table and set to work. I mixed the batter for bran muffins, put them into the oven, and laid the first batch of sausages in the frying pan.

By nine o'clock, all the guests had been served. Matt had left after slicing the fruit and finishing his coffee, and Edna was in the dining room, resetting the tables for tomorrow. I hadn't seen Rose this morning, and I still hadn't heard from the police in answer to my call.

Every time I reached for the sugar or glanced at the rows of canisters, I took a peek at the note. It never changed, but my sense of foreboding grew, so by the time I was alone in the kitchen, I was quite frightened.

It had clearly been meant as a threat, as had last night's visit. Would this person, whoever he or she might be, stop at issuing threats? Or were they prepared to take matters a step further?

"Good morning, love." Rose and Robbie came into the kitchen. She'd dressed in a purple velour tracksuit, tidied her hair, put on a touch of blush and lipstick, and covered her eyelids with blue shadow and her lashes with thick coats of mascara. She looked positively perky this morning.

I turned to her with a smile. "Did you manage to get any sleep?"

"Surprisingly, yes. When I got up, I had a peek out my window and saw the police tape around my flower beds. I found that somewhat reassuring. It means I wasn't imagining things."

I decided not to tell Rose about the note. She was a great deal tougher than she looked; she was probably a lot tougher than me, come to think of it. But I was worried enough for the both of us.

Edna carried a tray laden with dirty dishes into the kitchen. "Another lot done with. Morning, Rose."

"Good morning, Edna."

"Do you have any plans for today?" I asked my grandmother.

"The housekeeper says the condition of the wallpaper in room two-oh-four is getting worse. It's been torn for a while, but we hoped it would remain discreetly hidden by a carefully placed dresser until the end of the season. Apparently, such is not the case. She suspects some wayward child was amusing himself by tearing at it. I'll have a look at it later."

It was time for me to leave, and I hadn't heard from Detective Williams. I swept up the threatening note, still wrapped in its sandwich bag, called to Éclair, and wished Edna and Rose a good day.

"I'll have my tea now, Edna," Rose said.

"Kettle's over there," Edna replied.

Detective Williams didn't bother to come himself to question me about the paper I'd found. Instead, he sent a uniformed officer around to pick it up. He found me on my small porch, enjoying a second cup of coffee before plunging into the rest of my day, while Éclair sniffed around the yard.

"Aren't you going to fingerprint the plant pot I found this in?" I asked.

"I wasn't told to do that." I wondered if he was old enough to shave yet. Didn't look it. "The detective just said I was to pick up this note you say you found."

"The note I did find."

"If you say so."

"I do say so." I handed him the sandwich bag. "I touched the paper when I first found it, so my prints will be on it, but no one else did, and it's been in my presence ever since then."

"Thanks," he said. And he left.

Detective Williams was clearly not taking my concerns seriously. I wondered if he thought I'd written the note myself to throw suspicion off Rose or me.

No matter what he thought, someone had threatened Rose and me, and I didn't like it one bit.

I finished my coffee, called Éclair into the house, and went to work.

Bernie dropped into the tearoom in the middle of the afternoon. Earlier, I'd seen her car go by, heading up the driveway to the house, and I'd had no doubt she was on her way to consult with my grandmother.

"Rose filled me in on what happened last night." Bernie rubbed her hands together. "We're obviously getting close, and the person we're after is trying to scare us off."

"It might be obvious to them," I said. "I wish it was obvious to me. Something happened this morning I didn't tell Rose about." For the moment, we were alone in the kitchen. Cheryl and Marybeth were constantly bustling in and out, making tea, calling out orders, bringing in dirty dishes. I didn't want to talk in front of them, but I couldn't afford to take the time to go outside with Bernie. I took out my phone and showed her the pictures I'd taken of the note.

She let out a low whistle. "That sounds serious."

"It has me worried, all right."

"You need to tell Rose."

"No, I don't. And I won't. Nor will you. No point in worrying her. I can do more than enough worrying for both of us." I mixed pastry dough as I talked. I was again making strawberry tarts. Our berry delivery was back on schedule, and I'd been greeted by several boxes of the plump, glistening red fruit on the doorstep this morning.

"What brings you here this afternoon, anyway?" I asked.

"I needed to talk to Rose because I had something to report."

"Report?"

"Yup." Bernie snatched a piece of shortbread off a tray ready to be taken into the dining room and popped it into her mouth. She groaned with pleasure. "Oh my gosh. That's so buttery, it almost melts."

"Hey!" I said. "Don't be eating my food."

"You have more."

"That's for paying customers, not mooching friends. The shortbread's in that container over there. Replace the one you took, and don't you dare have another."

"Do you want to know what I learned?" Bernie said when the tray was once again complete.

"Not particularly, but you'll tell me whether I want to hear it or not, so you might as well go ahead." I put the pastry dough in the fridge to chill and took out an earlier batch, now ready for rolling out and filling.

Bernie eyed me. "This is serious business, Lily. The police are now officially calling it a murder."

I sighed. "I know it is. I just wish it wasn't our business. But someone made it our business, first by killing Jack

Ford on our property and then by threatening Rose. So go ahead."

I spread a sheet of parchment on the butcher's block island I use for making pies and tarts, floured it lightly, and then began rolling out the chilled pastry with a heavy marble rolling pin. I've had that rolling pin for years, taking it with me from job to job. It feels as comfortable in my hands as my own fingers.

"First thing this morning," Bernie said, "I was at town hall, checking zoning regulations. Jack Ford had a lot of enemies, and it's entirely possible one of those enemies followed him Saturday morning and knocked him over the cliff. If that's the case, it's possible we'll never be able to get to the bottom of it. But if the reason for his murder lies closer to home, then the sale of the Goodwill property, which will be facilitated by a change in the zoning, might be the key."

"If you say so," I said.

"I do."

"I know all that. What did you discover that's new?"

"What I learned isn't actually all that interesting. I went back through the town records for a few years. This will hardly be the first time residential property has been rezoned to allow for more development. Tourism is increasing by leaps and bounds, and the town wants to keep up. We might wish everything would remain the way it always has, but that's not going to happen."

"You got that right." Cheryl arranged teapots and cups on her tray. "All you have to do is mention jobs and some people'd sell their grandmother's grave to a developer. One order of afternoon tea for two and one for four. Can't blame them really. Young people need a reason to stay here and raise their own families. They can't do that without a job."

Marybeth began laying out the food on trays. "As long

as we keep the environment pristine. No point in developing the Cape so much the tourists have no reason to come here instead of going to New York or Boston."

Cheryl and Marybeth took their trays out to the dining room.

"All of which doesn't matter at this point," Bernie said. "In most cases, whenever the neighbors or other concerned citizens object to the zoning changes, they're overridden. But not always. I found examples of projects being stopped or scaled back because of public objection. Jack Ford and his company had sometimes been the ones proposing the rezoning, and a quick study of the records showed me he'd been more successful than some other developers, but even he didn't get his way every time."

"So?"

"Like I said, not all that interesting. What was interesting is who else was in town hall this morning, checking up on zoning patterns and regulations." She smiled at me.

I shook the rolling pin at her. "Bernie, can you possibly drag this out any longer? If you have something to tell me, tell me."

She leaned toward me. Instinctively, I leaned toward her.

"Matt Goodwill."

I straightened up. "So?"

"So? I find it interesting that he's looking up zoning regulations. All his talk about wanting to leave the property zoned as it is and keep it in the family. Ha!"

"Maybe he's just curious. Maybe he wants to know what he's up against, or is considering all possible options, like any sensible person would. Did you speak to him?"

"I did. I was very subtle."

I refrained from rolling my eyes. *Subtle* was never a word I used for the Warrior Princess.

"I pretended to be friendly and chatty. In return, he was cagey."

"If he was cagey, as you put it, it was probably because he knew you were up to something. What time was this?"

"The office opens at nine thirty. I was there right on time, and he came in a few minutes later."

I didn't tell Bernie that Matt had been at the house this morning. That would only make him look even more suspicious in her eyes.

Although I couldn't get rid of the niggling thought that he'd never shown up at our back door before. Might he have been wanting to see the effect his note had on me?

Now I was the one getting paranoid.

He'd heard about the trouble we'd had in the night and came over to check on us, like a good neighbor should.

Cheryl came back to replenish a teapot. I finished cutting the individual pastry shells and laying them on baking sheets. I'd bake the pastry blend, and then, when the shells were cooked and cooled, I'd add a puree made of the fresh berries, a touch of sugar, and a drop of lemon juice and top each tart off with a single perfect strawberry.

"Get the strawberries out of the fridge for me, will you please?" I asked Cheryl. "I might as well wash them while I'm thinking about it."

She turned around. Bernie ducked in barely enough time to avoid getting a teapot in the ribs.

"You need a bigger kitchen," Bernie said.

"Yes, I do," I replied. "But until I get one, I need fewer people in this one."

"I can take a hint."

I popped the tart shells into the oven and set the timer. "What have you got planned for the rest of the day?"

"I'm going to see what I can dig up about Matt Goodwill. I don't like that all my searching is not finding any source of income for him. If he's in need of money, I'll find out. Cheryl, do you know anything about Matt Goodwill?"

"Other than that he's Lincoln's son? Not really. He grew up around here but moved away some years ago."

The back door opened, and Simon's head popped in. "Sure is crowded in here."

We all laughed.

He looked from one of us to the other. "Everything okay, Lily?"

"All under control." I waved my hand around the kitchen. "Although it might not look like it."

"I meant about . . . uh . . . other matters."

"You know what's been going on?" Bernie said to him.

"What's been going on?" Cheryl asked.

"Don't you have customers waiting?" I said to her.

"Okay, okay." She left the room with a shake of her head.

"I know some of it," Simon said. "I've been keeping an eye on the house this morning. Rose sat outside for a while after breakfast on one of the benches overlooking the sea. The adjacent bushes are now pruned to within an inch of their lives."

"Thanks, Simon," I said. "But I'm sure we're safe during the day. People who sneak around in the night, making spooky noises at an elderly lady's window, aren't the sort to attack in broad daylight."

"I wouldn't be so sure of that," he said. "Catch you later."

He left, and Bernie grinned at me. "Nice! He's pretending to be worried about Rose, but that's just an excuse to pop in here and see you, Lily."

"Don't be ridiculous. He's not pretending about anything."

"Whatever you say." Bernie headed for the door and then hesitated. She turned to face me. "You'll take care, won't you, Lily?"

"Don't I always?" I said.

"No, you don't. But you know what I mean."

I nodded.

"And take care of Rose. It's nice that Simon's watching out for her, whatever his reasons might be, but he can't be there all the time. Do you think I should move in with her?"

"Move in? You mean into her rooms?"

"Yeah. Like a bodyguard. At least until this is all over."

"It might never be over. We might not even know when it is over if the killer slips away undetected. Other than that, Rose'll refuse to allow you to put yourself out, you know that."

"Offer's there if you need it."

I crossed the floor and gave her a hug. "I know. Rose knows, too."

She hugged me back. When we separated, I said, "You can have another piece of shortbread if you want it."

"Don't mind if I do," she said.

"Cheryl," I asked after Bernie had gone, "how long has Carla Powers been mayor?"

"Six years. She's in her second term now. She was a town councillor for several years before that. Why do you ask?"

"Just wondering. Has there ever been suspicions that she's in the back pocket of any developers?"

"As much as some people believe all politicians are crooked," Cheryl said, "I've never been one of them. My brother was on town council for a lot of years. He served the town of North Augusta because he cares about it. And he cares about the people who live here. That doesn't answer your question, but I'll say no. I've never heard any rumors of that sort about Carla. She won both of her elections by a good margin and got an even larger share of the vote the second time around. Now, if you were to ask me about her romantic entanglements, that's another story."

"I heard she was having an affair with Jack Ford."

"Jack Ford. John Doe. There's always someone. You

could make a soap opera about Carla and her husband. She threatens to leave him. He threatens to leave her. He moves out. She throws him out. He comes back. And then it starts all over again. They don't have any children, so I say it's no one's business but theirs. If she was having an affair with Jack, people would be watching her voting record on development issues pretty closely. Tell you the truth, Lily, I hope Carla stays on as mayor for many more years yet. She's honest, and that's not something you can say for all of them. Despite what I said earlier, plenty of politicians are out there who are eager to jump into developers' pockets. Enough talk. If I don't get this tea served, we'll have customers charging the kitchen."

She left, and I went back to my strawberry tarts and my thoughts.

I put my hands against the small of my back and leaned against them, trying to work some of the kinks out.

It had been an exceptionally busy day. The weather continued to be good, hot and sunny, perfect tourist conditions. At three o'clock, a line began forming. While waiting for a table, people toured the gardens or admired the house. Rose called to tell me she'd had several drop-ins: people inquiring if she had rooms available. Starting with tonight, the B & B was completely booked for the next three weeks.

"You won't believe who's here," Cheryl said to me at one point.

"Who?"

"Janice Ford."

"Jack's wife?"

"Yeah. I was serving tables in the patio when I saw her arrive. She left her car here and walked up to the house."

"Did she go inside?"

"Not that I saw. She went around the back. To where . . . well, to see where Jack died, I guess. She's now taken a seat in the patio and ordered a cream tea with Darjeeling. She's by herself. Just staring across the lawn at the house and the sea. Sad." Cheryl gave her head a shake and hefted her tray.

I briefly considered going out front and paying my respects to Janice but decided to leave her in peace. When I met her, I hadn't thought she was grieving for her husband, but people can be full of surprises. Perhaps she was remembering the good times. Presumably, she and Jack had had some good times together.

I hadn't heard from Detective Williams about the threatening note I'd found. I spent a lot of time wondering if I should call him to ask if they had any ideas about that or about last night's intruder.

I finally decided not to waste my time. For some reason, Williams was actively trying to discourage my interest in this case.

Which might be because he didn't like interfering civilians.

Or it might be something more sinister.

The oven timer dinged, and I turned my attention to more immediate matters.

At five minutes to five, I said to Marybeth, "I'm stepping out for some air. How's it looking out there?"

"Two tables on the patio are lingering over their tea, and that's it for today. Looks like we've been pretty much cleaned out."

"Which is a good thing," I said, "meaning money in my pocket. Not a good thing, as I have to spend this evening baking."

"I'd stay and help if I could."

"I know. Don't worry about it. I'm fine here on my own." Which was true. After all these years, I still love to bake. I don't love it so much when my staff are clamoring for orders, the dishwasher is overflowing and the pile of dishes in the sink is about to topple over, and I've just discovered the flour bin is almost empty.

But alone, by myself, in a neatly organized kitchen, surrounded by good, fresh ingredients waiting to be combined into something delicious?

Still my happy place.

I left Marybeth filling the sink with a fresh batch of hot, soapy water and went out the back door. I called Amy Redmond, and she answered.

"I heard about what happened at your place last night," she said. "The report says no one was harmed and nothing appears to have been taken."

"That's right. Rose had a fright, but nothing major. Unless you consider that any shock to a woman of her age can threaten to become something major."

"If you're calling me to ask what's happening, I have to tell you to talk to Detective Williams."

"I called Williams this morning. I left a message for him to contact me about the new development, and he hasn't."

"What sort of new development?"

"I found a note by the back door when I went to the B & B to start breakfast. It was a clear threat, telling me to mind my own business. I can only assume it had been left by last night's intruder."

"Where's this note now?"

"Detective Williams sent a uniformed officer around to get it."

"This is news to me," she said. "Although, I have to point out that as I am not on this case, there's no reason information would be shared with me . . ." Her voice trailed off. "But detectives shouldn't be keeping information to themselves. I'd like to see it."

"Then you're in luck," I said. "I took some pictures."

"Did you now?" she replied. "Are you at the tearoom?"

"Yes, and I'll be here for hours yet. I have to get tomorrow's baking started."

"I'll be around when I can." She hung up without saying good-bye.

When I bake things I've made a thousand times before, I have plenty of time to think. This evening, I thought. Bernie had drawn up her list of suspects for the murder of Jack Ford.

She'd missed one name.

Detective Chuck Williams.

I didn't believe, not yet, anyway, that Williams had killed Jack. I had no reason to suspect him, but it seemed to me his investigation into this case was on the sloppy side. I don't know anything about how police work, other than what I've read in mystery novels or seen on TV, and I've been told those are not always entirely accurate.

But reading between the lines, I guessed Amy Redmond was thinking along those same lines.

She, with more experience in major crimes than Williams, had been assigned to investigate trivialities. Williams wasn't interested in what Bernie found out or what Rose and I suspected. He still seemed to be focusing, despite the other suspects, on Rose herself as the killer.

I had to ask myself why.

Did he kill Jack Ford himself? Was he covering for someone else? Someone like Lincoln Goodwill, whom he'd known for many years? Or for Carla Powers, who was ultimately his boss?

Or was he simply as incompetent as he appeared to be?

Chapter 22

Over the next few days, we heard nothing more about the police investigation. Bernie continued checking into the records of all concerned, but if she came up with anything new, she didn't tell me. I asked her to find out what she could about Chuck Williams, and her eyes lit up.

"You think he's on the take?"

"I think it's worth looking into."

She found nothing of interest. He'd been born and raised in North Augusta. He'd lived in the same house for thirty years, and the mortgage had been paid off five years ago. Despite recent rumors to the contrary, he was still with the woman he married shortly after finishing high school. Mrs. Williams was a bookkeeper at an insurance company; they had three children, one of whom was a cop in Boston, one a commercial fisherman, and one a primary school teacher. Williams and his wife had gone on a very posh Caribbean vacation last year, but it hadn't been so expensive as to be totally outside the means of someone who'd saved hard for the trip. Bernie asked if I wanted to see pictures of Williams in his bathing suit, cavorting on the beach, and I assured her, with a shudder, that I did not.

She couldn't, she told me, find out anything at all about how Matt Goodwill made his living, and he had an almost nonexistent profile on social media. "Didn't I consider that interesting?" she asked. I did not. Even Bernie couldn't find out everything about everyone, and some people (probably wisely) stayed far away from social media.

Every day, Simon could regularly be seen creeping through the shrubbery, secateurs in hand, keeping an eye on Rose. If Rose noticed, and she almost certainly did, she didn't say anything to discourage him.

I wasn't sleeping well, and I could often be found in the gardens late at night, walking the dog and watching her carefully to see if she detected anything out of place.

She never did.

Williams didn't bother to tell me if they learned anything about the message that had been left in the geraniums, but Amy Redmond did.

The note, she told me, had been made by a cheap mass-produced printer on cheap mass-produced computer paper with standard ink-jet ink. No telltale watermarks or distinctive monograms to reveal the identity of the sender. One set of fingerprints had been found on it—mine.

Likewise, no identifiable prints had been lifted from Rose's windows or the windowsills.

Williams had concluded, Redmond told me, it had been a prank. Bored teenagers getting up to mischief at the location of a killing. She didn't say so in so many words, but her tone of voice told me what she thought of that.

The branch of the North Augusta grapevine that runs through Tea by the Sea via Cheryl told me that Mayor Carla Powers and Mr. Powers had recently been seen at the most expensive restaurant in town, staring deeply into each other's eyes and holding hands. Janice Ford had put her house up for sale. Bernie's digging revealed that Janice did indeed have a considerable amount of money in her own name, even after Jack had squandered much of it. Dorothy Johnson had been asked to move out of her retirement home after getting into a heated argument with the other residents over the placement of chairs around the stage for a musical evening.

Life carried on. I made breakfast in the B & B, had time for coffee and a quick walk with Éclair, and then baked all day and sometimes into the night in the tearoom. Another walk with the dog along the bluffs and to bed.

All very boring, but for the time being, I enjoyed the regularity of it, and I was happy in my new life.

The pattern broke on Monday, a little over a week since the death of Jack Ford, when after another glorious weekend, the sky darkened and rain moved in.

Some of the tables in the patio are protected by umbrellas, so they can be used in the rain as long as it's not too windy, but the bad weather reduces our available seating. Fortunately, the rain held off until Monday, after the weekend tourists had headed for home. The dining room was full most of the day, but we didn't have a line waiting outside.

At quarter after two, Cheryl told me Lincoln and Matt Goodwill had taken a table. "You should go out and say hi."

"Why?"

"Be neighborly. We're busy these days, but over the winter you'll need to rely on locals to keep business going."

"I'm thinking of expanding the menu in the off-season," I said. "Lunches, soup and salad, that sort of thing, along with desserts and afternoon tea. What do you think?"

"Good idea. North Augusta folk aren't likely to come out for a fancy, not to mention expensive, special tea in the middle of winter."

I took off my apron. "You're right. I'll make friendly."

I slapped a smile on my face and went into the dining

room. I stopped in the entranceway for a moment, enjoying a brief pause to simply take it all in.

My place.

People were chatting, drinking tea, and nibbling on sandwiches and pastries while the rain beat steadily against the windows. The scent of hot, fragrant tea filled the air, good china clinked, and a man laughed.

I should, I thought, get out of the kitchen more. Sometimes I got so busy baking, I forgot to stop and take a moment to appreciate the end product: satisfied customers enjoying my food.

Lincoln Goodwill, his son, Matt, and Roy Gleeson had taken a table in one of the alcoves. They'd ordered coffee and the light tea: sandwiches and pastries.

Lincoln and Roy were leaning close together, talking in angry whispers. Their posture was stiff, and both men's color was high. In contrast, Matt leaned casually back in his chair, cradling his coffee mug, glancing idly around the room.

He leapt to his feet when he saw me approaching. Lincoln and Roy stopped arguing and half rose.

"Lily!" Matt said. "Nice of you to join us." He gestured to the one empty chair at their table. "Please have a seat."

"Thank you, but—"

"I'm sorry," Lincoln said. "Don't mean to be rude, but this is a business meeting."

"That is rude, Dad." Matt gave me a smile. "Don't pay any attention to him. Everything's business to my father, all the time. I haven't seen you around for a few days. Is everything okay? You seem to be busy in here. How's your friend?"

"My friend?"

"The one with the red hair. What's her name again?"

As if he didn't know.

"Bernadette. We call her Bernie."

"The nickname suits her."

"I have to get back. I just wanted to say hi."

"You might as well sit down if you want," Roy said, not at all graciously. "I came here because Lincoln asked me. I didn't know we were going to keep going over the same ground one more time. I told you, Lincoln, I'm still hearing arguments for and against your rezoning. The public meeting is tomorrow night, and you're welcome to attend and say your piece like anyone else."

I knew about the meeting: Rose intended to go, and she'd ordered me to come with her. I was dreading it.

"The council votes on the matter on Wednesday," Roy continued. "You'll find out what I decide at the same time as everyone else."

Lincoln threw up his hands. "I don't understand what's changed, Roy! You were on my side before Jack Ford died."

"Speaking of Jack Ford," Matt said, "are the police getting anywhere in discovering who killed him?"

"No," Lincoln said. "Bunch of Keystone Cops, that lot."

"That's not fair. They're doing their best. Not all murders are solved." Roy glanced quickly at me. "Charlie says—"

"Whatever," Lincoln said. "I don't need Ford. Plenty of other developers out there. I have a prime piece of oceanfront property that's begging to be put to use."

"As I keep telling you, Dad," Matt said, "I will put it to use. You have to give me time."

"I've given you enough time," Lincoln snapped.

"Where does the mayor stand on this?" I asked.

"She's in favor," Lincoln said. "Always has been. Nothing's changed there. She knows what's best for this community, but she's only one vote on council. She's not some Luddite who's trying to preserve the glory days of North Augusta as a—"

"I assume you're calling me the Luddite, Dad, so I'll take my leave," Matt said. "May I escort you back to your domain, Lily?"

"All of ten yards? Sure. Nice, uh, talking to you, gentlemen." Not that they'd been at all interested in talking to me.

Matt escorted me to the kitchen.

"Your dad's not going to let you have your way?" I asked.

"He can be stubborn like that. Always has been. I have some ideas. I'm working some angles, but I'm running out of time. To be fair to Dad, he's getting desperate to unload that property. If that rezoning goes ahead before I've . . ." He broke off. "Not your problem, Lily. Have a nice day."

He walked away, and I went back to my tea-, sugar-, and cinnamon-scented comfort zone.

I'd tried my best to put the death of Jack Ford out of my mind over the past few days and get on with life, but murder has a way of hanging over everything. As long as questions remained unanswered, my mind couldn't stop trying to find the answers.

The one person who clearly didn't stand to benefit from the death of Jack Ford was Lincoln Goodwill. He'd sounded confident that another developer would take on the project—if it went ahead—but I wondered if that was true. Developers didn't like controversy, and some local people were opposed to the golf resort idea, Rose chief among them. I wouldn't want to be building a resort against Rose's wishes.

I wondered what sort of angles Matt had been talking about.

Had Matt Goodwill killed Jack Ford to delay the project long enough for these angles to happen?

Matt said he hadn't been in North Augusta at the time of Jack's murder. Didn't mean he wasn't. It's easy enough for people to travel long distances and back without being discovered.

Ultimately, nothing had changed since the death of Jack. The rezoning debate was going ahead.

Nothing had changed. . . .

But wait, something had changed. A thought flew through my mind. I grabbed at it. I almost had it. . . .

I stuck my head out of the kitchen and peered into the dining room. Matt had left. Lincoln and Roy Gleeson were getting to their feet, leaving empty plates behind them.

They looked across the room and saw me watching. Lincoln lifted his hand and forced out a stiff smile. Roy stared at me through narrow eyes.

Something had changed. . . .

"A bus tour's just pulled up outside." Cheryl ran up to me. "Sixteen people. They say they have a booking."

"Sixteen! That can't be right. We're not expecting them."

"The bus driver showed me the reservation request. I asked to see the confirmation, and he didn't have one."

"The reservation must have gotten lost last week, when the web page was down for a few hours. What are we going to do? I don't want to turn them away."

"We don't have space inside for sixteen people, not right now, but the rain's letting up and the clouds seem to be moving off. I told them to enjoy a stroll around the gardens while we get the tables ready. We can fit them outside. I'll have Marybeth start wiping down the tables and chairs. They've ordered the traditional afternoon tea. Do we have enough food?"

I ran into the kitchen as I called over my shoulder, "I can manage if I raid the freezer."

Sixteen unexpected orders of the full tea, just when I was getting ready to relax for the rest of the day. I could have turned the bus tour away, telling them their reservation request hadn't been confirmed, but that was not the way to build connections in the community. If I did so, I'd never get business from that tour company again.

One of the complications in serving afternoon tea, as opposed to a regular restaurant menu, is that everything has to be ready at once: scones, sandwiches, and sweets go on the same tray and come out of the kitchen at the same time as the tea itself.

I had scones in the freezer and enough cupcakes, macarons, and tarts to make a nice presentation. Sandwiches were going to be a challenge, as some of my ingredients, including the poached chicken, were almost finished.

Simon ran into the kitchen. He was dressed in his gardening overalls and mud-spattered boots. Thick gloves dangled out of his pockets. "What do you need?"

"I need help, but how did you know?"

He washed his hands at the sink. "Cheryl waved me over. Something about an unexpected rush."

"I need sandwiches made. Use the last of the chicken, and then use up the roast beef. I'll get started thawing the cupcakes and icing them."

Simon stuck his head in the refrigerator and began rummaging around. "Is this all the beef you have left?"

"Oh, dear. It is. Use what we have. I've plenty of cucumbers and cream cheese, so we can make that, and some cans of salmon are in the pantry. We can mix tinned salmon with mayonnaise, a splash of lemon, chopped celery, and chives and serve it on white bread."

Marybeth and Cheryl came into the kitchen and began preparing pots of tea.

"I told them that with such a large group, we can't take individual orders for tea, so I gave them a choice of Creamy Earl Grey, English breakfast, or jasmine green," Cheryl said.

"Thanks." I went to the freezer and got out containers

of scones. We should have just enough. Hopefully, these people weren't big eaters.

"What's the age group of our tourists?" I asked Cheryl.

"Seventy and up. Only two are men, plus the driver."

"Excellent." I pulled out my phone and made a call.

"Hey," Bernie said when she answered. "This isn't a good time. I'm writing up a storm. I've had the best idea. Instead of Rose going to—"

"Drop everything. I need an emergency run to the store." Without waiting for her to agree—or not—I rattled off my list. Aside from what I needed to prepare for our sudden influx of guests, I'd be working late into the night, restocking for tomorrow and the rest of the week.

"Got it," Bernie said.

With Simon's help, I soon had enough beautifully arranged trays of scones, a variety of dainty tea sandwiches, and tarts, cookies, and pastries to get us started. Cheryl and Marybeth served the tea and then began taking the food out.

Bernie's car drove up, and she came in the back door, lugging bags of groceries. I grabbed a loaf of sandwich bread out of one before she'd put the bags down, and tore it open. Bernie helped Simon slap together more sandwiches, and I piped icing onto cupcakes.

When we were finished, I leaned against the counter with a sigh.

Simon grinned at me. He lifted his right hand, and we high-fived.

"Glad I could be of help," Bernie said. "Looks like you've got everything under control here. I have to get back to Rose. My Rose, that is."

"Thanks. You really were a lifesaver. And you, too, Simon."

Cheryl came in with teapots for refilling, and I glanced at the clock over the stove. "It's quarter to five. If we get any new customers, tell them we're closed. We've barely enough left to offer a family of mice a tea party. You can go, too, Simon. I'm fine here now."

"Are you sure?" he said. "You must have more to make to get ready for tomorrow."

I smiled at him. "Thanks, but I'm fine. Barring any more disasters. Bernie, would you mind checking on Éclair and letting her out for a couple of minutes? Maybe look in on Rose, my Rose, too."

"Sure." She and Simon left.

The bus tour departed precisely at five, and Cheryl and Marybeth tidied the dining room and patio, laid the tables for tomorrow, and cleaned up the kitchen. As they were hanging their aprons on hooks, I said, "You guys really are the best."

Cheryl smiled. "We enjoy working here."

"Never a dull moment," Marybeth said. "See you tomorrow, Lily."

By five thirty, I was alone in the tearoom.

I selected music off my phone to play through the Bose speaker, made myself a pot of English breakfast, which I poured into my personal Royal Doulton cup, and set to work. Scones were the most important item. I can make sandwiches out of next to nothing and can shuffle desserts around, but if there's one thing that has to be perfect at afternoon tea, it's the scones. The pastry for the tarts ideally needs time to chill before being rolled out, so I'd prepare the pastry first and do the scones while it was in the fridge.

I assembled the ingredients and set to work. My mind drifted.

It was nice to have friends. I never would have managed without Simon's help, and we wouldn't have been able to complete the last of the trays without Bernie's emergency shopping trip. Not to mention that without her I'd have had to drive into town myself to shop before I could get started on the night's baking.

Something had been on my mind before that busload of unexpected tea drinkers arrived. It was important, but I'd lost it in the rush and panic.

Something about Jack Ford. And changes.

I mixed the pastry dough and formed it into flattened disks, wrapped the disks in wax paper, and put them in the fridge to chill. I made raisin scones next, and while they were baking, I started on batches of cupcakes, one of which would be coconut and one vanilla. I worked quickly and efficiently, listening to music, occasionally licking the inside of an empty bowl or a mixing spoon. I'd hoped to get a chance to try some new recipes this week, but tonight was all about restocking, so I stuck to my tried and true favorites.

I spread a sheet of parchment paper on the butcher's block and spread a light coating of flour on it to prevent sticking, took the pastry dough out of the fridge, and unwrapped the first disk. I laid it on the prepared surface, sprinkled the top with more flour and picked up my marble rolling pin.

I started at a knock on the back door. It wasn't locked, so I called, "Come on in."

I assumed it was Bernie, having another bout of writer's block and needing to talk it through. Instead, a man's voice said, "Hope I'm not disturbing you."

I turned around to face Roy Gleeson, town councillor. The sun was low in the western sky, and the shadows behind him were long. More time had passed than I'd realized. I let go of the rolling pin and said, "This isn't a good time. I'm very busy."

He shut the door behind him. His eyes flicked around the kitchen. I saw them settle on the block of knives on the far side of the stove. He stepped farther into the room so he was standing between the knives and me. He kept one hand in the pocket of his pants, and he did not smile.

Chapter 23

All my fragments of scattered thoughts suddenly meshed together into one cohesive whole, and I knew.

Lincoln kept saying he didn't know what had changed to cause Roy to no longer be enthusiastic about the rezoning proposal.

One significant thing had changed: Jack Ford had died.

Whereupon Roy immediately changed his mind.

Janice Ford had out and out told us that her husband paid kickbacks to Roy Gleeson, but we'd been focusing on reasons why she might have killed him. The first time I'd seen Roy, when he and Jack came into the tearoom, Jack had been quick to say a cup of coffee wasn't a bribe. He'd made the comment sound like a joke, but it hadn't been. He'd been reminding Roy who was the boss here.

"I'm busy." My voice cracked, and I coughed to cover it. "What do you want?"

"Just a chat."

"Sorry. Too busy. Why don't you come back tomorrow?"

"It's quiet out here," he said. "When your restaurant's closed and your staff have gone home."

"Not so quiet. Cars drive past all the time on the road or going up to the B & B."

"A few cars, yes. Your gardener's motorbike's gone, and I saw your red-headed friend drive away earlier. Most of the B & B guests have gone out to dinner."

"You've been watching my house."

He shrugged. "Let's say I'm interested in what you've been up to."

I reached into my pocket. I wrapped my hand around the solid case of my phone.

"Keep your hands where I can see them," Roy said.

"Why would I want to do that?" My heart pounded. My hands were drenched with sweat.

"You shouldn't interfere in things that don't concern you."

"The death of Jack Ford wouldn't have concerned me," I said, "if you hadn't killed him on our property and caused the police to suspect my grandmother."

"You're not as dumb as you look, are you, with all that blond hair and that sweet, innocent smile? When I saw the way you were staring at me earlier, I knew you'd figured it out."

I hadn't actually figured anything out, although I had my suspicions, half formed and nebulous though they might have been. But as it says somewhere: *The guilty run when no one pursueth*. "There's no point in threatening me, Roy. After you and Lincoln left, I called the police and told them everything I know."

He shook his head. "No, you didn't."

"I don't mean your pal Charlie. The man everyone else calls Chuck." Charles . . . Chuck . . . Charlie. "Charlie told me," Roy'd said earlier. He knew I'd been asking questions, because Chuck Williams—Charlie—had told him.

"Charlie's what we called him in school," Roy said. "When he grew up and joined the police, he decided Chuck was a tougher-sounding name. I never could get used to it."

"I spoke to Detective Redmond."

"You didn't do that, either. Unlike my old pal Charlie, she's not just filling in time until retirement. I might have hinted to Charlie that it wouldn't look good for his high-profile murder case to be solved by a hotshot, big-city *female* detective. I arranged for a couple of minor break and enters to give him an excuse to keep her otherwise occupied."

"Including creeping around in the night and trying to frighten my grandmother? That wasn't nice."

He blinked and shrugged. "I don't know anything about that."

Keep him talking. Keep him talking.

I didn't know what Roy was fingering in his pocket, but it was unlikely to mean me any good. He stood between me and my knives, but there must be something else in here I could use as a weapon. A cast-iron frying pan would do the trick, but I don't have one. This is a tearoom: I never fry anything.

My eyes flicked toward the door. No point in simply running. By the time I got the door open, he'd be on me. My only hope was to keep him talking until someone arrived to check on me.

Not that I was expecting anyone at this hour.

"You were a strong proponent of the rezoning application for the Goodwill property," I said. "But when Jack died, your position suddenly changed, and you told everyone you were undecided. What did he have on you?"

"Jack was a wealthy man, although most of that was his wife's money, but he was not a nice one. I did him a few small favors over the years. In return, he hired my son, Grayson, to work at his company, and . . . well, let's say he entertained me lavishly whenever I was out of town. I can manage, if I have to, without Jack's largesse, but although Grayson means well, he's not the most dedicated of workers. He'll never get such a high-paying job anywhere else.

"Jack threatened to let Grayson go if I didn't get the Goodwill property rezoned. I said I'd do what I could, but it wasn't entirely up to me. That made him angry, and he said if the rezoning didn't go through, he'd do more than just fire Grayson. He was going to tell the newspapers about our . . . arrangement. It was time for me to get out from under his thumb once and for all. I couldn't risk the damage to my reputation, never mind a charge of bribery. When your grandmother's letter threatened—"

"My grandmother's letter? What letter?"

"The one she wrote to the newspaper. If she knew, soon everyone would know Jack had been paying me to make a few small changes to the environmental assessment in order to push his rezoning application through."

I had no idea what he was talking about. Rose's letter hadn't said any such thing.

"I didn't want to kill anyone," he said. "And I really don't want to kill you. But you and your grandmother just can't stop interfering, can you?"

He pulled a length of rope out of his pocket. Tough, sturdy hemp rope, of the type a gardener would use to tie bushes in burlap for the winter or bring plants home from the nursery.

"Your gardener should learn to lock his equipment shed." Roy stretched the rope between his hands and took a step toward me. The vacant look in his eyes sent a shudder down my spine.

"You'll never get away with this."

"I have so far." His breath was sour on my face, and his eyes gleamed with madness.

I had nowhere to go. I leaned backward, pressing myself into the butcher's block. All my lovely sharp knives were on the other side of Roy Gleeson. My phone was in my pocket, but I'd never get it out and call for help in time.

"Good-bye, Lily." He lifted the rope. At that moment, the timer next to the stove went off, and the rooster announced it was time to take the latest batch of scones out of the oven. Roy jumped and glanced around, searching for the origin of the sound.

My right hand reached behind me and closed on the familiar shape of my marble rolling pin. I grabbed it, let out an enormous yell, leapt forward, and swung the heavy implement as hard as I could. I hit Roy smack on the side of his head. He yelled in pain and surprise and fell back. His legs buckled, and I kicked him solidly in the right knee. He collapsed, and one end of the rope fell out of his hand.

I raced for the door. He scrambled across the floor and grabbed for my ankle. I was still holding the rolling pin, and I brought it down hard against his outstretched arm. He screamed.

I wrenched open the door and ran outside, yelling as loudly as I could. Behind me, Roy grunted with pain as he staggered to his feet. I dared a peek over my shoulder. He was up and running now, coming after me. I headed for the welcoming lights of Victoria-on-Sea.

A car turned off the road into the driveway and screeched to a halt. Bernie was behind the wheel; Rose next to her. Two pairs of round eyes stared at me, and two mouths opened in shock.

"He killed Jack Ford!" I yelled and waved the rolling pin. "He's trying to kill me." I headed for the car, aware that Roy was only feet—inches maybe—behind me.

Bernie swung the car around and came toward us in a spray of gravel and sand. I leapt to one side, and Roy broke off the chase. He headed for the dark hulk that was the Goodwill house, where his SUV was parked.

Bernie reversed and gunned the engine again.

"No!" I yelled. "No! Not with Rose in the car!"

She didn't hear me, and it probably wouldn't have mattered if she had. No doubt Rose was encouraging her to continue the chase.

I dropped the rolling pin, fumbled for my phone, and

called the emergency number. I shouted our address. "He's after my grandmother!"

Actually, Rose and Bernie were after him, but I didn't bother to mention that.

Roy cut across the yard, Bernie hot in pursuit. I followed on foot.

Bernie's car came to a sudden shuddering halt. Her wheels spun uselessly. She was stuck in a patch of sand.

"Let him go! Let him go!" I yelled as I ran. "The police are on their way."

A motorcycle roared past me. It left the pavement, leapt over the sand, and tore through the beach grasses. A car horn sounded behind me, and I spun around to see Matt's BMW convertible fast approaching. I leapt out of the way. He screeched to a halt next to me, leaned over, and threw open the passenger door.

"What's happening, Lily?"

I jumped into the car. "Roy Gleeson. He killed Jack Ford. He tried to kill me."

Matt threw the car into gear without waiting for me to close my door. He saw Bernie, engine grinding, wheels spinning, firmly trapped in the sand, and stayed on the driveway.

Bernie abandoned her car and ran toward the Goodwill house, her long legs flying and her hair streaming behind her. Her wild red hair was illuminated by the headlights behind her, and it looked as though she carried flames within her. *She really does*, I thought, *look like a warrior princess*. Rose, thank heavens, made no attempt to follow. She'd gotten out of the car and was yelling into her phone and waving her cane in the air with her other hand.

By the time we reached the Goodwill house, Simon was off his bike and had Roy backed up against the SUV, hands in the air. I leapt out of Matt's car before it came to a complete halt.

"I didn't do anything," Roy yelled. "I went to talk to her, and she attacked me. She hit me with a rolling pin, for no reason whatsoever! That woman's a lunatic."

I probably didn't look all that much better, but Roy Gleeson truly did look like a lunatic. Rage filled his eyes, and spittle flew from his mouth. A thin trickle of blood dripped down the side of his face from where my trusty rolling pin had struck him.

"He tried to kill me!" I yelled.

Matt, Simon, and Bernie formed a semicircle around Roy.

"Get out of my way," he said. "If you try to stop me, I'll have you all arrested."

The welcome sound of sirens in the distance, getting closer.

"Why don't we wait for the police," Matt said, "and let them sort everything out?"

"Good idea." Bernie flexed her fingers and glared at Roy. "You make one move, buddy, and I'll crack your skull."

Chapter 24

A cruiser pulled to a halt, and two uniformed officers got out. Roy Gleeson screamed that we were attempting to kidnap him and ordered them to arrest us, but as it was him against the three of us, they slapped the cuffs on him.

More blue and red lights broke the twilight, and screaming sirens tore down the long driveway.

Amy Redmond was with them, and she marched up to me demanding to know what was going on. I told her, my words tripping all over themselves in my haste to get them out. Roy, meanwhile, was screaming that he'd been set up; and Bernie, Simon, and Matt chimed in—all at the same time—with their versions of events.

Finally, Redmond lifted a hand and calmly said, "I'll take your statements in a few minutes." She turned to one of the officers. "Take Mr. Gleeson into town. I'll be along to talk to him after I've found out exactly what's happened here."

Screaming abuse and threats, alternating with offers of a bribe, Roy Gleeson was led away and unceremoniously stuffed into the back of a cruiser.

"One at a time, please," Redmond said while my

friends gathered around me. "Lily, did Mr. Gleeson tell you he killed Jack Ford?"

I let out a long breath as I tried to remember his exact words. "He said he'd had enough and he needed to get out from under Jack's thumb."

"Sounds like a confession to me," Simon said.

"Not quite," Redmond said, "but enough for us to get started pressing charges."

"There was nothing indeterminate about him threatening me," I said. "He came into my kitchen because he knew we were closed and I'd be alone. He brought a length of rope with him and was going to use it on me." I shuddered and touched my throat. "He really did intend to kill me." My legs gave way, and I would have fallen had Simon not grabbed one arm and Matt the other.

"She needs to sit down," Bernie said. "She's had a terrible shock."

"You can go up to the house," Redmond said. "I'll take your statements there. Roy Gleeson can cool his heels in a cell for a while."

"Where's Detective Williams?" Matt asked.

"He's been taken off the case," Redmond replied. "When the call came in and Gleeson's name was mentioned, I contacted the chief and pointed out that the suspect and the investigating detective are cousins."

"Are they now?" Bernie said.

"Which is why Roy knew we'd been asking questions," I said. "Williams told him."

"And that put you in danger," Matt said.

Rose and Bernie were the ones who'd been asking questions, not me. They wouldn't have stopped asking questions if I'd been killed, but Roy thought I knew he'd murdered Jack, and thus I was the one who had to be silenced tonight. I could only assume Rose and Bernie were next on his hit list.

Matt, Simon, Bernie, and I walked across the lawn to the house in a tight group. Redmond stayed behind to give quick orders and then caught up with us. All the lights were on in the B & B, and guests had gathered on the verandah to watch the activity.

Police cars were parked next to the tearoom, and more officers were walking slowly up and down the driveway, studying the ground in the glow of their flashlights.

"What's going on over there?" I asked.

"You said you were attacked in your kitchen," Redmond said. "We need to gather evidence."

"Not my food! Please, I've been baking for hours." Then I remembered. "Oh, no! The rooster."

"The what?"

"The rooster timer crowed. That's what scared Roy so I was able to make my move to get away. I didn't take the scones out of the oven. They'll be ruined. They'll burn the tearoom down!"

She pushed a button on her radio. "I'll see the oven's turned off, but it's unlikely you'll be opening for business tomorrow."

I groaned.

"Consider yourself lucky," Bernie said. "You might have lost more than one batch of scones and a night's work."

"Lucky, yes, but it was more than lucky that you all arrived at the right time. Where were you and Rose, anyway?"

Bernie flicked her eyes toward Redmond. "Tell you later. There's more than one mystery here."

"No mystery about me," Simon said. "I ran into Matt in town. We went for a drink, and talk naturally came around to you two."

"Simon told me you had work to do tonight, but I hoped you'd be finished soon, and we could put our heads together and maybe try to figure out what was going on."

Matt turned to Bernie. "I was going to suggest Lily give you a call and ask you to join us."

"Were you now?" she said.

"I was." He grinned at her. It might have been a trick of the light, but I thought she grinned back.

Rose was waiting for us in the drawing room, Robert the Bruce standing guard by her chair. A hotel guest, she told us, had seen her making her way cautiously back from the Goodwill property and had hurried out to help her.

Over her protests, Redmond hustled my grandmother out of the drawing room, saying she needed to interview each of the witnesses in private.

"If I must," Rose said. "Bernie, why don't you make tea for our guests? Lily must have something in the pantry you can serve them. I'm going to my room. All this excitement has been most exhausting."

"I'll take you," Simon said.

"No, no. Not necessary. I can manage in my own house. You run along with the others." She made shooing gestures. "Off you go."

She gave me a wink, and I followed Redmond into the drawing room.

As I gave my statement, I tried not to speak too directly to a painting on the wall. The one showing an eighteenth-century ship heading out to sea, sails spread in all their glory.

Chapter 25

"And that," Rose said, "will teach you not to keep things from me."

"So there," Bernie said.

"I consider myself to be suitably chastised," I said. "Won't happen again." If I were five years old, I'd have crossed my fingers behind my back.

As I'd talked to Amy Redmond in the drawing room, trying to recall every moment of what had happened in the tearoom kitchen, fatigue began washing over me. Fatigue and a substantial dose of shock. Redmond called Bernie and asked her to take me to bed, and Bernie had done so.

I'd been aware, all through the night, of Rose and Bernie in the living room, taking turns watching over me.

I'd awakened when the morning sun touched the edges of my drapes. I had a moment of panic, recalling all that had happened, but then I lay back against my pillows with a contented sigh. It was over. Life would return to normal. I glanced at the clock. Quarter to six. Time to go to work.

Éclair snoozed at my feet, and the cottage was quiet. I threw the covers off, climbed out of bed, and peeked into the living room. A tangled mop of red hair stuck out from beneath a blanket on the couch, and the blanket moved up and down with Bernie's rhythmic breathing.

I felt a lump in my throat and tears in my eyes.

I let Éclair out and went for my shower.

Murder and attempted murder might have happened, but we still had guests, and guests needed to be fed.

When I next went into the living room, showered and dressed and ready for the day, I found Bernie folding the blanket.

"You didn't have to stay all night," I said. She was dressed in the same clothes she'd had on yesterday, now seriously rumpled.

"Someone had to in case you woke up frightened and confused. Simon offered to sleep over, but Rose was shocked."

"I doubt that very much."

"Okay. She wasn't shocked. She wanted to be the one to watch over you. I managed to persuade her to go back to her own bed by telling her I'd call if you needed her."

Éclair yipped at the door, asking to be let in. Bernie did so, and I gave the dog her breakfast and filled her water bowl. Bernie went to the bathroom and made some attempt to tidy herself up, and then we walked to the house, Éclair trotting at my heels.

"How long did Matt stay last night?" I asked.

"Who? Oh, Matt." She turned various shades of red and pink. "I don't remember."

"Give it up, Bernie. You like him. You can admit it now that we know he's not a killer."

"I will confess he has a certain rakish charm. And those dark eyes—good heavens a woman could drown in them. But she could use his eyelashes as life preservers."

"I hope you don't use that line in your book."

"Why do you say that? I like it. Let's change the subject. You going to be okay to make breakfast?"

"I'm fine. Really. I slept well, and I feel good."

Éclair let out a sudden excited yip and ran ahead. Simon and Edna waited for us by the kitchen door.

"You're early," I said.

"Frank was up all night," Edna said, "preparing this morning's edition to have the big news on the front page. Roy Gleeson has been arrested for the murder of Jack Ford and the attempted murder of Lily Roberts. Imagine that. I want to hear every sordid detail."

"Which I can't tell you," I said, "as the sordid details can't be reported in the paper before the case goes to court."

"I can keep a secret," she said. "Actually, I can't, so don't tell me. I wanted to see if you're okay."

"As you can see, I am."

I put the coffee on to brew and plugged in the kettle for tea. Bernie sat at the Formica table, while Edna set to work laying out the breakfast things in the dining room. Éclair curled up on the floor under the table, rested her face between her paws, and watched me.

"Is there anything I can do to help?" Simon asked.

Despite all the excitement of the previous night, Rose had remembered to leave a note with the numbers for today. A full house.

"I've got a coffee cake in the freezer. I'll use that today. I don't feel like baking."

Bernie shot me a worried look. "That's like me saying I don't feel like breathing. Are you sure you're okay?"

"Physically, I'm fine. Don't worry. I keep thinking about what happened, though, and what led to it. I simply can't understand why someone would believe killing another person would solve their problems."

"Don't try to figure it out," Simon said. "That you don't understand is a good thing."

I put melons and bananas on the table. "If you want to help, you can slice the fruit, please."

Éclair leapt to her feet as Robert the Bruce ran into the kitchen. The *tap-tap-tap* of Rose's cane sounded on the floor, and she followed him in, dressed and made up.

"You're up early." I gave her a kiss on the cheek, and when I pulled back, she put her hands on my arms and stared up into my face with those eyes, so much like mine, full of love. "I'm fine," I said. "Really."

"Glad to hear it. I assumed you'd all be gathering here this morning." She took a seat at the table. Robbie jumped onto her lap.

"Rose," Edna said, "can I make you a cup of tea?"

My grandmother's mouth fell open. When she'd recovered her wits, she said, "Why yes, you may. Thank you, Edna."

I put the coffee cake into the oven to warm and then poured coffee for Simon, Bernie, and myself and took a seat. "Okay, now you can tell me what you two were up to last night. Something about another mystery?"

Bernie and Rose exchanged glances. Rose nodded, and Bernie said, "We paid a call on Janice Ford."

"Why?"

"After dropping off your groceries, I took Éclair for a walk, like you asked me to, and then called on Rose. I asked Rose if there'd been any more signs of intruders after that one time, and she said no. I then might have accidentally let slip something about the note left under the geraniums."

Rose wagged her finger at me. "That came as news to me." Edna put a cup of tea in front of her. Robbie stood on his hind legs and sniffed at it. "If you'd told me about this threatening note, love, that little puzzle might have been cleared up a lot earlier."

"How so?"

"Thursday afternoon I was in room two-oh-four, checking the condition of the wallpaper."

"I remember you saying you needed to do that. What of it?"

Rose lifted her cane and pointed it at the ceiling. "Room two-oh-four is directly above here. A deluxe room with a balcony and sea view. While I was examining the paper, which incidentally will have to be completely removed and replaced, and I have no idea when we'll be able to get that done, I observed Janice Ford at the rear of the house."

"She came to visit the spot where Jack had died," I said, "and then she stayed for tea on the patio. I thought maybe she wasn't as indifferent to him as she'd pretended."

"Really, Lily. You can be so naive sometimes. She wasn't here to pay her respects. She was here to see what had happened to her note."

"Her note?"

"I stood at the window, watching her poking around and trying to be unobtrusive about it. When she thought she wasn't being observed, she lifted the leaves of the geraniums in the pot by the kitchen door and checked underneath. At the time, I thought she might have an interest in geraniums, and ours are particularly fine, if I do say so myself."

"They are that," Simon said as he peeled an orange.

"She was checking to see if her note had been found," I said.

"Exactly. When Bernie told me about the strange incident of the geraniums in the nighttime, I naturally remembered Janice's visit."

"Rose and I decided to pay her a call then and there," Bernie said.

"Why didn't you tell me?"

"Because I knew how busy you were baking for tomorrow Which is now today. You won't be able to use what you made, anyway, because the police took it all away as evidence."

"That's one night's work that'll never be seen again." The glass bowl in front of Simon was filling up with sliced fruit. "It'll all mysteriously disappear from the evidence locker."

Edna chuckled. I groaned. Bernie helped herself to a piece of melon.

"Janice didn't even try to pretend it hadn't been her creeping about that night and planting the threatening note," Rose said.

"She thought it dreadfully funny," Bernie added. "She's got a screw loose somewhere."

"Why?" I said.

"She's rich, spoiled, and bored," Rose said. "And she enjoys making trouble. She denied having anything to do with her husband's death. I believed her, but in the unusual event that I might be wrong, I planned to give Detective Williams a call when I got home and let him know what we'd learned. Obviously, that almost immediately became unnecessary."

We sat in silence for a few minutes. Rose poured a small amount of tea into her saucer, and Robbie helped himself.

Matt Goodwill stepped into the kitchen. "Is this a private party, or can anyone join?"

"Come on in," I said. "The more the merrier. Coffee?"

"Thanks."

Bernie jumped up to pour it. Matt gave her a warm smile, and she returned it. Rose caught my eye and wiggled her eyebrows.

"I have news," he said. "Anyone want to hear it?"

"I do," we chorused.

"I bought the house."

"What?"

"What house?"

"You don't mean the one next door?"

He grinned at us. "Yup. When I got home last night, the email I've been waiting for had arrived. I called my dad and told him I want the house and I'm prepared to pay full value, cash up front. He wisely decided to take what he can get now rather than hope for more if the property is rezoned and if a developer wants to buy it."

"We'll be neighbors," Rose said.

"We will. I plan to move in right away, as soon as I can get the water and electricity reconnected. Maybe even before that. Parts of the house are habitable enough for now, although living conditions are a bit rough. I intend to restore the house and the grounds to their full and former glory, but that's going to take a long time. Years probably. Maybe decades. I'll get it done as time and money permit. I can do much of the work myself, and I'll hire contractors as and when I can afford them." He smiled at Bernie. "You can come and visit anytime."

"I'm not very good with a hammer," she said.

"Then you can sit on the porch and watch me work. I'm rather good with a hammer."

"You know, I might just do that." Bernie's cheeks threatened to turn as red as her hair, and she buried her face in the coffee mug.

"What sort of email would you get that would enable you to buy yourself a house?" Rose asked. I'd been wondering that myself but thought it too much of a personal question to ask.

"A contract I've been expecting came in. I couldn't make my move before it was a sure thing, but now it is. I'm a writer." He grinned at Bernie. "Same as you. Last night I was offered a seven-figure advance for my newest book."

Bernie sucked in a breath. "But . . ."

"But you've never heard of me. Which is understandable, as I write under a pseudonym and don't make public appearances in America. I write true-crime books, stuff about serial killers and mass murders, and the name Goodwill isn't exactly suited to that. My pen name is Lincoln Badwell. My dad wasn't entirely pleased that I took his first name, but I thought it would work. And it has."

"I've heard of you," Simon said. "Those books are huge in the UK. My dad loves them."

"That's nice to hear," Matt said. "Thanks."

"Did you know about this?" Rose asked Edna.

"Of course I did. Matt has occasionally used back issues of the paper to do some research. Remember when I told you I couldn't keep a secret? I lied."

Voices came from the dining room, and Edna and I got to our feet. Time to get back to work.

Simon had finished preparing the fruit. He stood up and handed me the bowl. Our fingers brushed, and I smiled at him.

He smiled back, and then he turned to Matt. "If you need any help on your new house, mate, give me a call. I know my way around a hammer, too. And next time we go round the pub? Drinks are on you. Cheers." He left to start his day's work.

Bernie cradled her coffee mug. "I've had the best idea ever!"

"I hate to ask." I put sausages into the frying pan. Éclair's nose twitched. "But I will. What idea might this one be?"

"Rose—my Rose—and Tessa have to join forces when one of them is accused of killing the local magistrate who's in the pocket of the evil landowner. It's going to be a historical mystery! Isn't that great?"

"Marvelous," Rose said.

"I'm going straight home to get started. I suppose I'll have to learn something about policing back then. I wonder if Matt knows about things like that." She ran out the door.

"Edna," Rose said, "I'll have another cup of tea."

"Don't push your luck," Edna said.

Chapter 26

I didn't enjoy my forced day off. We had reservations for a full house again today, and I didn't fancy turning people away, but I had no choice. The police had closed the tearoom kitchen as part of their investigation. Yellow tape was strung around the back door and the patio gate, cruisers still filled the parking lot, and forensic officers were crawling around the driveway, searching for evidence.

I also didn't like doing Cheryl and Marybeth, particularly Marybeth, who I knew didn't have much in the way of extra money, out of a day's wages, even though I'd have no incomc today.

Once everyone except Edna had left and I was furiously attacking a bowl of innocent eggs prior to making scrambled eggs, I called Marybeth. I told her briefly what had happened and asked her to take a seat by the patio gate and tell guests when they arrived we were closed and to give them a sanitized version of the reason why.

Better that way, I thought, than have the rumor mill in overdrive. I wouldn't want anyone thinking the police had closed my kitchen because someone had died in there.

When breakfast service was over, I left Edna to clean up

and headed into town in Rose's Ford Focus. If I wanted to open the tearoom tomorrow, I had a heck of a lot of baking to do today. I couldn't get into the tearoom to get my ingredients or my equipment, but I could do some work in the kitchen of Victoria-on-Sea.

Which reminded me that my marble rolling pin, the one I'd carried with me all around Manhattan, the one that might have saved my life, had last been seen lying in a field somewhere. Now it was probably in the police evidence locker.

On my way into town, I waved at Marybeth, relaxing in the shade under the oak tree with a thermos, a lunch box, and a book. I stopped the car next to the back door of Tea by the Sea, told Éclair to stay, and got out. I asked the young officer guarding my premises if anyone had seen my rolling pin. He raised one eyebrow at me and grunted something that might have been, "Ask the detectives."

It might also have been, "Got any more of those cookies?"

At twelve o'clock, I was balancing trays of scones, trying to figure out how best to rotate scones, cupcakes, and tarts—all of which baked at different temperatures for different times—in the one small oven of the B & B, when Éclair leapt to her feet. A fraction of a second later, Rose came into the kitchen, followed by Robert the Bruce.

"Detective Redmond is here," Rose said. "She wants to talk to you."

"If I must," I said. "I gave my statement last night. I hope Roy Gleeson isn't still saying I attacked him for no reason."

"I don't know what he's saying."

I slipped the baking sheet of scones into the oven. "Can you keep an eye on these scones for me? They come out in twelve minutes."

"No," she said.

"No?"

"I'm not going to be left out." She left the kitchen.

I took the sheet out of the oven, washed my hands, and followed Rose and Robbie into the drawing room. Éclair followed me.

Amy Redmond was standing at the big bay window, looking out into the garden. She turned and smiled at us, and I assumed she wouldn't have smiled like that if she were here to arrest me.

"Would you like a cup of tea, Detective?" Rose asked as she settled herself into her chair. "Lily will be happy to get you one."

"I will?"

"Yes, you will." Robbie leapt into her lap, and Rose stroked his long fur. Éclair jumped onto the window seat next to the detective and gave her a thorough sniff.

"Thanks, but no." Redmond bent over and gave the dog a hearty pat. "I've been up all night, and I'm on my way home. But first, I thought you might like to know what's happening."

I sat down. Over Redmond's shoulder, I saw Simon climbing the steps to the verandah, a bag for garden refuse in his hands. "Has Roy confessed to the killing?"

"He says it was an accident. That Jack leaned on the gate and it broke and he fell."

Rose snorted. "An accident, yet he didn't run for help and pretended to know nothing about what happened when he showed up all calm and collected and so innocent."

"Not to mention," I said, "that he actually accused you of killing Jack."

Redmond grinned at us. "Yup. So he's going down, one way or another. He was supposed to meet with Ford and Lincoln Goodwill at nine o'clock on the Goodwill property. Jack Ford's phone records show that Roy called him at eight that morning. Roy said, when originally questioned, that he'd called to confirm the time. He now says he wanted to have a private chat with Ford before Lincoln Goodwill arrived. Ford had threatened him if the rezoning didn't go through, and Roy was worried it wouldn't. He needed to talk it over."

"I assume that talk didn't go well." Rose rubbed the fingers of her right hand together in that absentminded way of hers.

"No, it didn't. The two men went for a walk—Roy says he was too restless to talk in the car or on the porch of the Goodwill house. So they walked and ended up here, on your property."

"I'm thinking of getting a guard dog to keep the riffraff out," Rose said. "Maybe a team of armed guards to go with it."

"That will certainly help our family-friendly, home-away-from-home image," I said.

"I suppose it would be like closing the barn door after the horses have escaped. Continue, please, Detective. What happened after they took this companionable little stroll into my yard?"

"They argued," Redmond said. "And we intend to prove in a court of law that Roy Gleeson struck Ford with his hiking stick, forcing him into the fence and over the cliff. His failure to then try to offer assistance, or at the very least call for help, means it's manslaughter at a minimum."

"About the hiking pole," I said. "You're sure it was his, then?"

Her face twisted, and she turned her attention to Éclair. She stroked her fur, not looking at us. Outside, Simon moved slowly along the railing, trimming the plants in the flower boxes.

"We've been checking outdoor-equipment stores all over the Outer Cape in a wild-goose chase. Mr. Gleeson is divorced and lives alone. We searched his house and garage last night but didn't find the pole's partner. No doubt it's currently resting at the bottom of the bay. We hadn't released the information about the pole, so no one had reason to tell us Gleeson used them. Detective Williams says he wasn't aware Roy was an avid hiker."

"Should be easy to find out if that's true, if they were ever seen together in the presence of these poles."

Redmond lifted her head. She studied my face. "That line of inquiry, I've been told, is not to be pursued."

"Understood," Rose said. "Police incompetence doesn't look good in the newspapers."

Redmond pushed herself away from the window. "We'll be in touch as things go forward. Roy has also been charged with the attempted murder of you, Lily, so you'll have to appear in court."

"I can do that," I said.

Rose and I, accompanied by Robert the Bruce and Éclair, walked the detective to the door. Outside, Simon was deadheading the purple and yellow petunias in the baskets hanging over the verandah railing. He threw me a questioning look, and I gave him a nod in return. He grinned, touched his finger to his forehead, lifted his bag, and moved on.

A car came tearing down the driveway. It screeched to a halt at the foot of the steps. Bernie almost fell out.

"I have just had the best idea ever! Even better than my other one. Rose—my Rose—and Tessa are going to set up a detective agency together!"

Recipes

Traditional British Afternoon Tea Scones

Makes 12 scones

These are small light scones that Lily serves with jam and thick cream. I adapted the recipe from a traditional English one. My Canadian mother calls these "tea biscuits," and they are very different than what are often called "scones" in North America.

Ingredients:

2 cups all-purpose flour, plus more for flouring work surface and cutter
4 teaspoons baking powder
¾ teaspoon salt
6 tablespoons unsalted butter, cut into cubes
3 tablespoons granulated sugar
¾ cup milk
1 teaspoon pure vanilla extract
½ teaspoon freshly squeezed lemon juice

Instructions:

Preheat the oven to 425°F.

Combine the flour, baking powder, and salt in a large mixing bowl. Add the butter cubes to the flour mixture and rub them in with your fingers until the mixture looks like fine crumbs. Add the sugar and stir it in.

Heat the milk in a small bowl in a microwave oven for about 30 seconds, or until warm, but not hot. Add the vanilla extract and the lemon juice to the milk and stir until blended.

Place a baking sheet into the oven to heat it.

Make a well in the flour-butter mixture, add the milk, and combine quickly with a spoon. The dough will seem very wet at first. Sprinkle flour on a work surface and place the dough on it. Sprinkle the dough with flour and then fold it over 2 or 3 times, or until it is smooth. Pat it into a round about 1½ inches thick.

Dip a 2-inch smooth-edged cutter in flour and cut the dough into circles. Rework the remaining dough and cut it into circles.

Place the dough circles on the preheated baking sheet and bake for 10 minutes, or until the scones have risen and are golden on top. The scones should be eaten the day of baking, accompanied with jam and clotted cream. Or freeze the scones the day of baking and serve them later.*

*These freeze well. Be sure to cool the scones before freezing. Defrost them in a low oven for a few minutes before serving.

Coconut Cupcakes

Makes 1 dozen cupcakes

Lily includes a mini-version of these cupcakes in her dessert selection, but this recipe makes full-size cupcakes.

Ingredients:
1¾ cups all-purpose flour
2 teaspoons baking powder
½ teaspoon salt
½ cup packed shredded sweetened coconut
6 ounces (1½ sticks) unsalted butter, softened
1⅓ cups granulated sugar
2 large eggs, plus 2 large egg whites
1½ teaspoons pure vanilla extract
¾ cup unsweetened, full-fat canned coconut milk
2 cups of your favorite buttercream vanilla icing*
1⅓ cups large-flake unsweetened coconut (optional)

Instructions:

Preheat the oven to 350°F. Line the cups of a 12-cup standard muffin tin with paper liners.

Whisk together the flour, baking powder, and salt in a medium mixing bowl. Pulse the shredded coconut in a food processor until finely ground, and then whisk it into the flour mixture.

With an electric mixer on medium-high speed, cream the butter and sugar in a large mixing bowl until pale and fluffy. Gradually beat in the whole eggs, egg whites, and vanilla, scraping down the sides of the bowl as needed.

Reduce the speed of the mixer to low. Add the flour mixture to the butter mixture in three batches, alternating with the coconut milk and beating until combined after each addition.

Divide the batter evenly among the lined cups of the muffin tin, filling each three-quarters full. Bake, rotating the muffin tin halfway through, for about 20 minutes, or until a cake tester inserted in the center of a cupcake comes out clean. Remove the cupcakes from the oven, turn them out onto wire racks, and let them cool completely. Cupcakes without frosting can be stored overnight at room temperature, or freeze them in airtight containers for up to 2 months.

Frost the cupcakes by spreading a generous dome of icing onto each cupcake with a small offset spatula. If desired, garnish the frosted cupcakes with flaked coconut. Store them at room temperature until ready to serve.

*Lily uses a splash of coconut milk rather than plain milk in her vanilla icing. If you don't normally add milk to your icing, you can also replace a little bit of the butter with coconut milk.

Tea-Scented Bath Salts

For 1 bath

Lily sells these bath salts at Tea by the Sea, but they couldn't be easier to make at home.

Instructions:

Mix ½ cup Epsom salts with 2 teaspoons of your favorite loose tea leaves or two tea bags.* Pour the bath salts into a hot bath and relax!

*If you're concerned about the tea leaves clogging the drain, wrap the bath salts in a piece of cheesecloth and secure the top before adding to the bath.